D0209572

Lean on Me

Lean on Me

LESLIE GOULD

Guideposts
New York, New York

www.guideposts.org
(800) 932-2145
Guideposts Books & Inspirational Media

Cover design and illustration by Lookout Design, Inc.
Interior design by Lorie Pagnozzi
Typeset by Aptara

Printed and bound in the United States of America
10 9 8 7 6 5 4 3 2 1

For Peter, Godspeed.

Chapter One

JAMES BELL PUSHED THE ARM OF THE OVERHEAD light away from the operating table as Dr. Drew Hamilton stepped away from their sixty-eight-year-old patient. They'd just completed a stent placement.

"She'll be playing with her grandkids in no time." Dr. Hamilton's voice was muffled by his mask, and his eyes twinkled under his blue cap.

James nodded. There was nothing more rewarding than changing the course of a person's life, and he hoped that working as the lead nurse in the new Holistic Cardiac Program with Dr. Hamilton would turn out to be a change in the course of his life too. The doctor had requested James specifically, which meant James had to resign his old position and sign on with the new program, which had come together in record time. Although Hope Haven had been offering heart surgeries for several years, Dr. Hamilton felt this new program would enhance treatment, education, and rehabilitation at the hospital. James was only one week into his new job, but he hadn't regretted the move for one nanosecond.

"I'll wheel her down to recovery," James said as his pager went off. He squinted in the dim light to read the message. The CEO of Hope Haven, Albert Varner, wanted James to stop by.

Dr. Hamilton pulled his pager from the waistband of his scrubs at the same time. He glanced down, pushed a button, and then lifted his head toward James. "Albert Varner."

James's pulse quickened. "Does he want to see you too?"

Dr. Hamilton nodded. "I'll head down in a few minutes."

"What do you think he wants?" James gripped the end of the gurney.

"Probably to tell us what a great job we're doing." He patted James on the back. "See you soon."

James tried to smile, but an uneasy feeling settled in his gut. The chief executive officer of Hope Haven wouldn't ask to see them to tell them that.

Twenty minutes later, after having delivered his patient to recovery, James headed down the staircase to the administrative offices. Penny Risser sat at her desk flanked by pots of two-feet-high plants, thick with leaves. Her lacquered fingernails clacked out a rhythm on her computer keyboard as she talked on the phone. James stopped a few feet from her tidy desk and waited. Photos of Hope Haven through the years lined the wall. The first one had been taken in 1907 soon after the hospital was built. Founder and doctor, Winthrop Jeffries, stood on the front steps of the hospital, wearing a top hat. With him were four nurses, all dressed in dark dresses, white aprons, and white head coverings.

The last photo had been taken a few years ago. Staff members, including James, stood in front of the main entrance—a sea of white lab coats, blue scrubs, and casual wear.

"What can I do for you?" Penny asked as she hung up the phone.

"Mr. Varner paged me."

She looked down at a sheet of paper on her desk.

"About twenty minutes ago," James added as Varner's door swung open.

"There you are. Where's Drew?" The CEO stepped forward, scanning the waiting area. His dark hair needed to be combed, his tie was loose, and the sleeves of his white dress shirt were rolled to his elbows.

"He's on his way," James said, hoping the good doctor would show up, not wanting to face Albert Varner by himself. It wasn't that the man was intimidating; it was that he could be scattered and sometimes seemed to have a bad memory.

"Come on in," Varner said.

Penny cleared her throat as James headed toward the door. Varner turned toward her. "Yes?"

"The meeting isn't on the schedule until Monday," she stated.

He rubbed the back of his neck. "Well, I wanted to deal with it as soon as possible."

Penny rose and stepped around the side of her desk, her face more serious than usual.

Varner put up his hand as if to stop her. "I have this under control."

Penny's face fell, but Varner didn't notice. He'd already spun around and was stepping into his office. James followed and passed through the door into a virtual jungle of plants, all thanks to Penny's green thumb. Bamboo grew in pots under the window. A hanging basket filled the far corner and three smaller plants—a fern, a zebra plant, and a tropical lily—graced the front of Varner's desk, partially hiding the mess of papers and files.

"James," Varner said, running his fingers through his thick hair as he sat down, "how are you doing?" The man was usually outgoing and gregarious, though disorganized, but today he seemed more out of sorts than usual. He settled into his stately office chair behind the desk and rolled forward.

"Just fine, thank you," James said. He wanted to tell the CEO how much he liked working in the new Holistic Cardiac Program, but James—who usually could carry on a conversation with anyone whether it was professional, personal, or casual—felt ill at ease.

Just then Dr. Hamilton stepped through the doorway, saving James from having to say anything more. "Sorry to keep you waiting."

Varner stood and extended his hand, saying, "Drew, welcome."

Dr. Hamilton shook it enthusiastically and then settled into the chair beside James. "I have to tell you, Albert," he said, "it was genius of you to approve the new program. We've been busy all week, and next week is already booked. Patients who would have gone to Peoria are now staying in town for their procedures. And the health of the whole town will improve with more consistent treatment and education."

Varner ran his fingers through his hair again. "Actually Drew—and James—that's why I called you in. It turns out"—he cleared his throat—"that we made the decision prematurely."

Dr. Hamilton scooted forward on his chair. "Say again?"

"You know," Varner said, pulling his chair closer to his desk. "Zane should really be here to explain the ins and outs of all of this." He picked up his phone and punched a couple of buttons. Seconds later he said, "I need you in my office to go over some numbers." He glanced from James to Dr. Hamilton as he spoke but didn't smile. "On the Holistic Cardiac Program. Why it's not sustainable." Then he hung up the phone.

"He'll be right in," he said.

James's heart began to race.

"Albert,"—Dr. Hamilton moved to the edge of his chair— "we went over the numbers. There's the government money to help fund it."

"It turns out there are other standards that are being required of us sooner than we had thought."

"April Fool's Day was last week." Dr. Hamilton sat on the edge of his chair, glancing at his watch as if double-checking. "But this is still a joke, right?"

Varner shook his head solemnly.

Before Dr. Hamilton could say any more, there was a quick rap on the door as it swung open; Zane McGarry, chief financial officer of Hope Haven, strode into the office with a file in his hand.

"Drew. James," he said, shaking both of their hands as the men stood. "Albert." He faced his boss and then sat in the chair closest to the door. He was an intelligent man, which was evident in his clear brown eyes. He sat tall and waited.

"Zane," Varner said, "I was just telling Drew and James that we're going to have to cut the new program." The

CEO was usually charismatic. James was surprised at his bluntness.

McGarry nodded, a look of empathy on his face. "The timing is most unfortunate," he said. "We've just been notified of new national electronic-charting standards we need to meet, and our budget can't weather both the new requirements and the new program."

"But we'll lose business," Dr. Hamilton said, leaning forward.

"Yes, I'm aware of that." McGarry looked the doctor in the eye.

"How can Hope Haven survive if patients are going to Peoria for procedures and surgeries?"

"Frankly," McGarry said, "the hospital won't survive the way things are. At this point, we're just trying to keep afloat and last as long as we can."

Varner's head jerked forward. "Wait a minute, Zane. That's strictly your opinion." He shot a stern look at McGarry. "And I've already told you, it's an opinion I don't share."

McGarry met the CEO's gaze but didn't say anything.

"How can surviving as long as possible be a goal of yours?" James asked, addressing McGarry. "Deerford needs Hope Haven. Without it, the entire community is at risk."

McGarry nodded. "I couldn't agree more. Listen, I'm just trying to be realistic and stay on budget."

"What happened to the numbers you presented when the program was approved?" Dr. Hamilton asked.

McGarry opened his file. "First of all, the government grant for the program turned out to be a quarter of what we expected.

They had to readjust because of the new standards that have taken priority."

Dr. Hamilton whistled.

"Those new standards we're required to meet are expensive."

"And they are . . . ?" James asked.

"Updated electronic charting that meets national expectations."

"Surely there's funding for that," James said.

"We don't qualify." McGarry looked straight at Varner.

The CEO grimaced. "That's out of my hands," he said. "But I do want to reiterate this: Zane was just sharing his opinion. I'm certain Hope Haven will survive." He shot McGarry a steely look and then continued. "There's no reason to be pessimistic. We're closing one program—not the entire hospital."

"What's the timeline on the Holistic Cardiac Program?" Dr. Hamilton asked.

Varner shook his head. "There isn't one. We had to pull the plug, no pun intended, today. Right now."

"What about the patients who are scheduled for next week?"

"The regular surgery team will incorporate what they can. The others will have to go to Princeton or Peoria." Varner stood. "Drew, you'll go back to your previous position."

James stood. He'd be going back to the floor, and that would be fine. He was just happy to still have a job.

"And you, James." Varner's face reddened as he spoke. "According to human resources . . . I'm sorry, James. You've been terminated."

"Pardon?" James knew there had to be a mistake.

"I'm sorry," Varner repeated.

"But..." James felt completely blindsided. "I've worked at Hope Haven for twenty-one years."

Varner rubbed the back of his neck and turned his head toward McGarry. "Do you remember exactly what HR said?"

McGarry stood. "I wasn't at that meeting."

Varner motioned to the door. "Drew, would you ask Penny to come in here for a moment?"

To James, it felt like an eternity before Penny joined them. She lingered at the doorway, barely entering the room.

Varner's face was beet red now. "Penny, what were the details on James's new job?"

Penny's face was full of compassion, but she sounded like a robot. "This was all in the Holistic Cardiac Program paperwork. Because of the federal funding, it was a contractual job."

James nodded. He knew that. With the new job had come a higher salary—all of which went to cover his family's medical insurance that he had to purchase through the hospital.

"So," Penny said, "you gave up your seniority at the hospital. And since your previous job has already been filled, the hospital regrettably has to let you go since the contract is being terminated."

James stumbled and then sat down in his chair.

Varner sank back into his. "It has nothing to do with your job performance—"

"This is outrageous!" Dr. Hamilton's voice was loud and firm. "Hope Haven has never treated a loyal employee this way."

Varner shrugged. "He can apply for the next available job."

McGarry was obviously distressed. Beads of sweat had gathered around the hairline of his closely cropped hair. He stood as he spoke. "Albert, if you don't need me any longer, I have work to finish up." He slipped past Penny before Varner responded.

Penny pulled a dead leaf from the plant near the door. "Check in with HR—with Leila—first thing Monday morning, James. She'll discuss with you the settlement for the early termination of your contract and your benefits." She dropped the dead leaf in the wastebasket by the desk and then, with her back to Varner, made eye contact with James and mouthed, "Sorry."

He nodded. Leila was the nursing administrator. Surely she could see a mistake had been made.

"Albert," Dr. Hamilton said, "what's going on?"

Varner rubbed his forehead. "This has nothing to do with you and James. It has to do with keeping Hope Haven open." He pushed back toward the window. "Even so, James, I have to ask you to gather all of your things and refrain from discussing this with any of the staff as you leave. I don't want a mutiny on my hands before I can address this in a civil way. That will happen Monday."

Dr. Hamilton shook his head. "If you think I'm not going to talk with anyone about this, you're mistaken. I'm not going to let this go," he said. "I'm not convinced we can't find a solution that could save the Holistic Cardiac Program and, if Zane's correct—which I suspect he is—the hospital, as well." He turned to James. "Don't you agree?"

James did agree and he nodded, indicating he did, but all he could think about was telling Fern that he'd lost his job, unless Leila could secure a position for him ASAP.

Upstairs in the staff lounge, James didn't have much to gather from his locker—just his coffee cup, the jeans and sweater he'd worn to work that morning, and his stethoscope, penlight, and clamps. He changed out of the hospital's scrubs and back into his street clothes, took the stairs to the first floor and then hustled down the hall by the ER and out the back door to the staff parking lot into the chill of the afternoon, hoping he wouldn't see anyone. But of course that wasn't possible.

"James!" Anabelle was standing beside her car. "How are you?"

His minivan was parked a couple of spaces away. He willed himself not to tell her what was going on. He had never understood the power a company had over someone who had been terminated, until now. He wanted—he needed—to work at Hope Haven. He would comply with Albert Varner's instructions to a tee and hope Leila Hargrave could save the day come Monday.

"I'm good," James called out to his friend. "How are you?"

"Glad it's Friday," she answered. "What a week. You and Dr. Hamilton kept the floor hopping with all of your surgeries. I might have to hire some nurses just to keep up."

James grimaced at the irony of her statement.

Anabelle smiled. "What do you have planned for the weekend?"

"Oh, you know, the usual." *Praying.* "Catching up on laundry. Cleaning." *Updating my résumé.* "Playing basketball with Gideon and Nelson. Hanging out with Fern." *Fern.* His heart skipped a beat. "How about you?"

"I get to spend time with Lindsay Belle tomorrow." Anabelle beamed. The woman was crazy about her one-year-old granddaughter.

They said good-bye, and as James climbed into his van, he thought about the layoff scare Hope Haven had experienced just over two years ago. Then, everyone was in the same boat. Now, he felt like a lone, isolated target. He took a deep breath and came to his senses. Thank goodness it was just him. He hoped McGarry was wrong and there wouldn't be a ripple effect.

Frustrated, James pressed his forehead against the steering wheel. It had been less than two years ago that it looked like the hospital was going to close, and he'd considered moving his family to Peoria. And not long after that, the staff took a 10 percent pay cut to keep the hospital in the black. Surely Varner was right that the hospital wasn't facing such dire straits again. Closing the Holistic Cardiac Program would be bearable as long as Leila could put him back to work on Monday. If not, he could look into home health care, he supposed, but he knew that was about it as far as options in Deerford. He could look for a job in Princeton and commute, but they'd decided two years ago that relocating the family wasn't an option. As far as he was concerned, that still stood. Not to mention that they'd just moved into a new house in Deerford—Fern's dream home. No. Moving was definitely *not* an option.

James turned his eyes toward the hospital. The sun was low in the early spring sky, but it cast a shimmer of light over the bricks and windows. He turned on the ignition and let it idle for a minute before turning on the heater.

At least their previous home had sold last month. He'd begun the paperwork for a loan to buy their new place. If he really didn't have a job, he was pretty sure they wouldn't be approved for the house.

As he drove away from the hospital, he prayed, "What now, Lord? What do You have planned for me and Fern and our boys?"

Chapter Two

AFTER FINISHING THE DINNER DISHES, JAMES watched Fern for a minute. She rocked gently in the comfortable living room next to the fireplace, her walker just a couple of feet away. Her eyes were closed as she listened to an audiobook, her earphone buds firmly in her ears. Her short hair was held back with two barrettes, and she wore a nice pair of sweatpants and a jacket. The room was warm enough that she didn't have a blanket wrapped around her legs. Sitting there, she didn't look as if she had MS, as if she was fighting a disease that was slowly but surely attacking her central nervous system.

She was happy in the new house. God had provided what they needed, from the single-level layout to the hardwood and tile floors that made maneuvering from room to room so much easier than it had been in the old house with its wall-to-wall carpet. Having enough rooms for an office and exercise room was a big bonus, and the jetted tub in the master bathroom as well as the larger hot tub and the half basketball court in the backyard were more than James—and their boys—had ever dreamed.

He stepped next to her and touched her arm. Gideon and Nelson were settled in their rooms, and the main work of the day was done. He pressed his hand against her arm more firmly and said, "Sweetie."

Her eyes opened slowly and she smiled.

"I need to speak with you," he said, pulling a straight-backed chair beside her.

"What is it?" Looking concerned, she pulled the earbuds out and turned off the MP3 player. "Is it one of the boys?"

He shook his head. "It has to do with work—turns out I gave up my seniority when I took the lead-nurse job for the new Holistic Cardiac Program."

"James?" Her eyes were wide. She'd guessed at what was coming.

"Hope Haven cut the program today."

"Oh dear." She reached for his hand. "How are you doing?"

He smiled. That was so like Fern to be concerned about him before anything else.

"It hurts." He paused a moment. Talking about it with her brought his emotions to the surface. "But I'm going to speak with Leila on Monday morning to see what advice she has for me. And we'll trust God. Right?"

"But won't you get your old job back?" She squeezed his hand.

He shook his head. "I'm going to appeal it—talk to Leila like I said. In the meantime, I can apply for the next open position and anything else I can find in town. I'll check in Princeton too."

Fern exhaled. "Oh my."

Now it was James's turn to squeeze her hand. "I could use some help updating my résumé tomorrow."

"Of course," she said.

James leaned forward and kissed her cheek, and she reached up and pulled him close, hugging him tightly.

The phone began to ring but stopped quickly. Either it was a wrong number or one of the boys picked it up. A minute later, Nelson sauntered into the room. "It's Dr. Hamilton." He held the cordless phone out to James.

As James reached for it, Nelson glanced from his father to his mother and said, "What's up?"

James shook his head and mouthed, "Tell you later."

Nelson lingered for half a moment and then headed back to his room, and James said hello to the doctor.

After a quick greeting, Dr. Hamilton said he'd contacted the hospital board president, Bernard Telford, and found out that there had been an emergency meeting last evening. "I'm afraid the majority of the members are in agreement with Albert about our program," he said. "But I'm not sure any of them have done their homework. It's a travesty."

They chatted for a few more minutes, and then Dr. Hamilton said that he'd requested authorization to form an advisory committee of health professionals and it was granted. "Would you join me on the advisory committee?" Dr. Hamilton asked.

James headed through the dining room on his way to the kitchen, knowing it would be obvious to Fern that he no longer wanted her to hear the conversation. "Thank you," James said, stepping onto the tile floor of the kitchen. He kept walking and stopped at the back windows. "But I need to pass." He explained that because he would have much to gain if the program was saved, it felt like he would have a conflict of interest on the committee. Besides he was afraid it would only add more stress to Fern if he were gone evenings. "But I was wondering if I could use you as a reference on my résumé."

Dr. Hamilton groaned. "I'm going to get you back to Hope Haven ASAP. In the Holistic Cardiac Program if I have my way. There's no reason for you to work on your résumé."

"In the meantime . . ." James hoped his voice sounded upbeat.

"Of course you can use me as a reference."

James leaned against the kitchen counter. "Anabelle would be great on the advisory committee."

"She's next on my list," Dr. Hamilton said.

After he hung up the phone, James peered into the darkness of the backyard, again wondering how they'd qualify for a loan if he didn't have a job. He would play basketball with the boys tomorrow. And every day thereafter for as long as they still had the house.

Anabelle lobbed a tennis ball to Sarge and then stepped onto the deck. She'd been playing catch with her dog—a shepherd mix—for at least fifteen minutes, and her arm was growing sore.

"Come on, boy!" she called as he scooped it into his mouth and zigzagged across the backyard. "Come on!" Finally he ran up the steps to the deck and dropped the ball at her feet. The evening sun had set, and the icy chill of night had descended. She picked up the ball and dropped it in the plastic box of dog toys on the picnic table.

Anabelle's husband Cameron slid open the patio door. "The phone's for you."

"Who is it?" Anabelle patted Sarge's head.

"Dr. Hamilton." Cameron handed her the phone.

Anabelle's heart raced as she answered it. The doctor rarely called her at home. She hoped there wasn't some sort of emergency.

Dr. Hamilton quickly explained what had happened with the Holistic Cardiac Program and that James had lost his job.

"What?" Anabelle stepped into the house.

Dr. Hamilton added a few more details.

"That's absolutely ridiculous." She sank onto the window seat.

"I know. But it's where things are." Then he told her about the advisory committee and asked her to participate.

In a heartbeat she answered, "Of course." If James could be laid off just like that, then none of them were safe. They were all at the mercy of the CEO and the board. After ending the call, Anabelle dialed James. Just when she thought her call was going to go into voice mail, James answered.

Anabelle blurted out what Dr. Hamilton told her and said she was horrified by what had happened. James told her it was okay, that things would work out for him and his family. Then he said he couldn't talk, that he and Fern had just told the boys, and that he needed to get back to them.

"What can I do for you?" Anabelle asked.

"You could pray for us," he said, and then chuckled a little. "Because quite frankly this trusting thing is moment by moment—one minute I am doing it, and the next it's a struggle."

"Of course," Anabelle responded. "Tell Fern I'm praying for her too."

After the call, Anabelle rose slowly from the table. Sarge peered at her through the patio door, his nose against the glass, his dark eyes curious yet sympathetic. He tilted his head.

"What's going on?" Cam stood in the entryway to the dining room.

"James got laid off, and Dr. Hamilton's forming a hospital advisory committee."

Cameron shook his head. "Poor James. What about your job?" Cameron had been asking her lately when she planned to retire.

Anabelle shrugged. "Maybe I'll find out Monday." She could always retire and create an opening for James. He wouldn't qualify to be the nurse supervisor of CCU, but if one of the other cardiac floor nurses took the job, that would leave an opening for James. She hoped it didn't come to that. She wasn't quite ready to retire. And James had been perfect for the new cardiac position.

She sighed as Cameron stepped toward her with his arms open. "How about a hug, lass?" he said, using one of his many terms of endearment for Anabelle.

She nodded. That would help, for now. She relaxed into his arms and held him tightly.

As Candace started the dishwasher, she glanced at the kitchen clock. Nine forty-five. Both kids were down for the night, although Brooke probably wasn't asleep since she'd taken a book to bed with her. Candace yawned. She'd check her e-mail and then turn in herself. She'd offered to take the Saturday day shift the next day because two nurses were on vacation and one was out with the flu.

She settled down at the desk in the family room and then scanned her e-mail, deleting the junk messages as she went. As she skimmed down the FROM column, her cursor stopped on HEATH CARLSON. The message definitely wasn't spam. She clicked to open it.

I'm picking up a shift tomorrow too, he'd written. *How about lunch, if we can make it work?*

If we can make it work seemed to be the phrase the two of them lived by.

His e-mail continued. *I'll pop down to see you when I get a break in the morning—or at least try to call.*

He'd signed it *Love you. H.*

She couldn't help but smile as she e-mailed him back that she'd look forward to lunch, *if we can make it work*. She added a smiley face, then *Love, Candace* and hit Send. It was so nice to be writing *love* and *I love you* again.

Even though the house was growing chilly Candace felt warm inside as she clicked through her other messages. A newsletter from Brooke's school. Several advertisements. That was it.

She logged off and shut the computer down and then wandered around the house, turning off lights and turning down the heat the rest of the way. Light shone under her mother Janet's door. She was probably reading and would be up late. She didn't seem to need much sleep, but she did enjoy her alone time in her room.

Candace checked on Howie first. He was on his stomach with his blankets pushed down to the bottom of the bed and his legs tangled in his top sheet. She kissed the back of his head, her lips brushing his brown and copper hair, as she breathed in his sweaty, little-boy scent. He stirred a little and turned his head toward her, smiling slightly but not opening his eyes. She gently tugged the sheet straight and then pulled the covers back over his little body, knowing in a few minutes everything would be undone again. Thankfully his internal heater seemed to keep him warm at night.

Next she stepped across the hall to Brooke's room. As she opened the door, a light flicked off.

"Brooke?" she said.

Her daughter didn't answer.

Candace stopped at the edge of her bed. The book *Black Beauty* was by her head, and Brooke faced the wall, her blonde hair a wave of curls. Candace backed out of the room, sure there was a flashlight tucked under the blankets. She remembered doing the same when she was Brooke's age. She smiled. No harm done. After all it was a Friday night.

She made her way down the hall, illuminated by the night-light, and slipped into her bedroom, thinking about Heath again until she flicked on the light to her bedroom. On the table beside her sleigh bed was her wedding photo. Dean smiled down at her, his blue eyes bright with adoration. Dean.

She walked around to the other side of her bed and sank down on the mattress, facing the photo. "What do you think of all this?" she whispered. Inhaling, she stood, her eyes still on the photograph. She loved the picture. It had comforted her through the years since his death. But tonight, for the first time, she wondered if she should move it to the living room. It was too much to be thinking about loving Heath one minute and grieving Dean the next.

Elena turned off the news at ten fifteen. The house was completely still. Rafael had a gig with his band in Peoria, and Cesar was working late. She'd intended to wait up for him but wasn't sure if she'd make it. She padded down the hall.

She'd had a busy few hours with Izzy before bedtime. Her granddaughter had fallen asleep on the couch before dinner and then was a bundle of energy for the rest of the evening. They'd played Twister, made peanut butter cookies, and worked on the kitty puzzle on the card table in Izzy's room. And then read a stack of books at bedtime.

As Elena reached the half-open door to Izzy's room, she heard a faint, "*Buela?*"

"Yes," Elena said. *The little stinker*, she thought with a smile. *If she sleeps at all during the day, she's up half the night.*

"Would you read me *Madeline* again?" Her voice was louder now.

Elena stepped into the little girl's room and kissed her forehead. "No. You go to sleep."

"Please," Izzy said.

Elena shook her head. "I'm too tired to read another word. I'm going to bed."

"How about if I come tuck you in?" Izzy's sparkling eyes were evident even in the dim light.

"Nice try," Elena said. "Now go to sleep."

As she reached the doorway, Izzy's sweet voice filled the room, reciting, "'In an old house in Paris that was covered with vines, lived twelve little girls in two straight lines. . . .'"

Smiling as she recognized the first sentence from *Madeline*, Elena stepped out of the room, leaving the door half open. Izzy's voice followed her down the hall. It seemed she had more than the first bit memorized. Elena realized she was still smiling as she got ready to wash her face. That granddaughter of hers was so, so smart.

At eleven thirty, Elena awoke to Cesar slipping into bed. "How are you?" she muttered, reaching for his hand.

He seemed tense.

"What's the matter?" she asked.

He scooted toward her. "I'll tell you in the morning."

"You can tell me now." Light from the streetlamp shone through the curtains. Cesar's brow was creased. She cuddled against him.

"They were short of officers, so I took a drunk to the ER tonight. Nice man—very apologetic but really a mess. All worried about how his wife and son were going to react." He wrapped his arms around Elena.

"That's too bad." She had seen patients like that before. Life had gotten away from them and they knew it and were ashamed, but seemed to have no inkling on how to turn things around.

"There's more." He exhaled slowly. "When I was at the ER, I heard there's a rumor going around that the administration's closing departments at the hospital."

"Really?" Elena hadn't heard anything earlier in the day. They wouldn't be closing the ICU, that was for sure, but she wondered who might be affected. Then again, it could just be a rumor.

"And the ER secretary said that James was laid off this afternoon."

"James?"

"Yep." Cesar started to relax and settle into the mattress.

"Are you sure?" That couldn't be.

"That's what I was told." Cesar's voice faded as he spoke.

"What else did she say?"

Cesar waited a moment to answer, and when he did his voice was practically a whisper. "That was pretty much it."

"Cesar?"

He responded with a gentle snore. His brow was smooth now. His worries gone.

Not again, Elena thought as she stared at the ceiling, wide-awake. *What in the world is going on at Hope Haven this time?*

Chapter Three

SATURDAY MORNING, ANABELLE PARKED IN HER daughter Ainslee's driveway, sure Doug had already left for his office. He had a design project he needed to finish, and Ainslee was going to work at the antiques store Once Upon a Time for a few hours. It thrilled Anabelle to be able to help them out and spend time with Lindsay Belle. She collected her purse and stepped into the bright sunshine of the spring morning. It was supposed to get up to sixty-five degrees by afternoon—the warmest day of the year so far. Maybe she and Lindsay Belle would go for a walk. The little girl was starting to toddle around. In no time she would be running.

Ainslee's yard wasn't exactly neglected—the girl's father was a retired landscaper after all—but it wasn't in the tiptop shape it had been in previous years. Her daffodils bloomed alongside last autumn's leaves that had been raked into the flower beds as mulch in the fall but not cleared out yet this spring. Anabelle smiled. It was obvious her daughter and son-in-law had other things to keep them busy besides yard work. Anabelle knocked on the back door.

"Come in," Ainslee called out.

Anabelle stepped into the kitchen. The black granite counters were covered with bowls, a few glasses, and several mugs. A box of whole-grain cereal sat on the table, next to the high chair.

"We're in the living room."

Anabelle heard a squeal and then a thud as she turned the corner.

"Lindsay Belle." Ainslee's voice was full of exasperation as she stood with the baby's shoes in her hand.

"Where is she?" Anabelle looked around the room.

Ainslee pointed as Lindsay Belle's head popped up between the sectional and the coffee table, which was covered by a lime-green and pink beach towel clipped with tablecloth holders, like one would find at a picnic, to the glass top. The towel clashed garishly with the sectional and the modern art piece above it.

Lindsay Belle grinned when she saw Anabelle. The little girl's thin auburn ponytail bobbed around atop her head.

"She wants to play in here all the time." Ainslee sat down on the couch and picked up Lindsay Belle, but the baby arched her back and squealed again. Ainslee nodded at the table. "Why didn't anyone tell me this thing was a really stupid idea?"

Anabelle pursed her lips together. She'd known all along that the minimalist coffee table was going to be a problem with a toddler, but Ainslee wouldn't have believed her back then.

Ainslee let out a groan as Lindsay Belle arched her back again.

"I'll do the shoes when we go out," Anabelle said. "You should go on to work."

"Thanks." Ainslee sounded relieved. "The stroller's in the garage. Lindsay Belle could use the fresh air."

"I could too," Anabelle said. "We'll have fun."

Ainslee put the shoes on the coffee table and stood, slinging the baby to her hip. "Her lunch is in the fridge, and there's sandwich stuff for you."

Anabelle nodded as her daughter relinquished her granddaughter. "Try not to have too much fun." Ainslee smiled.

"You know me; I won't be able to help myself." Anabelle hugged her granddaughter, forgetting that her reading glasses were around her neck; Lindsay Belle had them nearly to her mouth before Anabelle grabbed them.

Ainslee scurried around, stepping over blocks and balls and teething toys, grabbing her teal scarf off a dining room chair, her boots from the entryway, and her black blazer from where it had fallen off a hanger looped through a slat of the open staircase. Anabelle tried not to gloat. The house, thank goodness, was no longer the immaculate showpiece it had once been.

Ainslee kissed Lindsay Belle on the cheek and waved good-bye.

"Bye-bye!" Lindsay Belle made a fist and opened and closed her fingers, toward herself.

"Thanks, Mother!" Ainslee called out from the kitchen just before the door slammed. A moment of silence fell over the house.

And then Lindsay Belle began to cry. Big crocodile tears formed in her pale blue eyes and then rolled down her cheeks. "Mama," she wailed.

"She'll be back," Anabelle cooed. "She has to work, and then she'll be home. We'll have fun together while she's gone."

Anabelle gathered up a collection of blocks by kicking them together with her foot and then sank down to the floor, balancing Lindsay Belle as she did. "Let's play," she said, handing a red block to her granddaughter.

The baby shook her head, sending her little ponytail bobbing around again.

Anabelle placed a blue block on top of the red, and Lindsay Belle smacked her hand against them.

"How about a walk?" Anabelle said, struggling to her feet with the baby in her arms.

Lindsay Belle smiled at Anabelle and clapped.

"Yes." Anabelle stood up straight. "But we have to put your shoes on."

Lindsay Belle's lower lip jutted out.

Anabelle's cell phone began to jingle in her jacket pocket.

Elena. Maybe she had more information about the situation at Hope Haven.

The women chatted for a minute. Elena had heard what was going on from Cesar but that was all. Anabelle filled her in with what she knew.

"Actually, I was calling to see if you and Lindsay Belle wanted to go to the park."

"*Ooh*, a play date," Anabelle said, squeezing Lindsay Belle. The little girl clapped her hands together. "That sounds great." Playing with Izzy would be the distraction she needed.

Elena and Anabelle decided to meet in fifteen minutes, and Anabelle knew Elena would probably be there in ten. The woman was never late.

Anabelle stocked Lindsay Belle's bag with diapers, a container of cereal, a bottle, and an extra set of clothes. Then she put on the little girl's shoes, coat, and hat. "Bye-bye!" Lindsay Belle said.

Anabelle was delighted at the words her granddaughter already knew. "That's right, sweetie. We're going to see Izzy at the park!" Anabelle slung the diaper bag over one arm and picked up Lindsay Belle with the other.

Anabelle headed through the kitchen and into the garage, poking the opener for the overhead door and then pushing the stroller with one hand in a curvy line out to her car. She was grateful she had a baby safety seat now. She strapped Lindsay Belle in and then wrestled the stroller into the trunk, feeling like she'd had a workout by the time she'd fastened her own seat belt and started the engine.

Ten minutes later they were at the park. Izzy came running from the swings toward them, her pink fleece jacket unbuttoned and billowing around her, her long curly hair in corkscrew pigtails flying around her head. Elena walked after her granddaughter, her long legs covering the distance quickly. The morning sun was doing its best to chase away the spring chill. Tulips were nearly ready to bloom in the flower beds on the other side of the playground and the sweeping lawn of the park was beginning to green.

Anabelle lifted Lindsay Belle out of her car seat.

"Hiya!" Izzy called and then came to an abrupt stop, gasping to catch her breath.

Lindsay Belle squealed in delight at the sight of the older girl.

Elena lifted the stroller from the trunk, Izzy held the diaper bag, and then Anabelle lowered Lindsay Belle into the stroller. By the time they reached the play structure, Lindsay Belle was whimpering to get out and walk. Anabelle lifted her to the ground and then kept hold of her hand, directing her to the toddlers' section. Izzy quickly took her other hand, and Lindsay Belle let go of her grandmother and toddled along with her little friend. Anabelle stepped back, watching the two head for the kiddie structure. Lindsay Belle kept looking at Izzy and smiling.

"Isn't that cute?" Elena said, pushing the stroller out of the way and moving the diaper bag to the seat so the whole contraption wouldn't topple over.

"Izzy's a natural," Anabelle said.

Elena chuckled. "She'll be babysitting in no time."

Izzy had an arm around Lindsay Belle now, guiding her forward. The little girl plopped back on her padded bottom, and Izzy gently helped her up; then the baby toppled over onto Izzy, and they both went down, giggling as they did. Together the girls stood and then made their way over the little bridge that led to the slide. No part of the structure was more than a couple of inches off the ground and had been perfectly designed for toddlers.

The two women sat down on the bench adjacent to the playground and watched their granddaughters.

"I talked with Cesar about the advisory committee," Elena said. "I'm going to call Dr. Hamilton when I get home."

"Oh good," Anabelle said. Having Elena on board would contribute both energy and intelligence to the committee.

"Cesar said he'd heard that departments were being closed— not just one. Is that what you heard?"

Anabelle shook her head. "Dr. Hamilton said that just the new Holistic Cardiac Program was cut. He said McGarry seemed concerned about the overall health of the hospital, but Varner seemed confident we'd carry on."

Elena tapped her foot. "I'm more apt to trust McGarry on this."

"But it's unbelievable that the hospital could be in trouble again, after what we've already gone through," Anabelle said.

Elena agreed. "Unbelievable and frustrating."

Lindsay Belle began to toddle toward them; Anabelle stood, ready for her granddaughter, when the little girl took a wide turn. Two bigger boys were on the big-kid swings across the park and calling back and forth to each other. Lindsay Belle began to toddle faster, heading toward the cement curb around the playground.

"Wait!" Izzy yelled, coming around the side of the toddler play structure.

"I'll get her," Anabelle said, striding toward her granddaughter. Lindsay Belle was moving pretty quickly for a baby that hadn't been walking long.

Izzy began to run, and she hadn't seemed to hear Anabelle. Lindsay Belle turned and started to laugh, as if she thought it was a game. Just as Izzy reached her, Lindsay Belle plopped down on the cement curb and Izzy swerved to miss her, tripping and then falling onto the little girl.

Anabelle lunged toward the children with Elena right behind her. Lindsay Belle screamed as Izzy rolled off her. Already the older girl was saying, "Are you all right?"

Anabelle scooped Lindsay Belle up. There was blood on her cheek. She swiped at it quickly but couldn't see a wound.

"Is she okay?" Elena asked.

Lindsay Belle arched her back as she screamed. Anabelle checked the back of her head but couldn't see a cut.

"Buela?" Izzy was behind both of them. "Buela," she said again. "Look."

Both women turned around. Izzy held her hand. It was covered with blood. Elena stooped down. "Sweetie," she said.

Blood gushed from Izzy's lower lip.

Elena stepped out into the hall of the Emergency Room and tried Rafael on his cell phone one last time. She had a medical power of attorney form he had signed that she always kept in her purse, giving her permission to approve medical treatment for Izzy. He'd gone off to Springfield with a bandmate to look at a new sound system.

The call went into voice mail for the fourth time, and Elena hit End. There was no reason to tell him one more time that they were in the ER, that Izzy was okay but probably needed stitches.

Elena stepped back into the cubicle. Izzy held an icepack against her lip, her big gray eyes dry now. They'd smarted with tears at the park, but she'd been amazingly calm, more worried about Lindsay Belle than herself. "You're doing so well," Elena said, putting her arm around her granddaughter.

"Is Daddy coming?" Her words were muffled behind the ice.

Elena shook her head. "I still couldn't reach him. He is going to be so surprised when he gets my messages." She smiled at her granddaughter, trying to be positive. "And he's going to be so proud of how brave you've been."

"When's the doctor going to get here?" She sounded a bit forlorn.

"Soon," Elena said, caressing the girl's hair. They'd been in the ER for half an hour. She wondered if Anabelle and Lindsay Belle were still in the waiting room or if they'd given up and gone home.

Elena sat down in the chair beside the bed, her hand on Izzy's leg. A minute later Dr. Weller walked in. His smile and goofy disposition, accentuated by his lanky build, put Izzy at ease.

"How about if you hand over the ice and let me take a look," the doctor said.

Izzy inched the pack away from her lip. It was swollen and the gash was wide. The ER nurse had already cleaned the wound, removing the gravel and dirt. Poor Izzy had been brave, but Elena knew it hurt.

The doctor slipped gloves onto his hands and tipped her head, taking a closer look. As a mom, and a nurse, Elena was sure Izzy needed stitches. She'd had quite a run of ER visits with Rafael when he was a boy: a slash on his thigh from a barbed wire fence, a cut on the back of his head from falling off the top of the swing set and landing on a rock that he had thrown onto the lawn, a cut on his arm from an encounter with his skate boarding ramp. It had been one thing after another.

"This definitely needs to be closed up," Dr. Weller said, letting go of Izzy's chin. He turned toward the supply cabinet and opened the top drawer. Elena expected him to pull out a suture and needle, but instead he had a tube in his hand. "Have you used super glue before?" he asked Izzy.

"I'm not allowed," she said, seriously.

"Of course not." He chuckled. "Thankfully I am. This is a super glue for skin. It means you don't have to have stitches."

Of course. A wave of relief passed through Elena. No straight-jacket. No holding Izzy down. No keeping her from screaming while the doctor stitched just below her mouth. Or maybe they would have had to sedate her.

"It will just take a minute," the doctor said.

He directed Izzy to lie back on the table, and Elena stood and held both of her hands and whispered encouraging words to her.

"I'll hold the skin in place," Dr. Weller said. "And then I'll squirt."

Izzy smiled.

"Here's the deal," the doc said. "You smile one last time and then no more smiling, okay? Not until I'm done. If you can do that, your grandma will—what do you like? Candy? Soda?"

"Ice cream!" Izzy said.

"Okay. She'll take you out for ice cream."

"Can Lindsay Belle come too?" Izzy asked.

"We'll see," Elena answered. Perhaps the little one was home taking a nap by now.

The doctor worked quickly and in no time the job was done.

"Will she need to see a plastic surgeon?" Elena asked, helping Izzy to sit back up.

Dr. Weller pulled off his gloves. "There's actually less scar-ing with this. It will hardly be noticeable. I don't think a plastic surgeon could have done any better." He extended his hand to Izzy, and she shook it sweetly and then said a polite thank-you.

As Izzy and Elena waited for the nurse to come in with instructions on keeping the wound clean, Izzy started picking out letters around the room. "E," she said pointing at the sign above the door. "X-I-T."

"That's great," Elena said. "How about over here?" She pointed to the sign by the oxygen line.

"O-X-Y—"

The nurse waltzed in. "Oh, someone's learning her letters," she said and then grinned. She pointed to her scrub top that looked like a colorful version of alphabet soup, and then zeroed in on the letter *C*.

Izzy put her hand up to her eyes.

"Careful, Iz," Elena said, "don't bump your lip."

"How about this one?" The nurse pointed to an *N*. Izzy shook her head.

"Oh, come on," the nurse said. "I heard you reciting those other letters."

Izzy peeked out from behind her fingers but wouldn't respond. The nurse sighed. "I tried," she said as she turned to Elena and began to explain how to care for the wound. As Elena listened, she wondered at Izzy's sudden attack of shyness. It wasn't like her.

Anabelle sat in the cafeteria with Lindsay Belle, feeding her bits of steamed vegetables. The little girl yawned and rubbed her eyes. It was definitely nap time, but Anabelle didn't want to leave until Elena and Izzy were done.

"Anabelle?"

She turned, expecting Elena, but it was Candace, standing with a tray of food. "What are you doing here?"

Anabelle motioned for her friend to join them and then explained what had happened with Izzy at the park.

"Oh dear," Candace said, dipping her spoon into her minestrone soup. "How's Elena holding up?"

"Well, you know. She's a tower of strength. But it was pretty unnerving." Anabelle handed Lindsay Belle a piece of steamed carrot. She couldn't imagine if it had been Lindsay Belle injured. Just that first second of thinking that Lindsay Belle was bleeding had about undone her. Not that she was thankful it was Izzy who had been hurt, but she hoped that, by the time Lindsay Belle was six, she would be able to react as calmly as Elena had.

"How are things around here today?" Anabelle asked. She'd been tempted to go up to the Cardiac Care Unit and see if anyone was gossiping about James's being laid off but had refrained.

"There are rumors and more rumors," Candace said. "The latest being that they're going to close the Birthing Unit."

"They wouldn't do that," Anabelle said. "That would be ridiculous."

"That's what I said." Candace took a spoonful of soup. "But it isn't a big moneymaker."

Anabelle gave Lindsay Belle another bite of carrot. *It seems like that's what health care's coming down to—money,* she thought. *Sure, a hospital's a business, but health isn't a commodity like coffee or—*

Lindsay Belle sputtered, and orange mush came flying out of her mouth. Anabelle grabbed a napkin and swiped it across her granddaughter's face.

Many of the other nurses, including Candace, didn't have the option of retiring or depending on a husband like Anabelle did. Relocating at this time would be a huge challenge for both Candace and her kids. Anabelle quickly told her friend what Dr. Hamilton had said, that only the one program had been targeted. Candace didn't seem entirely convinced.

Lindsay Belle laughed and another piece of carrot flew, landing on her arm. Anabelle wiped it up with a second napkin. She smiled at her granddaughter, but inside she was thinking of James again. What would his family do?

Lindsay Belle was grinning at Candace now and bobbing her head around, the little ponytail on top of her head fanned out like a palm tree atop a tropical island.

"She's adorable," Candace said. "And to think she's almost one. How did that happen so soon?"

Anabelle smiled, remembering Lindsay Belle's birth. Candace had been there too, giving Ainslee the best care available. "First the kids grow up in a flash and then the grandkids." Anabelle tried to laugh but it came out a little hollow.

"You're telling me," Candace said. "It seems like life has been on hyper speed since Brooke started middle school. Here she is, already a teenager...." Her voice trailed off and Anabelle followed her gaze.

Heath Carlson, wearing blue scrubs, headed toward them. It looked as if he was picking up a Saturday shift as well.

"Hi," Candace called out, scooting toward the wall. "I was afraid you weren't going to be able to get away."

"Me too." It was obvious the two had hoped to meet for lunch. Heath sat down and quickly said hello to Anabelle and Lindsay Belle.

"We should be on our way," Anabelle said as she started to gather up Lindsay Belle's dish, sippy cup, and container of cereal. Neither Candace nor Heath protested. Once she had the diaper bag over her shoulder and the baby in her arms, she turned to the couple and said, "See you soon."

They smiled and said good-bye, but by the time Anabelle was across the cafeteria and stole a backward look, the two were deep in conversation, still sitting side by side, looking intently into each other's eyes.

Chapter Four

"THANK YOU FOR STICKING AROUND," ELENA SAID to Anabelle, as they walked toward their cars, each carrying her granddaughter. Lindsay Belle was asleep in Anabelle's arms and Izzy's head was nodding. The poor thing had to be exhausted from her ordeal. "We were going to stop for ice cream, but I think we'll wait for that," Elena added.

"Are you sure you don't want me to follow you home?" Anabelle asked.

"Positive," Elena said. "We're doing fine. Izzy will sleep." She smiled. "And I might too."

By the time she reached the house, Izzy was asleep. Elena eased her out of her booster seat, careful not to bump the little girl's lip, and lifted her into her arms. Without waking, Izzy wrapped her legs around Elena's waist. As she reached the back door, she heard a car stop at the front of the house and by the time she was ready to head down the hall, the doorbell rang.

She switched directions, figuring if she didn't answer the door whoever was there might keep ringing. When she eased it open, there was Sarah, Izzy's mother, wearing an old gray sweatshirt that matched her eyes—and Izzy's.

"I was in the neighborhood," she said. "And thought I'd stop by."

Izzy stirred a little and flopped her head to Elena's other shoulder, presenting her face toward her mother.

"What happened?" Sarah gasped.

"She's fine," Elena said, her voice a whisper, trying to downplay the wound and the bruising that was turning a dark purple. "Just a little playground accident."

"It looks awful!" Sarah's pitch was high and her voice loud.

"*Shh.*" Elena couldn't help herself. She didn't want Izzy to wake up to her mother overreacting. And it didn't look that bad—swollen, sure, and discolored—but not nearly as bad as if she'd had stitches. "Come on in," Elena said. "I'm going to put her down for a nap, and I'll be right back."

But Izzy woke up when Elena eased her onto her bed and refused to nap. "I'm fine," she said to Elena. "I'm not tired at all."

In a minute Sarah was in the hallway. "I heard voices," she said.

"Is that you?" Izzy asked, scrambling off the bed. "Is it Sunday?"

"No, silly," Elena said. "It's still Saturday."

Izzy giggled as she headed toward the hall. "I thought maybe Mommy had come to go to church with us."

Sarah met Izzy in the doorway and gave her a hug; the woman's blonde hair fell against her daughter's dark curls. "Sorry about your boo-boo."

Izzy touched her lip cautiously and then shrugged. "Are you going to church tomorrow?" The little girl led her mother toward the living room.

"Not tomorrow," Sarah answered. "I have to work." She was employed in the cafeteria at Hope Haven and needed to take every shift she could get.

"How about some lunch?" Elena asked. "Tomato soup? Grilled cheese sandwiches?" Izzy could sip the soup through a straw.

"Okay," Izzy answered.

"Thanks," Sarah said, brushing a stray strand of hair away from her face.

Elena left the two in the living room with a stack of books and headed into her kitchen, to the pantry. By the time she had the soup started and the sandwiches frying in the pan, Izzy was at her side.

"Buela," she said. "Maybe I should take a nap after all." She looked up and rubbed her eyes. Sarah stood in the doorway.

Elena kneeled beside her granddaughter. "What's the matter, sweetie?"

"My head hurts."

Elena put her arm around Izzy. "Maybe you're hungry."

The little girl shrugged.

"Let's have lunch."

Izzy had been given a dose of children's pain reliever at the hospital, and it would be another couple of hours before Elena could give her more.

Sarah and Izzy helped set the table and then they all sat down. Elena said a blessing, and they began to eat, but Izzy only picked at her food. After a few minutes she excused herself to go lie down, giving Sarah a quick hug on her way.

"She doesn't have a concussion does she?" Sarah asked after Izzy headed down the hall.

"No. They checked for that." Elena felt amused at Sarah's question. "But she could still have a headache from the fall. She landed pretty hard."

Sarah looked concerned but didn't say anything more. Elena wondered if she was blaming her for the accident, thinking she hadn't watched Izzy carefully enough, but she chased that thought away. Accidents happened.

Sarah thanked Elena for lunch and then left a few minutes later, and Elena decided to clean up later and check on Izzy. The little girl was fast asleep. Elena curled up beside her granddaughter, breathing in the little girl's sweet scent as she guided a strand of long wavy hair away from her face. Izzy stirred a little and scooted toward Elena, fitting her body against her grandmother's. Elena wrapped her arm around the little girl and breathed a sigh of relief. Thank goodness the injury hadn't been worse.

Izzy's head still hurt a little after her nap but by the next morning, as she got ready for Sunday school, she declared that the headache was gone. She wore her green princess dress, a white sweater, and her white dress shoes with the slick bottoms that Elena was constantly reminding her not to run in. Her mouth was even more swollen than the day before and more discolored, but Izzy didn't seem self-conscious about her wound.

As Elena drove to church, the wind picked up and dark clouds scudded in from the east.

"Why do we need spring showers when we already have April flowers?" Izzy gazed out the window at the daffodils and tulips bending in the breeze.

"It might not rain," Elena answered.

"Really?" Izzy sounded like a teenager. "'Cause that's what it looks like to me."

"You're probably right." Elena sighed. Two days of sunshine and then back to the rain. What else did she expect in early spring in Illinois?

After she checked Izzy into her Sunday school class, Izzy carefully explained to the teacher what had happened. Izzy said matter-of-factly that she'd had a playground accident and had to go to the hospital. The teacher patted her shoulder and that was all. Elena was pleased that the teacher had handled the situation with such little drama, but when she picked up Izzy after class, she was surprised to find her granddaughter quiet and withdrawn. They followed her friend Mateo, flanked by both his parents, down the hall. When the little boy turned around and smiled at Izzy as he skipped along, she frowned in return. Elena pulled her aside and asked what was going on, but Izzy stared at her shoes.

"Did Mateo tease you about your lip?"

Izzy shook her head.

"Sweetie, you need to be polite to people." They continued walking down the hall, now at a distance from Mateo and his parents. It wasn't like Izzy to be rude or moody.

In the fellowship hall, Elena asked if Izzy wanted a cookie or muffin. She politely said, "No, thank you," and then backed up against the wall, watching the other children and adults. Elena poured herself a cup of coffee, surprised that Izzy was feeling self-conscious, sure something must have happened during Sunday school.

Ten minutes later, they settled into a pew in the middle of the church. Light streamed in from the stained-glass windows that lined the walls of the church. Christ on the cross with His mother Mary weeping below was to Elena's right. To her left was a benevolent angel gazing at the empty grave, and beyond that was Christ, in a red robe, knocking on a wooden door, a halo around His head and a purple sky above Him. Izzy usually stared at the windows every Sunday, taking in the story of each, but today she cuddled next to Elena. As the singing began she wiggled closer, and Elena decided she was tired. Yesterday had worn her out. She thought her granddaughter might fall asleep, but when the children were excused for children's church, Izzy was ready to go.

Elena enjoyed the service, listening intently to the teaching. It was about living in right relationships with both God and others. She thought of Sarah and the healing that had taken place in her life. She then thought of Rafael and how it was evident, in little ways, that he was learning to forgive Sarah. He wasn't as hostile to her as he used to be. Elena was thankful that her son was a devoted father to Izzy and would do anything for his little girl. And she'd been impressed the night before when he'd been so gracious to her about Izzy's hurting herself. He'd been concerned and loving to his daughter and then joked with Elena that Izzy took after him, saying she was a regular chip off the old block. That had made Cesar laugh and he joked with Izzy that if her dad was right, that meant she'd have quite a few more trips to the ER before she grew up.

Cesar. How Elena wished he was sitting beside her. *Please, Lord, do whatever it takes to bring him to You*, she prayed.

As the last song ended, she slipped out of the pew and out the back of the church, heading down the stairs to the large classroom where they held children's church. If Izzy was feeling overwhelmed, it would be better to get her outside before the crowd of people began milling around, but when she reached the room full of kids, Izzy was smiling as she colored at a table with Mateo. And when Elena told her it was time to leave, Izzy asked if she could stay a couple of more minutes.

Elena agreed and gathered her granddaughter's sweater from the hook across the room. Then she sat down carefully in a little chair at the shortened table and began tucking her A-line dress around her legs.

Izzy held up her coloring sheet and pointed to the words at the bottom. "Want to hear our verse for the day?"

Elena nodded.

Izzy turned the paper around so she could read it. "'Delight yourself in the Lord, and He will give you the desires of your heart,'" she read.

"Oh, Izzy," Elena said, "what a wonderful verse, and what great reading. Do you know what *desire* means?"

"My teacher said it means 'wants.'" The little girl beamed and then winced. Clearly smiling was painful. She said good-bye to Mateo as his parents arrived, and, together, grandmother and granddaughter walked out to the parking lot.

As Elena fastened her into her booster seat, Izzy said, "Buela, do you want to know why I was sad after Sunday school?"

Elena looked in the rearview mirror. "Yes, of course."

Izzy let out a little sigh. "Well, all the other kids have parents that drop them off and pick them up. I was feeling bad that Mommy couldn't come today and that Daddy doesn't come at all."

Elena started the car. "What happened during children's church that made you not feel as sad?"

"The verse."

Elena turned around and looked over the top of the headrest.

"God knows what my heart wants, right?" Izzy had both hands on the padded bar of her booster seat. "And He'll give it to me."

Elena hesitated for a moment and then said, "Sweetie, what exactly does your heart want?" A few months ago it had been that her parents would get back together. Was she hoping for that again? "Izzy?"

Finally the little girl said, "I can't say."

Elena backed out of the parking space, trying to think of how to talk with her granddaughter about balancing faith and reality. As she pulled onto the street, she said, "Izzy, prayer isn't like a wish. Telling someone what you prayed for doesn't have any bearing on whether your prayer is answered or not. The answer is up to God."

"I know." Izzy's voice was light and carefree. "And God cares about what I want, right?"

"Sure," Elena said. "But what we want isn't always what's best—we have to leave that up to God. And if there are other people involved—" She was ready to launch into a talk about free will when Izzy started waving.

"Look! There's Mateo!"

The boy was walking hand in hand with his parents, but he dropped his father's hand to wave at Izzy. He was all smiles—and so were his mom and dad.

Chapter Five

ONDAY MORNING, JAMES SAT AT HIS DESK IN his home office and talked on the phone with Leila Hargrave. She confirmed he was out of a job and suggested he come in for the financial settlement from the early termination of his contract as soon as possible.

"Believe me, you will be the next hired, but it might take at least a few weeks, possibly months. I wouldn't blame you if you looked for something else in the meantime, just in case," Leila said.

He agreed that was the prudent thing to do. Next he called the hospital in Princeton and asked for the nursing administrator. He was transferred to her voice mail, but before he could leave a message, a recording came on saying there was a hiring freeze. James left a message anyway, saying he would send in a résumé and asked the supervisor to contact him.

Next he found the Web site of Tender Loving Health Care. No job openings were listed, but there were instructions to call about current listings. The agency had branches in Princeton, Peoria, and Deerford. He could travel to Princeton for work but Peoria, at over an hour away, was out of the question. That would be two additional hours a day that he would be away from Fern and the boys.

James picked up the phone and dialed the number. It rang and rang and just as he anticipated that call going into voice mail too, the line clicked and a harried voice said, "Hello, Tender Loving Health Care. Missy speaking."

"Hello, Missy. My name is James Bell. I'm a registered nurse, and I'm calling to inquire about available jobs," James said.

"I'm in the middle of a . . . crisis. Could you come down to the office in about an hour?" Before James finished saying he could, she said, "See you then. 'Bye."

He heard Fern's walker in the hallway, and moments later she stood in the doorway, asking, "What did you find out?"

He quickly filled her in on what he'd learned in the last few minutes, then said, "The home health place in town is interested in talking with me." He hoped his voice sounded optimistic. He knew Fern was trying to put on a brave front, but she seemed down.

She made her way into the room and sat down on the love seat, pushing the walker to the side. Her cat, Sapphire, jumped up beside her. "I can help you target your résumé for home health."

"Thanks," he said, turning back to the computer and going into the word processor program to open the file. Then he stepped away, and Fern made her way to the office chair. She tweaked a few words. "We should emphasize the wide range of patients you've cared for over the years. Accident victims. Stroke patients. People with cancer. Cardiac patients. The kind of people who most need home health . . ." She did a little more typing, and James read the changes over her shoulder. They were perfect. It was too bad he didn't have actual home health experience, but the truth was that he didn't.

"Thanks," he said to Fern. "It's ready to go."

She clicked Print as James scanned the document again. At the bottom of the page, medic in the US Army was listed. That was how his career had started.

He looked down at his sweatshirt and jeans. He needed to go change, to look presentable. He placed his hands on Fern's shoulders. "It will work out."

Fern nodded and spun around in the chair toward him.

He placed his hands on her shoulders again. "God has proven He is faithful, over and over."

She nodded again. James touched his forehead to hers.

"Thanks," she whispered.

He lifted his head and gazed intently into her eyes. "For?"

"Taking such good care of all of us."

What she didn't understand was that her presence was what motivated him. He couldn't imagine his life without her. She was the reason he worked as hard as he did. She was the reason he kept moving forward.

Though he didn't want to, he left her and went to their bedroom to change clothes and then go over to the home health place.

An hour later, he was still waiting in the outer office of Tender Loving Health Care staring at his khaki trousers. Missy, the office manager and the person he had spoken to on the phone, had greeted him quickly and said she would be with him as soon as possible. There was a receptionist's desk but no receptionist.

James decided to wait another ten minutes. He picked up the news magazine on the chair beside him, again, and flipped through it, searching for anything he might have missed the first two times through it. The magazine was the only reading material in the office. He stopped at a small article about the job sector toward the back. The subtitle read: "Companies not looking to hire jobless." James cringed as he read that some HR companies were tossing the résumés of those not currently employed.

"Come on in." The woman stood in the doorway to her office, looking even more harried than she had an hour and ten minutes ago and much more than she'd sounded on the phone. "Things aren't usually so crazy around here." She pushed her long dark hair away from her round face. "We have a new client." She chuckled. "Anyway. So you're an LPN?"

"RN," James answered.

"Oh. I thought you said LPN on the phone."

He shook his head.

"Sorry," she said, then frowned. "I've been getting a lot of things wrong today." The woman looked about forty years old and had an open, sweet smile even though she was clearly agitated. She invited him into her office and then motioned for him to take a seat at a small table. She sat across from him.

James took the opportunity to slide his résumé across the tabletop.

The woman took it in her hand. "I hate to say this." She held it up. "But I have a whole stack of these. The economy has brought every RN out of the woodwork."

James's heart sank, and he hurried to explain what had happened at the hospital that led to him losing his job, hoping she could read between the lines that he was surprised to find himself looking for a job. "Feel free to call Dr. Hamilton to corroborate my situation or the HR department or Albert Varner himself. They'll verify what happened and vouch for my experience."

The woman had her reading glasses on now and was scanning the résumé. "Oh, I can see you have a lot of experience." She peered over the top of her lenses. "Any tech skills?"

"As in health care informatics technology?"

She nodded.

"No." He wished he could say yes.

"Too bad. We need to convert all of our charting. I'm applying for a government grant to do it." She stood. "I would love to hire you if"—her phone began to ring—"I had an opening." She held up her index finger. "Hold on just a moment. I'd better take this call."

She sat down at her desk and swung around in her office chair, her back to James. After saying hello, she listened for several minutes and finally said, "I understand. I'll have another assignment for you in a day or two."

After hanging up the phone, she picked up James's résumé again. "Did I see a reference to military experience on here?"

"Yes, ma'am."

She smiled. "Desert Storm."

He nodded, feeling hopeful for the first time all morning.

"I'll keep that in mind," she said.

A moment later, she walked him to the door. As she started to extend her hand for him to shake in farewell, her phone rang again. With a wry, nettled expression she turned and disappeared back into her office.

As James stepped out into the overcast spring morning, he couldn't help but sigh. "Lord," he prayed again, "I wonder what You have planned for me."

Instead of heading home, he pulled his van into a space in the front lot of Hope Haven, since he couldn't park in the back employee lot anymore. As he walked toward the hospital, the sun peeked out from behind a cloud. Daffodils bobbed and bowed in full-blown splendor in the front flower beds, the tulips looked ready to pop open any day, and he noted how welcoming the brick building appeared. Instead of going in the front door, he stepped around to the side of the building and peered at the stained-glass window of the chapel. The royal colors brightened as the clouds parted for the sun, causing the emerald green and royal blue geometric shapes to shimmer in the morning light.

"James!" Eddie Blaine walked toward him, wearing coveralls and a stocking cap and carrying a push broom in his hands. "How come you're not working today?"

James hoped Eddie didn't see him grimace. There was no reason not to be concise. "I'm headed to the HR department. I was let go on Friday."

Eddie stumbled a little and almost dropped the broom. "Say what?"

"It's true," James said. "The hospital ended up cutting the new Holistic Cardiac Program."

"But why didn't they give you another job?"

"There aren't any other jobs right now."

"But you'll be hired back, right?" Eddie leaned against the broom handle.

James tried to smile. "I hope so."

The custodian shook his head. "Unbelievable," he muttered, and then, "Well, best of luck."

James walked back to the front door and through the lobby of the hospital. There were a few visitors sitting in the comfy chairs but no one he knew. He took the first right and headed down the hall toward HR.

Leila Hargrave greeted him in her usual cool manner and directed him into her office, closing the door behind her. He towered above her even though she wore pumps.

"Frankly, I'm really embarrassed by all of this," the nursing supervisor said, scooting her chair toward her desk. "Legally, the hospital has the power to terminate your contract. Ethically, it's inconceivable for the administration to let a nurse go who has worked here for twenty years." She shook her head and then patted her signature gray bun that was nestled at the nape of her neck, as if to make sure it was still in place.

James felt as if he needed to comfort her. "Things will work out," he said.

Leila nodded. "I know they will." She let out a sigh. "Probably the larger question is, 'Will things work out for the hospital?'" She pulled a file from her side drawer and then made eye contact with James. "Don't tell anyone I said that."

"Is it that bad?" James had been hoping that McGarry had been overreacting about the hospital's being in a bad position—again.

"Yes and no," she answered. "Sure, things are tight but if the administration keeps making knee-jerk—" She slapped her hand over her mouth. "Okay, I'm going to stop now." She opened the file and divided the stack of papers in two. "Here's your copy." She handed the document to him and continued speaking. "We'll freeze your retirement account so when—or if—you come back, it will pick right back up again." She flipped the page of her packet. "As far as insurance . . ."

This was the biggie.

"COBRA will be available to you."

"When does the insurance we have now end?"

"You're paid up through the end of April."

James nodded. *Yikes. With Fern's preexisting condition, it will be impossible to find another company that will accept her. I was a fool to take the contract job.* But then he recalled that the hospital had offered him the same health insurance they'd had for years, and it had never occurred to him that the Holistic Cardiac Program would be cut. "How much will COBRA cost a month?"

Leila shook her head. "You'll have to contact them. I can't even give you an estimate."

"But a lot, right?"

She nodded solemnly.

James had read recently that Americans spent 20 percent of everything they made on health care. He thought about Fern. The money they spent on her was definitely worth it. Sure, life was hard, but she had a relatively good quality of life. What would their family be like without her? Even twenty years ago, she would have been completely bedridden by now with her MS.

But without insurance, the cost of her care would completely break the family's finances within a few months.

Next, Leila had James fill out paperwork to be put on a list of nurses approved to work at Hope Haven in case they needed someone to pick up extra shifts when the hospital was shorthanded.

"Please," Leila continued, "put me down as a reference on your résumé. I want to say that there will be an opening here before the month is over and as soon as one appears, I will call you. But I'm beginning to fear that the hospital may even put a freeze on hiring within a few days."

James felt as if the wind had been kicked out of him. "P-p-pardon?" he stammered.

"We're looking at a hiring freeze. That's the next piece of bad news in all of this."

James managed to stand and extend his hand to her. "Th-th-ank you." He was aware that he was still stammering, something he hardly ever did anymore.

Leila shook his hand. "This is simply a matter of you being in the wrong place at the wrong time. It's as simple as that."

James knew Leila was right, but it didn't make her words any more comforting.

Monday after work, Candace sat at the kitchen table reading the *Deerford Dispatch* while her mother played the baby grand piano in the living room and Brooke and Howie focused on their homework.

"Mommy," Howie said, "what's five plus seven?"

"Sweetie," she said gently, "it's your homework. You figure it out."

He stared off into space for a minute, his lips moving.

Candace was in the middle of an article on Hope Haven. CEO Albert Varner was quoted as saying the financing for the Holistic Cardiac Program didn't come through and that was why it wouldn't be implemented. There was no mention of cutting the Birthing Unit.

"Twelve!" Howie shouted.

Brooke groaned. "Quiet! I'm trying to finish my social studies so I can go on the hike."

"What's twelve?" Candace whispered.

"Five plus seven," Howie answered and then beamed, his green eyes dancing. She patted his head, her hand resting on his thick hair for a moment. Maybe they needed to dig out the addition flash cards she bought a couple of months ago. First grade was almost over, and Howie was still struggling with his simple addition.

Candace turned her attention back to the article. At the bottom, in a sidebar, was a notice about the advisory committee of medical professionals that was being formed. She'd volunteered to be on the committee at work today, and the first meeting was tonight . . . at seven thirty, according to the paper.

Heath had volunteered to serve on the advisory committee too and offered to give her a ride after he took her and the kids, if they finished their homework, on a short hike and picnic at Bass Lake. The afternoon turned out to be so nice that they both thought it would be great to soak up some of the sunshine.

It was a lot to fit into the late afternoon and evening, but it was worth it to get some fresh air. Rain was predicted again for the next day.

She folded the newspaper. Her mother had agreed to watch the kids that night and any other nights the committee met, if she could, because they both felt it was important for Candace to be involved in what was going on at the hospital. Her mother had her retirement pension and contributed to running their home, but they all depended on Candace's job at Hope Haven.

"Mom, what's a malpractice suit?" Brooke asked, tapping the eraser of her pencil on the tabletop.

"What's the topic?"

"Health care and what it's going to look like for our generation. Our teacher said it's important."

Candace smiled. The seventh grade at Deerford Middle School was dealing with contemporary issues, which was fine with her, as long as they were concentrating on the basics of social studies too. "A malpractice suit is when a patient sues a doctor, or other medical provider, for doing something wrong in the care of the patient."

"Like?"

"Well, let's say we have a patient in the hospital who has been in labor for thirty-six hours and the baby is breech and the heart monitor shows it's in distress. If the doctor didn't order a C-section and something happened to the mother or the baby, the patient could sue. They'd hire a lawyer, and it would go through the court system."

"Oh." Brooke tapped her pencil a few more times. "So that's one of the reasons health care costs are so high?"

"That's exactly right," Candace nodded with pride and Brooke began writing.

It was also one of the reasons other small hospitals had closed their obstetrics wards. A huge malpractice suit could totally wipe out a place like Hope Haven. Candace folded the paper. Having been the target of a spurious malpractice suit not too long ago, Candace didn't want to think about that eventuality. "Are you two almost done with your homework? I'm going to make sandwiches, and Heath will be here in a few minutes."

"Done!" Howie jumped from his chair.

Candace reached for his worksheet. "Let me check."

He had several wrong answers, and she marked those mistakes and slid it back to his place. "Good effort. But redo these," she said.

Howie groaned as he climbed back on his chair.

Forty-five minutes later, they strolled down the pathway along the lake with Howie running ahead and Brooke skipping after him, her curls bouncing up and down on her back.

"I just can't believe we're worried about the state of the hospital again so soon," Candace said.

"Let's just take it a step at a time," Heath said calmly. "We should find out more tonight, but remember just because the hospital can't sustain a new program doesn't mean Hope Haven is in a bad situation again."

Candace nodded, but she couldn't help thinking of the worst-case scenario. A fish jumped in the lake and the breeze picked up a little, playing with the branches of the weeping willows on the other side of the path. Howie turned back toward Candace and Heath and pointed to a hawk circling above the tree line.

Heath gave him a thumbs-up and called out, "Attaboy!" Then he lifted the binoculars around his neck and watched the bird for a moment. "Want to look?" he asked Candace.

She took the binoculars from him. She could see the hawk's beak and eyes. The feathers on the crown of his head stuck up a little and the ones on his wings were so perfectly laid out and arranged that she couldn't imagine anyone looking at them and not believing in a Creator. She handed the binoculars back to Heath. "That's really cool."

A wave of peace swept over her. The kids were farther ahead now—hurrying along, stopping to pick up a rock or a stick and then rushing on. For the moment, Brooke seemed more like a little girl than a thirteen-year-old, and Candace liked that.

Heath took her hand and gave it a reassuring squeeze. She liked that too. She playfully bumped into him, and he put his arm around her, pulling her close. She breathed in the warm scent of his aftershave, thankful for how he calmed her. Those were just a couple of the things she loved about him: his steadfastness in the face of adversity and the manly way he smelled.

"There's an article in the paper about the hospital," Fern said to James as he stepped into the living room. "It mentions the suspension of your program."

He sat down beside her on the couch.

"Did you know about the advisory committee?"

He nodded.

She pointed to the sidebar of the article. "How about the meeting tonight? Had you heard about that?" Her caring eyes met his.

"No."

"It's at seven thirty. I could go with you if you'd like."

James put his arm around his wife. "I don't plan to go. I don't think it will make a difference." He certainly didn't want Fern to go. It was apt to be emotionally charged, and that would be doubly draining for her.

"There might be new information."

James sighed. "Probably not." If there were, Dr. Hamilton would let him know. Or Anabelle would.

"I think that you should at least go."

James stood. "I'll think about it. First, I need to finish dinner." They were having beans and rice, New Orleans style. The first of many budget meals in their future, he was sure. Fern had found the recipe on the Internet. He called down the hall to Nelson. It was his turn to set the table. Gideon was on KP. Afterward, James planned to play basketball with the boys.

Chapter Six

NABELLE HURRIED DOWN THE HALL OF HOPE Haven toward the boardroom. She'd arrived early, wanting to talk to Dr. Hamilton before the meeting began, but there was already a group of people ahead of her, filing into the room. She followed them and made her way to the front. Granted, it was a fairly small space, but she had not expected so many people to show up.

It looked as if the article in the paper had caused alarm. Cam had certainly reacted that way and asked her point-blank if she would consider retiring now. She had answered no. In her heart, she knew she wasn't ready—unless it was necessary for James to have a job again.

Heath and Candace sat at the table in the front of the room, and Candace motioned to Anabelle to join them. She made her way around to the back, next to Candace.

"We're supposed to sit up here," she whispered. "There's going to be a general meeting first and then the advisory meeting."

"Oh." Anabelle hadn't realized that from what Dr. Hamilton had told her or from the newspaper article. A moment later Elena made her way to the front of the room and sat next to Anabelle.

"Oh, goodie," Anabelle said, "I was hoping you would be on the committee."

Elena reached over and squeezed her hand. The room continued to fill, and at seven thirty sharp, Albert Varner checked his smartphone and then called the meeting to order. "After the article came out in the paper, we decided to allow the public to ask questions." Varner turned to Anabelle and said, "Do you mind taking notes?"

She nodded and pulled her grocery-list notebook out of her purse as Dr. Hamilton slipped into the chair at the end of the table.

As Varner asked for questions, Anabelle spied James slipping into the back of the room and leaning up against the wall. Anabelle turned her attention to her notebook, concentrating on what was being said.

James had given into Fern's concerns and agreed to go to the meeting, as long as she put the idea of accompanying him out of her mind. Now, standing against the back wall, he scanned the crowd and smiled at the sight of his colleagues sitting in the front of the room. If he had hand-selected an advisory committee, he would have chosen the same five people.

The mayor of Deerford, Donald Armstrong, stood and asked what departments were going to be cut. Varner answered that only one program was going to be cut—the new one—and that had already happened.

The school superintendent stood next and said he'd heard the Birthing Unit was closing. James glanced at Candace who was, of course, watching Albert Varner intently.

The CEO shook his head. "No, that's a ridiculous rumor. All of this has been blown out of proportion." He glanced down at his smartphone as if he had notes he was checking.

The superintendent countered with a statement. "I know of other small-town hospitals that have cut their maternity programs, and young families moved away in droves. In a matter of years the schools were gutted."

Varner began to stammer. "I already said—we're not making any more cuts." He looked toward the front row James stood on his tiptoes. Zane McGarry, the CFO, was directly in front of Varner. The chief executive continued, "We have no plans, whatsoever, to even make cutbacks to the Birthing Unit, let alone eliminate it."

Someone James didn't know, an elderly gentleman, asked when the hospital would reinstate the Holistic Cardiac Program, quickly adding that his wife had heart problems and they'd felt comforted to know when she had a procedure done that a state-of-the-art facility would be available with additional education and therapy. Varner dodged the question without answering it, saying the decision would be made in a couple of months. He hadn't said that on Friday.

James had been thinking about what Missy at Tender Loving Health Care said about the grant to add electronic record keeping to her business. Hope Haven had electronic charting, but the hospital wasn't up-to-date with its technology. Varner had said the hospital wasn't in compliance with the new electronic standards, and McGarry had said they didn't qualify for government grants to become compliant. He raised his hand.

Varner squinted as he searched the group. James raised his hand a little higher.

Varner cleared his throat. "James?" He crossed his arms as he spoke, his smartphone still in his hand.

"Thank you," James said, stepping away from the wall, praying his voice sounded even and that he wouldn't stammer. He did not want to add any drama to the evening. "I've heard lately about government grants for IT programs, and I wondered if Hope Haven has looked into those."

"Of course we have." Varner sounded both impatient and defensive and, even from the back of the room, James could tell that sweat was beading on the man's forehead.

McGarry stood. "As the chief financial officer for Hope Haven, I'd like to address James's question."

Varner gave him a nod, and McGarry turned toward James. "It's an excellent, ongoing question. We have applied for grants in the past but haven't qualified. We haven't applied for a grant this year however." McGarry paused, looked as if he had more to say, and then sat back down.

Clearing his throat, Varner stared at McGarry. James could make out the man shrugging his shoulders. There was obvious tension between the two executives. Varner gestured toward the table, then addressed the crowd. "That's an issue that the advisory committee will have to address."

Valera Kincaid, the reporter for the *Deerford Dispatch*, raised her hand.

Varner sighed and then acknowledged her.

"Is the advisory meeting open to the press?"

James didn't wait for Varner's answer. He slipped out the door, leaving his friends and colleagues behind. He had no hope for clear answers from the administration. The general meeting had simply been a public relations move. He hoped the advisory committee wasn't a similar ruse.

He strode down the hall, half regretting that he hadn't agreed to be on the advisory committee, but he couldn't imagine Varner's allowing it. The man seemed intimidated enough just having James at the meeting.

Feeling isolated and alone, James headed to the lobby. He shouldn't have come to the meeting. There no away around it. Getting laid off hurt, and being at the hospital and seeing the administration dodge important questions was painful too.

He rounded the corner. The lobby was completely empty as he crossed it. Before he realized what he was doing, he was in the hospital chapel, sitting in the back pew. A single lamp lit the altar area, but besides that, the room was dim and the stained-glass window was nearly dark, just muted tones of purple, scarlet, and emerald green.

He leaned back against the wooden bench and ran the numbers in his head. He had a little bit of a rainy-day fund set aside, and they had Fern's disability checks, but that was all. He'd need to apply for unemployment right away.

He'd always felt sympathetic toward the unemployed, but now he identified completely.

"What am I going to do, Lord?" he prayed. He waited a few minutes. No answer came.

He sighed and stood.

Persevere. That was what he was going to do. He didn't need to wait for God to tell him that. It had been the story of his life.

He smiled a little. Persevere and go play basketball with his boys. He couldn't change what had happened. He couldn't predict the future. But he could shoot hoops with his sons. That was here and now.

Anabelle leaned back in the comfortable boardroom chair and watched Varner out of the corner of her eye. Clearly he didn't feel comfortable having Valera stay for the advisory committee meeting. He'd dodged the questions during the public meeting, and now the CEO was consulting with McGarry in the corner of the room. Anabelle stood and stretched, taking a couple of steps closer to the two men.

"We don't have anything to hide," McGarry said.

She couldn't understand Varner's response. He was whispering as he glanced down at the screen of his smartphone. Maybe he was checking a document to see what his options were.

"Better safe than sorry," McGarry answered.

"Exactly." Varner looked please. He approached Valera, who sat in a chair in the back of the room.

"It's going to be a closed meeting," he said. "No media. No public."

"On what grounds?"

"The usual," he said.

"But this isn't a trustees' meeting. This falls under your own bylaws concerning open meetings."

Varner looked confused.

Valera opened her bag and pulled out a file. "I have it right here."

Varner turned toward McGarry and the CFO stepped forward. "Let's agree to have Valera attend tonight. We can re-examine the issue for future meetings."

Valera looked pleased.

Flustered, Varner called the meeting to order.

"What is the status of Hope Haven's compliance to technology standards?" Dr. Hamilton asked.

"I'll defer to Zane on that," Varner answered, wiping his forehead with the handkerchief that he'd been clutching in his hand for the last few minutes.

"James's idea of pursuing a government grant is great." McGarry leaned forward and looked around the table. "By planning to implement new technology, not only would we qualify for grants, but we'd also be eligible for ongoing government money." He paused. "Besides, if we don't pursue updates soon we'll be out of compliance, as I'm sure you suspected. The government is changing the laws about medical records."

Anabelle wrote down McGarry's words, verbatim, in her notebook. She'd read about the new technology standards in health care, but it gave her a headache to think about it even though she knew it was inevitable. She'd been resistant to e-charting and all it entailed long enough. It was the future.

"Why aren't we already on the bandwagon with this?" Dr. Hamilton asked.

McGarry glanced at Varner.

"Zane's working on it," Varner answered.

McGarry put his palms down flat on the table. "Actually, I'm not. I'm not qualified, nor do I have the time to educate myself about all of this and do my current job."

"Zane." Varner dabbed at his forehead with his handkerchief again.

"We've put off hiring a CIO long enough." McGarry's voice was low and firm.

"CIO?" Candace asked.

"Chief informatics officer. To implement and maintain the technology we need. Plus, the person would be responsible for writing grants."

Anabelle wrote down what McGarry had said.

"And what department would we have to cut to hire a CIO? They aren't cheap." Varner crossed his arms, his handkerchief wadded in his fist.

Valera sat in the first row of chairs, typing away on her laptop. Anabelle could imagine what Thursday's headline would be—maybe "Hope Haven Administers Squabbles."

Varner's voice rose as he spoke. "Because we'd have to cut something." He turned his attention to Heath. "How about the imaging department? Everyone could go to Peoria for their ultrasounds and X-rays. Then again . . ."—he turned his attention to Candace—"if we cut the Birthing Unit, we won't need as many ultrasounds. Or . . ."—he glanced from Dr. Hamilton to Anabelle—"We could completely gut the cardiac department and get rid of all vascular surgeries. That would greatly reduce the number of patients on the CCU floor."

Anabelle's cheeks grew hot as she turned her attention back to her notebook. Varner had made his point. Everything was important, as well as expensive.

"We could send all critical patients, not just the cardiac ones, to Princeton or Peoria." Now his attention was on Elena. Anabelle expected a sassy comeback from Elena, but her friend's face was frozen.

"Wait a minute." Anabelle had had enough. "Could we redirect the meeting? I don't see how threatening all of us is constructive."

Varner sank back in his chair. "You're right. It's not constructive. My hands are tied right now. The only thing I can see to do is ride this out and hope enough other small hospitals are facing the same problem and that the government comes to our rescue."

Anabelle wanted to groan. She realized that, despite Varner's drama, they really didn't know what the status of Hope Haven was, whether it was just the new program that needed to be cut or more.

Dr. Hamilton cleared his throat. "I propose that the advisory committee meet independently, without any executives present."

"I think that's an excellent idea," McGarry said.

"But we need more information." Dr. Hamilton sat ramrod straight. "About how serious the situation is. And how close Hope Haven is to closing."

Albert Varner's shoulders sagged and he glanced at McGarry and then at Valera Kincaid. "I need to close the meeting," he said. "If any of this gets out to the public, it will only make things worse."

She hesitated for a moment and then closed her laptop. "I'll call you first thing in the morning," she said to Varner, "with follow-up questions."

"Fine," he said.

It was as if the whole room held its breath as Valera walked toward the door. Once it closed, Varner let out a sigh. "As much as I've been trying to deny it, Hope Haven is in a bad spot," he said, placing his smartphone on the table. "Zane forced me to listen to him late this afternoon. I've been wanting to downplay the financial part of this—as a PR move. But Zane let me know we're past that now."

Zane nodded. "If we don't come up with an immediate solution, I'd say we have another month or two before we close the doors . . . unless we find a way to tap into the available grant money."

Anabelle scribbled McGarry's words into her notebook and then held the pen numbly in midair. She couldn't imagine Deerford without the hospital. She couldn't imagine her life without it. She couldn't imagine why God was allowing them to go through this again, not after what they'd already gone through.

"I need the numbers," Dr. Hamilton said. "For each department. I need everything you're going to give the board. I need all the government requirements concerning the new technology and predicted costs."

McGarry nodded. "My pleasure," he said. "I want the advisory committee to take a look at this and give us your input—especially concerning ways to secure a grant."

"We'll give you the numbers as long as I'm allowed to attend the advisory committee meetings," Varner interjected. "Suggestions have to be grounded in facts. We've already grappled with everything you'll see. You'll just waste your time if I can't clue you in on what we've already discovered."

Dr. Hamilton thought for a moment and then nodded in agreement.

Anabelle looked at the long faces around the table, from Candace, to Heath, to Elena. How were they supposed to be able to fix what hospital executives couldn't?

Dr. Hamilton stood and shook Varner's hand. "I know this has been a stressful evening for you."

The CEO wiped his forehead again and Dr. Hamilton turned toward McGarry. "And thank you for your effort in all of this too."

McGarry nodded. "It's a dire situation, but I don't think we're totally without hope."

Dr. Hamilton glanced around the table. "I'll get copies of all of the paperwork to the four of you ASAP. Then we'll meet again after that."

"And I'll have copies of these minutes to everyone by Wednesday," Anabelle said, closing her notebook.

"And we'll all pray in the meantime," Elena muttered under her breath. Anabelle nodded her head in agreement.

Chapter Seven

"WHAT ARE YOU GOING TO DO TODAY?" GIDEON asked James as he crammed his chemistry book into his backpack.

James swallowed the coffee in his mouth and put his cup down on the kitchen table. "Errands. Look for a job. Try to recover from our game last night." He smiled.

Gideon pretended to shoot a basketball and then pulled his arm down with a satisfying, "Yes." He'd won their one-on-one tournament the night before, and he was proud of it. But then his expression quickly morphed into a grimace. "I thought medical jobs were recession-proof."

"Usually they are." James stood and patted his son's shoulder.

"Come on," Nelson called out from the doorway. "Or we're going to be late."

James gave Gideon a hug and then stepped toward Nelson. His youngest son gave him a quick squeeze and then led the way to the front door. A few seconds later, he heard Gideon's car start and then sputter, so James stepped to the window. Gideon revved the engine and, after revving the engine a couple of times, backed out onto the street. It sounded as if the car needed a trip to the shop soon, but that wasn't in the budget. Maybe he could take a look at it after school.

After pouring himself a second cup of coffee, James headed down the hall to the office and logged onto the computer, finding the Illinois State unemployment Web site. He skimmed the text, stopping on benefits. It would take three weeks before payments began arriving.

He clicked on START AN APPLICATION and began scanning the questions. Soon, he was filling in his Social Security number, contact information, recent position, employer, gross earnings, schooling, and past pay.

"James?" Fern's walker wheels whispered against the wood floor in the hall. He might not have heard it if she hadn't spoken. "Are you still here?"

"In the office," he said.

She'd slept a little later than usual, which James was thankful for. He was afraid the extra stress might exacerbate her symptoms. Any additional rest she could get helped.

"What are you doing?" she asked, stopping in the doorway.

"Applying for unemployment." He smiled at her. "There's oatmeal for breakfast."

Fern headed for the kitchen. James could tell when she reached it because the sound of the wheels of her walker changed to a whir on the tile from the soft noise they made on the hardwood floors. Then the whir stopped, followed by the clank of removing a bowl from the cupboard. It started again and then stopped. Softer clanking sounds indicated she was at the stove dishing up her breakfast. He was tempted to go carry her cereal for her, but reminded himself that most mornings she got along fine without him.

The phone rang and James picked up on the first ring, hoping it was someone at Hope Haven. It wasn't. It was Valera Kincaid. After a quick hello she asked if she could interview him.

"About?"

"Hope Haven. Being laid off. What you think the hospital should do."

"I'm sorry, Valera, but I don't have any comment," James replied. He was certain it wasn't in his best interest to talk to the media about any of this.

"This is your chance to get out your side of the story."

"I'm sorry," James repeated. "I need to—"

She interrupted him. "Could I call you back in a few days?"

"—go." James quickly, but politely, said good-bye and hung up the phone, feeling out of sorts. He didn't want to become a spokesperson about Hope Haven when he didn't have a clear understanding of what was going on. He tried to focus again on the unemployment Web site. He could mail in a direct deposit request and a canceled check. That sounded like a good idea. He printed the form and kept reading. A form would arrive in the mail within a week stating what his unemployment would be. He would have to log on to the site and report on his job-search and work status every week. Payments would be made every other week. There would also be scheduled phone calls with a representative from the state to evaluate his job search and previous year's gross income.

James skimmed the application one more time to make sure he hadn't missed anything. When he'd thought about applying for unemployment, he'd imagined going to an office packed with waiting people, many of them down and out. Applying online was certainly more convenient.

James submitted the application, picked up his coffee cup, and headed to the kitchen. Fern was holding on to the counter, taking baby steps to the table, the bowl of oatmeal in her hand.

"Want a cup of coffee?" James asked.

"Just a half cup," she said.

He poured a half inch of milk into a mug and added the coffee—a little caffeine didn't seem to affect Fern's balance—and sat down at the table beside her.

"What do you have planned for today?" she asked.

"I need to stop by the bank. And go to the grocery store."

"I thought we could have split-pea soup with chunks of ham for dinner," Fern said. "And bread and a salad."

James nodded. It helped him immensely when Fern came up with meal ideas. It was such a relentless task.

"I'll put peas on to soak this morning," she said. "And start the soup this afternoon. We have the leftover ham that needs to be used."

He liked her economical menu ideas too. He had the hardest time keeping track of the leftovers, and he'd always admired how Fern could come up with ideas of how to use them.

They sat in silence for a little while as James scanned last evening's newspaper. Finally Fern said, "At least the old house sold last month. This would be even harder if we were still making that mortgage payment."

James agreed.

"And I'm so thankful we have the down payment for this house," Fern said.

James agreed to that too. He needed to call the bank and let them know he'd been laid off. He wouldn't share his concerns with Fern about not qualifying for a loan until he knew for certain what the outcome would be.

He thought about the old house and all the fix-it projects he'd had to do there, which was ironic since he would have plenty of time for projects on this house—although none were needed—if he didn't find another job. He took another sip of coffee and added *go by bank first* to his mental to-do list.

Though he needed to go back to work full time, he enjoyed sitting and enjoying his coffee with Fern. But real life called him away, and he headed out to take care of those things that just couldn't wait.

He deposited his settlement check and then waited to talk with Shelly Baxter, the loan officer he'd already consulted with. At that time, he'd planned to apply for a loan for the new house this week.

Shelly hung up her phone and motioned to James, stepping around her desk to shake his hand. She couldn't be more than thirty and wore her chestnut hair long and straight. She pushed her tortoise-shell plastic-framed glasses up on the bridge of her nose. More and more it seemed like the professionals around him were younger and younger.

"How are you?" she asked, sitting down behind her desk. "Ready to start the loan process?"

As he explained the situation he was in, the expression on her face grew more and more concerned.

"I'll be honest," she said, "it wouldn't be impossible for you to qualify for a mortgage since you have a substantial down payment, but your interest rate would be higher to offset our risk as the lender."

"So, it would be better to wait until after I've found another job?"

She nodded. "But you're a nurse, right? You'll have another job in no time."

James said he hoped so and thanked Shelly for her time, saying he would be back in to talk more about the mortgage soon. As he pushed through the door of the bank and stepped out onto the sidewalk, a light, cold rain began to fall. It would be ridiculous to get a mortgage with a higher interest rate right now. They'd either have to refinance as soon as possible or live with a higher rate. Either way they would lose money. He needed to call Cody Wyatt and tell her what was going on. He hoped she would be fine with renting for a few more months.

He started his van, deciding to stop by Tender Loving Health Care again.

He drove over to Smith Street and turned left, wondering if checking in with Missy again would annoy her or show her that he was really interested in working with the organization. He decided it was worth the risk and parked in front of the office, stepping from his van quickly. He'd just check in with Missy and tell her he would be willing to take an LPN position if necessary.

He would be willing to take anything that was available, actually. When he opened the door he was surprised to find a receptionist at the small desk in the outer office.

"May I help you?" She wore jeans and a Chicago Bulls sweatshirt and looked to be college age.

"I was hoping to speak to Missy," James said.

"She's busy." The girl kept her eyes on her computer screen as she spoke. "Come back after lunch."

James thanked the young woman, and she nodded without looking at him. As he reached the front of the office, Missy's door swung open.

"Can you believe it?" She was standing with her profile toward James, talking to the receptionist. "Another nurse has refused to take care of Joel Morris."

"Why don't you drop him?" the receptionist said. She still had her eyes on the computer screen.

James cleared his throat as he stepped forward.

Missy spun around. "Oh, it's you. You scared me!"

"Sorry," James said. "I just stopped by to check in, to see if you had any openings."

"Since yesterday?" She laughed.

James stepped backward. "I'll check back next week."

"Sure," Missy said. "Wait. You were in the army, right?"

"Yes, ma'am," James said.

The receptionist turned her head toward James for half a second and then looked at Missy.

The woman had a smile on her face, and her feet hopped in a little jig. "Come into my office," she said, gesturing toward the open door.

A moment later, as she and James sat down at the table, Missy said, "I have a veteran living just outside of town. He's waiting to get into a rehab program in Texas. He's . . . let's say difficult. I've had three LPNs withdraw their services in the last week and a half."

James cocked his head to the side. That must have been what all the phone calls yesterday were about.

"Would you be interested in giving it a try?"

"What's difficult about the client?" James couldn't imagine that the actual care could be that daunting, otherwise the man would still be hospitalized.

Missy raised her eyebrows. "He's angry. Acting out. He's thrown his bedpan against the wall more than once. That sort of thing."

James started to smile and then caught himself. He could handle flying bedpans. "Sure. I'd like to give it a try."

"I can't pay you what you were making at the hospital."

James nodded. "I assumed that."

"I'll pay more than I would an LPN though." She turned her attention to her computer and clicked her mouse several times. In a second her printer began to whir. "Can you start tomorrow?" she asked.

"Yes. Yes, I can," James answered, sitting up straight.

She pulled a stack of papers from her printer. "He's a sergeant in the army, a local kid who enlisted after high school and was stationed at Fort Stewart, Georgia, in an infantry division. They were deployed nine months ago and he was injured just before Christmas. He's scheduled to go to Brooke Army Medical Center in San Antonio—to rehab—in a few weeks."

James leaned back in his chair. Of course it was a temporary position. But maybe after that a position would open up at the hospital or Missy would have another assignment for him.

Missy slid the papers across the desk to James. "Here's the information you need—address, protocols, all of that." She turned her attention back to the computer. "I'll print out a contract . . ."

He skimmed the paperwork. Sergeant Morris had been driving a Hummer on December 21 when it was struck by an improvised explosive device. His back and legs had been injured, but he was regaining movement in his legs. His left arm had been shattered and he'd had three surgeries on it already. He'd also suffered a head wound.

James had read plenty about soldiers coming out of Iraq with brain injuries. They were called the "hidden wounded." Often it was months or years before the lasting damage could be assessed.

"What do you think?" Missy asked. "Still want to accept the assignment?"

James looked up from the documents. "Of course," he said. He couldn't imagine not wanting to care for Sgt. Joel Morris.

On Wednesday, Candace stepped into the courtyard of Hope Haven. It was cool but clear and dry. She and Heath had agreed to meet and have lunch together outside, hoping for some privacy.

It seemed like a long, long week so far, and she felt relieved that the weekend was just around the corner. She brushed a twig off the picnic table, sat down, and opened her lunch bag. She'd decided to start economizing wherever she could, just in case, and bringing her lunch instead of ordering a bowl of soup or a sandwich in the cafeteria would save a chunk of money each month. The kids were taking their lunch every day too.

"Hi." Heath stepped through the door to the courtyard with a tray from the cafeteria. "I brought you a piece of apple caramel pie."

Candace smiled, touched that he remembered how much she liked the specialty dessert that the cafeteria only offered occasionally. "Thanks." That was another thing she loved about him—that he remembered those little details.

He sat down across from her and slid the pie across the table. He had a burger and fries on his plate, which he could eat seven days a week and not gain a pound.

"Have you heard anything new?" she asked.

Heath shook his head. "I saw Varner talking to the nursing administrator this morning though. Neither looked happy."

No one had seemed happy at Hope Haven all week. Candace took a bite of her turkey on whole wheat. Varner had spoken with her boss, Riley Hohmann, the day before, but so far no one had heard a thing about the details of the conversation.

The door to the courtyard opened again and Anabelle appeared. "Mind if I join you?"

Heath turned his head and in unison Candace and he said, "Sit down."

Anabelle had a salad on her tray. "I was hoping I'd find you out here." She sat beside Heath. "Any word on the advisory committee?"

"Dr. Drew said he was gathering the last of the paperwork he wanted us all to have. Then we'll meet," Candace answered.

"Is it just me, or does it feel like the whole hospital is holding its breath?" Anabelle stabbed a cherry tomato with her fork.

"That's actually a nice way of putting it." Candace slid the second half of her sandwich back into her bag.

"Oh, I don't think things are that bad," Heath chimed in. "There's no use guessing what's going to happen."

Candace appreciated Heath's optimism—usually. That was something she loved about him too. But on this issue, she was afraid he was in denial. Obviously the hospital was in trouble.

The wind picked up a little, and the just-budding branches of the birch tree across the courtyard began to sway. A robin landed on the wall and bobbed its head around.

Heath stood and stepped toward the robin and then looked at the tree. "Look, there's a nest," he said.

Sure enough there was, in the crook of the branches.

"What are you looking at?" Elena had come through the door without anyone noticing.

"Bird-watching," Candace answered, nodding her head toward Heath. She liked how he turned into a little kid when a bird appeared.

Heath pivoted around slowly. "It's not spring until the robins begin nesting. Look." He pointed to the tree.

Elena clasped her hands together. "Oh, isn't that wonderful? And right here in our courtyard." She sat down beside Candace. "How is everyone?"

Heath sat back down, saying, "Fine."

"Well, I'm not so fine," Elena said. "I'm afraid of being replaced by a nurse's aide."

"Really?" Candace couldn't fathom that. Especially not in ICU.

"That's the rumor." Elena took a sip of her coffee—it was all she'd brought with her.

Candace exhaled. She pushed the pie away. She couldn't enjoy it.

"Rumors and more rumors," Anabelle said. "I'm anxious to figure this out."

The others nodded in agreement.

Anabelle put her fork down. "Could we pray? For wisdom for the advisory committee."

"And for James," Elena said. "I feel like he's been cozened."

Candace started to laugh. "And poor James isn't even here to appreciate your choice of words. What, exactly, does it mean?"

"Swindled." Elena was obviously pleased with herself.

"And the administrators and executives," Anabelle continued, "we should pray for them." Anabelle bowed her head and the others quickly joined her, except Candace who stole a look at Heath. His head was already bowed and his eyes closed.

"I'll start," Anabelle said. "Dear Lord . . ." She prayed for the hospital and that it would be saved. Elena prayed for James, and Candace prayed for wisdom for the advisory committee and the administrators and executives. Heath didn't pray out loud but concluded the other prayers by simply saying, "Amen."

There was silence for a moment and then Candace spoke. "How's James doing?"

"He's found a part-time home health position," Elena said. "And applied for unemployment."

Candace grimaced. But she had to admire James for his integrity to take whatever job was available.

"Well, James will excel at whatever he does," Anabelle said.

"They're lucky to have him," Elena added, wrapping her hands around her coffee mug.

Candace sighed. If James could persevere through his trial, surely she could continue on with a good attitude through her own uncertainty.

Elena and Izzy cuddled on the couch, a stack of books on the coffee table.

The back door banged. Heavy footsteps sounded through the kitchen. Elena looked over her shoulder; her son stood in the doorway, his cell phone to his ear. He waved at Izzy, and she scooted off the couch and dashed across the room to him. He lifted her up with one arm as he flipped his phone shut and then slid it into the pocket of his jacket. "What's *mi bonita* up to?"

She squealed as he bounced her higher in both of his arms and then said, "Reading. With Buela."

"How's it going?" His question was more for Elena than Izzy.

"Good," Elena answered.

Rafael lowered himself into the wingback chair next to the fireplace, with Izzy still in his arms. He looked at his daughter. "I'm so glad I got home before bedtime."

Izzy grinned.

"Would you read to me?" Rafael asked his daughter.

Izzy climbed down from his lap, picked up the first Madeline book, and then snuggled next to her dad and began reading it perfectly. When she finished the last line, Rafael praised her and then said, "Go put on your pajamas." Rafael lowered the little girl to the floor. "Then come back out, and I'll read to you."

Izzy smiled and scampered down the hall.

"She's doing well, isn't she?" Elena said.

"Not according to her teacher." Rafael scooted forward on the chair and clasped his hands. "She's concerned about her reading."

"Really?" Elena's thoughts raced. The teacher hadn't said a thing to Elena about the topic, and she picked Izzy up from school a few times a week, at least. And Izzy was reading, amazingly well. But besides that, she was only in kindergarten.

Rafael nodded. "I just had a message from her."

The teacher wouldn't call without a reason.

"She says she thinks Izzy's regressing in her reading skills—that normally whether a student reads or not isn't a big deal, since it's kindergarten. But she says Izzy was reading quite well and now isn't at all." Rafael stood. "I don't think the teacher knows what she's talking about though."

"Call her back and ask for more details," Elena said.

Izzy came running down the hall; she'd put her pajamas on in record time. "Can I have a piggyback ride?" she squealed at Rafael.

"Climb on." He dropped down and Izzy clambered onto his back.

"Be careful she doesn't fall," Elena said. Izzy's lip was healing nicely, but if she hit it again, it would reopen.

Elena headed into the kitchen to unload the dishwasher; otherwise, she'd probably keep nagging Rafael. But at least Izzy wasn't afraid to roughhouse after her accident. She really was a trouper.

A half hour later, Izzy was down for the night, and Rafael was raiding the refrigerator.

"I was thinking more about Izzy's reading," Elena said as she scoured the sink. "One of us should have her read to us out of a book she doesn't know." It had dawned on her that the little girl only read books to them that had been read, over and over, to her.

"I tried that when I put her to bed."

"And?" Elena rinsed out the sink.

"She said her head hurt." Rafael juggled roast beef, cheese, mustard, lettuce, and a tomato in his hands.

"Oh." Elena rinsed out the sponge. "It sure didn't seem like she had a headache earlier."

Rafael agreed.

"Didn't you eat at the restaurant?" Elena scanned the countertop.

"Nah," he said. "I didn't want to take the time."

She appreciated him wanting to get home in time to put Izzy to bed. "Make sure to clean up when you're done."

"Yeah, yeah." Rafael opened the breadbox. "I know."

Elena started to head back to the living room but then turned around. "You might do some research online about reading issues," she said. "It might give you a head start in talking with her teacher."

"Yeah, yeah," Rafael said again, looking up from spreading mustard on the bread. He smiled. "Actually that's a good idea. I'll do that tonight."

Relieved, Elena started for her room to put on her own pajamas. Sometimes it was hard to know how much advice to offer Rafael.

Chapter Eight

RIDAY MORNING, JAMES SLOWLY DROVE OUT the highway to the Morris home, his windshield wipers working furiously to clear the sheets of rain. It was his third day caring for Joel Morris. Wednesday and Thursday the twenty-three-year-old man had been sullen and moody and in pain each day and had taken his full amount of prescribed pain medication. He'd been mouthy and rude. James had told him several times to tone down his language.

On the bright side, he hadn't thrown the bedpan.

The first thing James had done was get rid of the thing, although he was pretty sure Joel's parents still let him use it. James had Joel up as much as possible and in the bathroom as much as needed. His plan was to never give the kid a chance to throw the bedpan at him, no matter how much he raged about not wanting to transfer into the wheelchair for a trip down the hall.

His mother Melanie Morris seemed detached, giving James just the amount of information that he needed. But each time he was getting ready to leave he sensed that she was getting ready to hover.

James helped Joel shower, checked his meds, and saw to his wounds, which were healing nicely. Joel was beginning to be able to use his left arm for the first time since his accident, but the young man was still weak.

James turned onto Willow Road. The Morris home was a 1950s ranch, which worked well for Joel's injuries since he was in a wheelchair. His hospital bed was in the middle of the living room since the doors to the bedrooms weren't wide enough for his chair. His father, whom James hadn't met, had taken the molding off the bathroom door so Joel's wheelchair would fit through it.

He parked in the driveway and stepped out into the pouring rain, hurrying toward the front door of the house. He rang the bell and waited. He heard voices inside, raised and loud. He rang the bell again. The voices grew more heated. He rang the bell a third time. Finally Melanie answered.

"Brace yourself," she whispered. "We're having a bad day." She stepped out onto the porch, wearing slacks and a blouse, looking as if she was ready to go into an office. Her shoulder-length hair was styled, and she wore lipstick and earrings. She was a small woman, not much bigger than Fern.

James kept his voice low. "What's up?"

"He's trying to cut down on his pain meds. Says he's tired of being numb, says I've been overmedicating him and treating him like a baby."

"Maybe I can help him figure out the dosage," James said. "Sometimes it's a hard balance to find." He followed Melanie into the house. She veered to the left, toward the kitchen, and James stepped into the living room.

Joel glared at him from the bed. "What? You're still coming around? I thought you would have quit by now too." The young man's dark curly hair was growing in on his left side where his head wound was and was just beginning to cover his scar. His face was hollow. He was a big-boned kid and tall.

Melanie had said Joel had lost thirty pounds since the accident, and James knew a lot of it had been muscle. The medical chart said the kid was six foot two; he was definitely too large for Melanie to transfer easily in and out of bed.

James took off his jacket and draped it over the straight-backed chair in the corner, ignoring Joel's comment. "Heard you're having some issues with your pain meds." James stepped around to the side of the bed.

"You heard wrong." Joel's brown eyes were bloodshot and red-rimmed.

"What's going on?" James picked up Joel's pillbox. He hadn't taken a pain pill since the one James had given him eighteen hours before. "Whoa, dude, you can't go this long. Besides making life unbearable, it's going to interfere with your healing."

Joel stared at the ceiling. "I don't want to get addicted to that stuff. I have a buddy who is. He was injured in Iraq just like me."

"That's a valid concern," James said. "But your injuries are serious, and you're early in your healing."

Joel's voice grew louder. "Well, addictions run in the family, if you know what I mean."

James paused for a second and then said, "Could you elaborate on that?" He hadn't read about any family addictions in Joel's medical chart. Those questions had been left unmarked. He had no idea what Joel meant.

"Joel, honey," Melanie said from the kitchen. "Don't get riled up . . ." Her voice trailed off.

"Joel?" James coaxed.

The young man turned his face toward the wall. "I don't want to talk about it."

"Your family medical history is pertinent, Joel. I need more information to help you."

James stepped closer, and Joel pulled something out from under the blankets, something metal and shiny. James saw it coming in slow motion, the bedpan coming at him like a Frisbee, or more like a flying saucer, flung with Joel's good hand. James ducked and the bedpan bounced off a chair and onto the floor, liquid splattering out of it onto the carpet as it did.

Melanie rushed into the room. "Joel Morris!" she shouted. "We've had enough of that."

Joel turned his face back to the wall and curled up into a fetal position. Melanie's hands flew to her face and her shoulders began to convulse.

James patted her back. "Where are your cleaning supplies?" he asked.

"Under the sink. The carpet cleaner's in the yellow can."

Fifteen minutes later, James stood beside Joel's bed, the daily pill dispenser in his hand. "We're having a do-over here. How's your pain right now? On a scale of one to ten."

Joel stared at the ceiling. "Eight."

"That's way too high." James opened the Friday flap on the pillbox. "I'll cut the pill in half. If your pain isn't down to a three in half an hour, you'll need to take the other half."

Joel kept staring at the ceiling, not responding.

James raised the hospital bed and then handed him the pain med, which Joel slipped into his mouth. James quickly passed him the bottle of water, before the young man changed his mind. Joel slowly swallowed the pill and then passed the bottle back to James.

"The lady from home health was out yesterday after you left. I think she was checking up on me."

James winced.

"She said you used to be in the army."

James nodded. "That's how I got into nursing. I was a medic during the first Gulf War."

"Boy, you had it easy."

James didn't answer. Joel was right. There was no comparing the two wars, none at all.

"How many soldiers did you lose?" Joel's voice was rough.

"From my unit?"

"No, your squad."

"None," James answered. Only one person died in his unit and that was from a Humvee rollover.

"So you were in Iraq?"

James smiled. "No, Saudi Arabia."

Joel snorted. "And you took a lot of fire there?"

"Not a lot, but there were a few Scud missile attacks." He'd been stationed in Dhahran. No one in his unit had been killed, but twenty-five soldiers from other units had died in all. It had been one of the worst nights of his life, but paled in comparison to what Joel had been through.

"No IEDs though?" Joel still wasn't looking at James.

Improvised explosive devices. The bane of the coalition in Iraq.

"Negative," James answered.

Joel snorted again.

James needed to get Joel's mind off the war. "Have you had breakfast?"

Joel shook his head. "Not hungry."

"Well, it's shower day. You need some food in your stomach and your pain under control. What would you like to eat?"

"Nothing."

"Then I'll choose." James headed into the kitchen. Melanie leaned against the counter, a cup of coffee in her hand, staring out the window over the sink. She'd retreated down the hall right after her reaction to Joel's outburst, and James hadn't heard her return. She startled when James stepped into the room.

"Sorry," he said.

"What do you need?" she asked.

"Breakfast for Joel."

"He said he wasn't hungry."

"He still needs to eat."

Melanie put her cup down. "He refuses nearly everything I fix for him."

"How about something easy? And a glass of juice."

Melanie opened the cupboard to her right, and James spotted a box of granola bars. "One of those would be perfect," he said.

"He was on a feeding tube at Walter Reed," Melanie said, handing a bar to James. "I keep wondering if he needs to go back on one."

James shook his head. "Let's see how he does in the next few days." He'd been getting most of his calories from supplement drinks, but he needed solid food too.

She opened the fridge and pulled out a small box of apple juice. "He used to like these when he was a kid." Melanie's eyes were teary as she turned to James. "I bought some the other day, remembering . . ." Her voice trailed off again.

"I know this is hard for you," James said.

Melanie sighed. "Compared to what Joel's going through, it shouldn't be."

"Life isn't like that," James answered. "You're all in this together."

"Both Gary and I took time off when Joel was injured—first we flew to Germany, and then we stayed with him at Walter Reed. Used up all of our vacation time. Now I'm taking a leave of absence." James already knew that Melanie was an accountant for the school district and her husband was a farm-equipment salesman who traveled a lot. "Gary's stressed out too. It shows in his job." Her eyes wandered back to the window. "And the VA has been slow to pay what they said they would."

James could imagine how disheartening it would be to wait for the US Department of Veterans Affairs to come through.

Melanie turned back toward James. "I'm sorry. You don't need to be burdened with our problems."

"No," James said. "I do. Knowing what's going on for all of you will help me take better care of Joel." Besides it put his own problems into perspective. "Joel mentioned something about addictions running in the family."

As he spoke Melanie turned away from him. "Like prescription drug addictions?"

"I'm not sure," James said.

She glanced back toward him. "Do you think he's concerned about getting addicted to his pills?"

"It seems that way. He mentioned a buddy—"

"Joel has always been a good kid." She interrupted him again. "He never even drank, let alone did drugs."

That was good to know. "I'll talk to him again," James said. "Try to see what he was talking about. I'll explain to him the difference between legitimate pain medication and substance abuse too. Controlling pain actually speeds the healing process."

Melanie nodded and whispered, "Thank you."

"Now about that bedpan."

Melanie grimaced. "I forgot he still had it. I've been trying to keep it in the bathroom and only give it to him when he needs it."

"Good," James said. He knew it was hard for her to help her son in and out of bed. "While I'm here, he won't be using the bedpan at all. We'll be working on the wheelchair transfers until he can do them by himself."

She nodded.

James continued. "How does your day look? Do you have errands to run? Things to do in town? It would probably be good for you to spend some time out of the house."

"What if he loses his temper?"

"I can deal with it." James had been reading up on post-traumatic stress disorder and knew it was a possibility Joel suffered from it. He knew to expect the unexpected. He smiled at Melanie, hoping to encourage her. "You should take some time for yourself."

She hesitated and then said she thought she would. "I have my cell. The number's on the piece of paper taped to Joel's bedside table. Call if you need me."

When he returned to the hospital bed, Joel had his eyes closed.

"How's the pain?" James asked, unwrapping the granola bar.

"Better."

"Here's some breakfast." James placed the bar in Joel's good hand. It was easier for Joel to eat than a bowl of cereal or eggs. The kid was probably tired of having his mom try to feed him.

Joel opened his eyes and ate half the bar and then handed it back to James, who placed the box of juice with the straw in place in his hand. He drained the juice in no time.

"Ready for that shower?"

Joel nodded.

"Need more pain meds?"

Joel shook his head, but James noted that the young man's jaw was clenched as he did.

An hour later, James pulled Joel's wheelchair backward over the small ramp that had been installed on both sides of the patio door. The rain had stopped and the clouds had rolled back, revealing blue sky. The Morrises' property was five miles out of town on an acreage that butted up against Crooked Creek. The hanging, budding branches of weeping willows swayed in the distance. Between the house and the creek was a sloping lawn with a plot for a garden on the side, which hadn't yet been tilled, and a rose garden on the other. The bushes were scraggly and overgrown and should have been pruned well over a month ago. Melanie and Gary Morris would have been at Walter Reed in Washington, DC, about that time, still hoping their son would survive.

"I used to play down by the creek for hours when I was a kid," Joel said. "Catching frogs. Pretending I was an Indian scout. Fishing."

James pulled a plastic chair that was tucked under the eaves of the house out by Joel's chair, pleased that Joel was sharing about his childhood. "Did you catch anything?"

"Frogs." A hint of a smile passed over his face. "Never any fish."

"How about your dad?"

"What about my dad?" Joel's eyes were focused on the creek.

"Did he catch any fish?"

Joel gave James a sideways glance but in a second his eyes were back on the creek. "You don't know my dad."

James waited for more of a response but none came. They sat in silence for a moment until James decided that now was as good a time as any. "About that bedpan this morning—"

"It didn't hit you. If I'd wanted it to, it would have."

"Okay." He'd assumed the other flying bedpans hadn't hit the other home health care nurses, but now he wasn't so sure. "Listen, Joel, no more of that. If you're frustrated, let me know."

Joel crossed his arms and dropped his eyes.

"Joel?" James tilted his head.

"I hear you, man." His voice was snarly.

"And the other thing we need to discuss—"

"What are you? The gestapo?"

"—is your pain medication."

"Hey." Joel whipped his head up and met James's eyes. "Believe me, I know. They went over it at Walter Reed, okay?"

"I need to be sure you're clear about the difference between abusing prescription pain meds and managing your pain."

"I know plenty of people who ended up with an addiction without ever intending to."

"Well, sure," James said. "But let's concentrate on your pain meds. Managing your pain will help you heal sooner."

"Blah, blah, blah," Joel said. "I've heard this before."

"So what exactly is your concern?" James asked.

"Who said I had a concern?" The expression on Joel's face matched his smart remark. Now he was messing with James, on purpose.

"Actually, you did."

Joel stared at James a moment and then shrugged, saying, "Take me in, would ya?"

After turning him around, James opened the patio door and wheeled him back into the house.

"My dad says I need to buck up and take this like a man." Joel balled his good hand into a fist as James transferred him back to his bed.

James took a deep breath. The young man was less than six years older than Gideon. "*Hmm.* That's one perspective. Another is that you need time to grieve everything you've lost. Don't minimize what's happened to you, okay, Joel? You've taken a hit. Grieve, but keep moving forward. Everything you eat, every hour you sleep, every positive thought that goes through your head will help you heal."

Joel's eyes flashed. "You know what I thought I liked about you?"

James couldn't help but notice Joel's use of past tense. "What?"

"I didn't think you were bossy and controlling like those other nurses. But you proved me wrong today." Joel turned his head away from James. After a few minutes his chest began to rise and fall rhythmically. James sat in the chair in the corner and wrote in Joel's chart. In a few more months, Missy said each nurse who worked for Tender Loving Health Care would carry a laptop and do all of their charting on it. It was a mystery to James why Missy could get a grant and figure out financing for the needed changes but Hope Haven couldn't. He sighed and hoped the advisory committee had made some progress.

When James was done, he stood at the patio door and watched the creek. It was running high from the spring melt and the rain. He could imagine Joel as a boy playing along the bank and splashing in the water. He'd always wanted acreage in the country for his boys, but it wasn't meant to be. He sighed. So many things in life weren't meant to be. But he was more than thankful for what was.

Joel slept for an hour and then at lunchtime, James made him a peanut butter and jelly sandwich and grabbed another juice box. The young man ate without comment and then took his meds without protesting, including the pain pill.

"Do you keep in touch with your unit?" James asked, taking the water bottle from Joel.

"Yep. They have two weeks left. My chaplain e-mails me every day." Joel smiled a little. "He keeps saying he's going to come visit as soon as he can."

When James heard Melanie come through the front door, he told Joel he would be back on Monday morning. "And your physical therapist will be here too."

"That sounds like fun." Joel's frown matched his sarcasm.

As James walked to his car, he noticed the front hedge that needed to be trimmed and the debris that had collected in the yard from the winter storms. He imagined that under normal circumstances the Morris place was in good shape. As he backed out of the drive, he wondered how many other families there were in the area with disabled vets. He didn't imagine there were many. In fact, the Morrises might be the only one. He hadn't heard of any others. The family had sacrificed so much and would continue to. Their whole lives had been changed.

On the way into town, his cell phone rang. He checked the screen quickly. It was Cody. He'd been waiting for her to return his call for days. He pulled over and flipped the phone open to speaker.

They exchanged hellos, and then Cody got right down to business. "I really need to get that loan paid off," she said. "It's eating up all my reserves." He knew his childhood friend was sincere.

"I understand, Cody. I really do." James rubbed the back of his neck.

"You don't know how much it pains me to say this." She stopped.

James could only imagine. She'd been nothing but generous with them.

She continued, "You can rent the house until I find a buyer." She paused and then added, "I just hope with all my heart that buyer will be you."

Monday, James left the Morris home before the physical therapist arrived because she was running late. He stopped by the grocery store and picked up spaghetti sauce and pasta for dinner. Thankfully they already had ground beef in the freezer. There was a special on French bread for ninety-nine cents a loaf so he picked up two of those. He'd use the second one for French toast in the morning.

He was thankful that Fern's MS had started in her forties, at a time when it was easier to handle traumatic changes, and not in her twenties when they were trying to establish themselves. They had been married for years and already had children. Both had good jobs.

Joel had all the uncertainties of life ahead of him.

As he drove home, he thought again about the needs of the Morris family. Tonight was Nelson's Boy Scout meeting. The troop needed to come up with a service project. Helping the Morrises would be good for the family and the troop. The war seemed so far away to the average American and even more so to the average teenager. Joel would bring it a little closer.

After supper, on their way to the meeting, James told Nelson about the Morrises and his idea for a service project. He didn't comment but listened intently.

At the meeting, Nelson, as troop leader, called everyone to order and then led the other Scouts in the Pledge of Allegiance.

James's heart swelled as the boys recited the words, ending on a louder note as they said, ". . . with liberty and justice for all."

"The first item on our agenda," Nelson said, "is to come up with a service project."

"How about selling donuts?" Shane Singh shouted out, pushing out his belly, which didn't need much help.

"That's not a service project." Nelson crossed his arms. "We need to help an old lady or clean up a public space, something like that."

The boys looked around at each other for a moment.

Finally, Nelson said, "My dad has an idea."

The boys all turned toward James.

He'd hoped Nelson would bring it up, if he wanted it considered. The idea was for the boys to take charge of the troop. It wasn't like Cub Scouts where the parents planned everything. James leaned forward in the chair. "I know of a family in the area with a son who was injured in Iraq."

"What happened?" Shane asked.

"IED."

"Improvised explosive device," Nelson explained.

Shane made a face. "Duh. Everyone knows what that is."

"Anyone else get hurt?" another boy asked.

"One of his buddies was killed," James said. "Two others weren't injured at all. The explosion broke the back of the man I know, tore up his left arm, and injured his head."

None of the boys commented.

"Right now he's in a hospital bed and a wheelchair."

"How old is he?" Shane asked.

"Twenty-three." James imagined it seemed old to the boys.

"I have a brother that's twenty-two," another kid said.

James nodded. Joel was actually younger than the average soldier in Iraq, which was close to thirty due to the heavy deployments of army reservists and National Guard soldiers.

"What does he need help with? Getting around?"

James smiled, imagining the entire troop trying to push Joel's wheelchair. "I think coming up with something to help his family would be better. His mom and dad took time off work to be with him in Germany and then at Walter Reed, and his mom is taking a leave of absence from her job right now."

"So, they need money?" Nelson asked. He'd been concerned about his own family's finances so James wasn't surprised that's what would come to mind for him.

"We could have a can drive," Shane said. "And give the family the proceeds."

"That's an idea," James said even though he knew it would only be a drop in the bucket as far as their overall expenses were concerned. "Or maybe they need some work done around their house."

"Like chores?" Shane groaned. "Cleaning toilets and stuff like that?"

James smiled. "That would be appreciated. But maybe you could come up with something longer lasting."

"Like?"

"I could ask the family what needs to be done. Maybe they have a house project you could do. Or yard work."

The boys groaned again.

"I'll send out an e-mail when I find out." James leaned against the back of the folding chair. Maybe the Morrises wouldn't be open to a troop of boys descending on their home, but hopefully they would.

When James broached the subject with Melanie the next day, tears filled her eyes. "It's not only that we don't have the time," she said, "we just don't have the emotional energy right now to tackle extra work. Does that make sense?"

James nodded. How many times had friends helped him and his family when they didn't have the energy to handle something on their own? "I'm thinking the boys could come on a Saturday in the next few weeks," James said.

"I'll talk to Gary," Melanie said. "I'll let you know tomorrow."

The physical therapist was coming at ten, so James hurried Joel through a shower. He heard voices down the hall as he positioned Joel's chair to transfer him back into his bed and assumed Melanie was on the phone.

"How long until you lose your job?" Melanie was clearly upset.

"They're fighting again." Joel's good hand was balled into a fist as James helped him stand and then pivot toward the bed.

"Who?"

"My parents. My dad took another day off work."

James swung Joel's legs onto the bed. Maybe he'd finally get to meet the illusive Mr. Morris.

The physical therapist arrived right on time. She was in her late twenties, short and small, with her blonde hair pulled back in a ponytail. She wore slacks and a sweater and seemed a little wary of Joel, making James wonder how the session had gone the day before. She stood at the end of his bed with her hands on her hips.

"I wondered if you'd come back." Joel had a mischievous look on his face.

She shook her head, just slightly. "So did I." She stepped around the bed. "Are you ready to work today?"

He nodded. "I was tired yesterday, that's all."

"You were rude." Her eyes sparked as she spoke.

"How about if my buddy James sticks around? He'll keep me in line."

James nodded at the woman and extended his hand. "James Bell. I'm the home health nurse."

"Polly Green."

Joel began to smirk.

The young woman shook James's hand, turning her back to Joel. "I can handle him teasing me about being a Polly Pocket but not the lashing out. Or the crude language."

James looked around her at Joel. He was still smiling. PTs at army hospitals were probably more accustomed to bad manners than a young woman doing home health care in Illinois.

"What are your goals for Joel?" James asked.

"Mobility. Strength." Polly pulled a file from her bag. "Preparation for his transfer to the army hospital."

"Sounds good. I'll take a seat," James said. He gave Joel a steady look and then watched as Polly maneuvered Joel's legs, one at a time, lifting them to a forty-five-degree angle and then lowering them slowly. James had made sure Joel took his pain meds to be able to handle the PT session.

Joel suggested Polly apply for a job with the CIA as a torturer, but the comment was made in good fun. She laughed and said she'd keep that in mind as a second career. Then she worked in silence, moving on to Joel's arm. He winced in pain and cursed.

"Use your words," Polly said, as if she were talking to a toddler.

"I was," Joel said and cursed again.

James stood and stepped to the end of the bed. "Use a number," he suggested. "If the pain's an eight. Say that."

"You guys are full of it." Joel turned his head toward the wall. "I'm done for the day." Joel's voice had turned mean.

Polly shrugged and unrolled the sleeves of her shirt. "It's up to you."

James wanted to remind Joel that the harder he worked the stronger he would be for rehab, but he knew the young man was aware of that.

"I'll see you on Thursday," Polly said. James walked with her as she headed to the door, opened it for her, and followed the young woman outside. "He was much better today," she said. "Thanks for staying."

"See you next time," James said, wondering just how bad Joel had been on the physical therapist's first visit.

As he headed back toward the house, a man hurried out the front door.

James introduced himself, and the man responded, shaking his hand and saying, "I'm Gary Morris. Joel's father."

James nodded. He'd assumed so.

He thanked James profusely for his work. "Melanie said that Joel's settled down a little, and she attributes it to you." Gary zipped his coat as they spoke. "She's too easy on him, but doesn't see it."

"I can only imagine how stressful Joel's injuries have been on your whole family." James could only guess how devastating it would be to have one's child so badly injured.

"Oh, we're doing fine." Gary Morris had an easy air about him. "Joel's doing great. He'll be off to rehab soon and then home again. In no time, things will be back to normal."

James wondered what the man meant by *normal*.

"It's been a pleasure to meet you," Gary said. "I've got to zip into the office for a few hours." He nodded his head toward the house. "We had a rough night. I didn't get much sleep."

"Joel had a hard time last night?"

"You could say that." Gary dangled his car keys in his hands.

"Did he take his pain meds?"

Gary shrugged. "All I know is I hardly slept. I was up half the night, trying to calm him down."

The man waved as he hurried toward his SUV, and James ambled back into the house. As he gathered up his things to leave, he asked Joel how bad his pain had been the night before.

"The same."

"Did you take your meds?"

The young man nodded.

"Your dad said it was a rough night."

Joel snorted. "For him. Not for me. He was being a pain in the—"

"Joel." Melanie stepped to the end of his bed with a half sandwich and a box of juice in her hands.

James excused himself, saying he would be back the next morning at nine. Melanie walked him to the door and thanked him, Joel's lunch still in her hands. He expected her to give an explanation about what was going on, but she didn't. He told her good-bye, hoping she didn't plan to help Joel eat.

As he backed out of the driveway, he prayed for the family.

Chapter Nine

NABELLE STEPPED OUT OF ROOM 3 AND nearly bumped into Leila Hargrave, the nursing administrator.

The two greeted each other warmly, and Leila said she'd walk with Anabelle down to the nurses' station. "I'm checking in with everyone this afternoon," she said. "Per the administration's orders, I need to make sure the supervisors are keeping their staff at the most efficient level."

Anabelle knew *efficient* was business talk for *bare bones*. It meant overworking the nurses to save the hospital money. Some years it meant piling on the patients so management could get a bonus. "I've been doing that," Anabelle said. "Within reason." It was a tricky balance to provide good care and stay within the department budgets.

"We've been asked to cut all costs again," Leila added.

"Really?" Anabelle stopped in the middle of the hall. A fluorescent light flickered above her. "They think we can squeeze that much more out of our departments?"

Leila frowned and said, "Yes. That's what they think. Starting today, they want any nurses who are not needed to be sent home immediately. Do your scheduling to utilize each nurse to the fullest. Reassign patients as often as needed to juggle the workload."

"Is this something the advisory committee is going to be consulted on?" Anabelle crossed her arms. Dr. Hamilton had scheduled another meeting, but it looked more and more like the group was strictly for show.

"You can certainly discuss it," Leila said. "In fact"—her voice was nearly a whisper—"it would be a wonderful idea if you did." She waved a farewell as she rounded the corner, her practical shoes clicking along the linoleum and her gray bun secured in its usual position.

Anabelle sank down into the office chair at the computer and then spun around to the whiteboard with the assignments on it. Marie's patient in room 5 would be discharged in an hour. Anabelle could take that patient and assign the one in room 6 to another nurse. Then she could send Marie, who had the least seniority, home. It would make for a hectic day for Anabelle, taking on two patients with all of her other duties, but she didn't think the situation would be unsafe.

She started down the hall to room 5 to tell Marie. At least Leila hadn't asked her to lay off anyone—yet.

Marie might be happy to go home early. She had a little boy in preschool and two children in elementary school. It would give her more time with her family.

Marie was anything but happy to go. Her eyes grew moist, and she asked Anabelle if she could let someone else leave early.

"I can ask if anyone would like to go home," Anabelle said, half expecting Marie to tell her why she didn't want to go, but the woman didn't elaborate.

Ten minutes later, Raina Levitt volunteered to go home when Anabelle asked if she was interested.

The afternoon continued at a high pace. Anabelle's patient in room 3 needed an angiogram, and the blood pressure of the additional patient she took on shot sky-high right before the shift change. Anabelle administered medication to bring it down and alerted Dr. Hamilton.

By the time she gave report to the next shift she was exhausted but took time before leaving to look at the next day's scheduling. If no new patients were admitted, she could get by with one less nurse. She stood and scanned the hall looking for Marie just as the woman walked around the corner, headed for the stairs.

Anabelle got the woman's attention. "I need to put you on call tomorrow," Anabelle said.

The woman's hand flew to her chest and she approached Anabelle in a couple of steps. "I already told you it's not a good time."

"Everyone's going to have to take turns."

The woman lowered her eyes and her voice fell to a whisper. "I don't know if I should tell you this, but my husband just left me."

Anabelle's heart sank.

"It turns out he'd been gambling—and now all the creditors are calling me."

"Oh dear," Anabelle said, feeling deeply for Marie.

"I can't afford to lose the time off work."

"I'll do what I can," Anabelle said. "But you'll have to take your turn sooner or later. There won't be any way to get around it."

Marie winced. "How about my job? Do you think I'm going to be let go?" She was the last hired on the floor.

"I hope not," Anabelle said.

Marie pulled her shoulder bag against her side. "I don't know what I'll do if I lose my job. It's the money sure, but also the health insurance. My youngest has asthma. You wouldn't believe how much an ER visit is without insurance."

Anabelle could imagine. "No one has said anything about layoffs, so let's just focus on the immediate. I'll ask Raina if she wants tomorrow off too. If she doesn't, I'll give you a call."

Marie thanked her and left. Anabelle picked up the phone and called Raina. Thankfully, Raina was happy to have another day off. Her grown daughter and grandchildren were coming for the weekend, and she had plenty to do to get ready. But Anabelle knew she was only delaying the inevitable. Marie, and other nurses who desperately needed the hours, wouldn't be getting as many as they expected, and, if it came to layoffs, there wouldn't be any way to save Marie's position. Anabelle pushed the office chair away from the phone and stood slowly. James needed more than anything to get rehired at the hospital, and things at Hope Haven were only getting worse.

Candace kissed both of her children good-bye, stepped through her front door, and waited on the stoop for Heath to arrive, the manila folder of paperwork Dr. Hamilton had given her last Friday in her hands.

Heath had called when he left his house and couldn't be more than a minute or two away. She breathed in the fresh air and stepped out onto the walkway to get a view of the sky. The night was clear and bright, studded with stars, and cold. A sliver of a moon hung low, just above the treetops.

Headlights appeared a block away and Candace walked toward the street as Heath pulled his yellow Jeep to the curb and jumped from the driver's seat to hurry around the vehicle to open her door.

She smiled and thanked him, noting his good manners were another thing she loved about him as she climbed up into the seat and set her folder of documents on top of his. As they approached the hospital, they chatted about Hope Haven. "I'm feeling really anxious about all of this," Candace admitted.

Heath reached over and took her hand but didn't respond. She liked that. She didn't expect him to have an answer. She just wanted him to listen. It was comforting to ride with him to the meeting. Over the last four years she'd gotten so used to handling things on her own that it was a relief to be facing all of this with Heath at her side.

He let go of her hand, downshifted, and pulled into the hospital parking lot where he parked in front. Candace spotted Anabelle's car and Elena's small SUV as she climbed out of Heath's Jeep.

She glanced at her watch. They had three minutes until the start of the meeting. "Let's hurry," she said to Heath who had grabbed both of their manila folders. They strode through the sliding doors and through the lobby.

All of the other advisory committee members were already seated at the large table of the boardroom, with Varner at one end and McGarry at the other.

Dr. Hamilton welcomed the two and then called the meeting to order. Candace slipped into the chair between Anabelle and McGarry, and Heath sat down across the table. Candace noticed that the reporter from the *Deerford Dispatch* wasn't present.

"Did everyone have a chance to go over the paperwork?" Dr. Hamilton asked.

Everyone nodded. It had been a daunting task and had taken Candace hours over the weekend.

The group discussed the reports at length, asking questions and gaining clarity on the problems, information that came mostly from McGarry. The grants that had been applied for last year had mostly been rejected due to errors in the paperwork.

"We hired a consultant to do the work," Varner said, "but obviously he didn't know what he was doing." After further discussion, Dr. Hamilton asked if everyone felt they had a general idea of where the hospital was as far as finances.

A sad sigh went around the table.

"Exactly," Dr. Hamilton said and then glanced down at his notes. "My thinking is that the first thing this committee needs to explore is hiring a chief informatics officer."

"I'll reiterate that we can't afford a CIO," Varner said, his voice tense.

"Plenty of small hospitals have CIOs," Dr. Hamilton countered.

"They have bigger foundations," Varner explained. "Or very wealthy benefactors. Hope Haven doesn't have the same resources as some of those other hospitals."

Dr. Hamilton crossed his arms. "We can't afford not to hire a CIO. We'll have to figure something out."

McGarry cleared his throat and the group turned their attention to the end of the table. "I've put out some feelers for a CIO, and Albert's right—we can't afford the salary. But, my executive assistant Quintessa has been researching government grants again. She also has a lead on a consultant who's had better success with actually securing grants. There's definitely money out there to help install a more sophisticated informatics system, but the irony of the situation is they all want a CIO in place to implement the program."

Candace leaned forward in her chair. "So what we need to do is find a CIO who will accept a lower salary."

Varner let out a sigh and Candace's face reddened, afraid the man saw her as an imbecile.

But McGarry smiled at her. "Something like that."

Anabelle came to her defense. "It could happen. Maybe there's a CIO out there who would like to relocate to a smaller town, someone who's looking to retire soon and would be willing to take Hope Haven on as a project."

"Any idea where we could advertise for such a person?" Elena asked.

Varner groaned. "This is the problem with these committee ideas. You people don't understand business."

Candace's face reddened more.

"Albert," McGarry said, his voice firm.

"You're nurses." He glanced at Heath. "And a technician."

"And a doctor," Anabelle said, nodding at Dr. Hamilton. "Who's happened to run his own business for years and years."

"It's not the same," Varner hissed.

Heath placed his hands down flat on the mahogany table. "I have a buddy from high school who works for an electronic charting company." He said it as if he hadn't heard a word Varner had said. "He does consulting, pro bono, for nonprofits. I also seem to recall that he has some experience with grants." Heath tilted his head as if trying to remember the particulars of the situation. "I'll contact him and see if he has any ideas for us."

Candace wondered where the friend lived. Heath had grown up in Washington State. She knew there were lots of high-tech companies located in the Seattle area. Maybe the friend lived there.

"He sounds like he could be a good resource," Elena said, her dark eyes focused on Heath.

"It's certainly worth a try," Anabelle chimed in, as she looked up from the notebook she'd been writing in. "All of us should ask around and see if we can come up with additional resources."

Varner crossed his arms. The discussion continued, but Candace didn't offer any more suggestions as she silently took in the discussion and the ideas of the players around the table.

Anabelle wrote in her notebook as quickly as she could, jotting down who said what and how others responded. She knew she couldn't record every word of the meeting, but she wanted to get the essence of the discussion. Tomorrow would be another busy day, so she probably wouldn't be able to type the notes up for a day or two. Then she would e-mail the minutes to the other members.

Dr. Hamilton was saying he was ready to go on to the next order of business. "Which is," he looked down at his notes, "cutting all budgets by ten percent."

A collective groan circled the table.

Varner was muttering, but his words were clear to Anabelle as he said, "This is another reason I hate committees."

"Respect and safety have to be considered in scheduling." Anabelle looked directly at Varner. "We all need to be aware of cutting expenses, but we have to be careful not to cut to the point of jeopardizing our patients or alienating our staff."

"We're not asking that," Varner said.

"I know," Anabelle replied, "but sometimes it's an uneven balance. We'll do the best we can, but we can't promise ten percent."

"I don't mean to jump the gun," Varner said, his gaze intent. "But HR will be contacting you tomorrow about a hiring freeze and further cuts, meaning positions."

Anabelle sank back in her chair. That was exactly what she'd feared. How many jobs would they want her to cut? Because letting one nurse go wouldn't save 10 percent of the budget, not even close.

"You people don't seem to understand that either we cut spending to the bone, cut more departments, or close the hospital." Varner looked around the table from one person to the next.

"But what sort of hospital will we have left?" Anabelle placed her pen next to the notebook on the table. "Will people even want to come to Hope Haven?"

Elena nodded. "You know how much easier it is for personnel to make mistakes when we're understaffed. If we have dissatisfied clients—and maybe even lawsuits because of minimal staffing—that's only going to hurt the hospital more."

"There's nothing else we can do." Varner's eyes sparked under his shock of dark hair. "Haven't I made myself clear?"

"But how did we get to this place?" Anabelle held her pen like a pointer. "It was just two years ago that it looked like the hospital might close—and yet it was saved. What's happened to put us in such a negative place again?" She couldn't bear to lose everything that they'd worked so hard to keep.

"I'll answer the question," McGarry said, and turned to Anabelle. "It's a combination of many things. You might call it the perfect financial storm. Our own staff insurance premiums just went up for the fourth year in a row, patients are choosing only basic health care procedures right now because of the economy, and there's a whole segment of the population that had insurance a few years ago and doesn't now, so that's another contributor. The hospital has had to eat more bad debts in the last year than since the 1930s."

"I get all that," Anabelle said, her voice clipped. "What I don't get is the change in attitude. I know the staff is willing to do whatever it takes, within reason, to keep Hope Haven open, but it feels as if the administration isn't very hopeful."

"Now that's not true." Varner sat ramrod straight. "We're doing all we can."

McGarry cleared his throat. "I'd like to answer that too, if I may."

Varner nodded.

"I think the administration is worn down. We're caught between government regulations, the current economy, the needs of the town, and the needs of the staff. Right now it feels close to impossible."

Varner grimaced in agreement.

"Impossible?" Anabelle looked up as she wrote. "It's never impossible. Right?" She looked around the table. Dr. Hamilton, Heath, and Elena nodded in agreement. Candace didn't look as sure.

McGarry cleared his throat. "I said 'close to impossible.' Please make sure that's correct in your notes."

Anabelle blushed as she reread what she'd written and then met McGarry's gaze. "That's exactly what I wrote."

"How about a piece of pie?" Heath steered his Jeep down Oak Street. "We could stop at the Parlor."

The clock on the dashboard read nine thirty. Candace was too keyed up to go home to bed. "Sure," she answered. "That would be great."

Heath parked across the street from the restaurant.

"It's a beautiful night," Heath said, taking her hand.

Candace agreed.

Kerri Lane met them inside the door of the restaurant, two menus in her hand.

"We're here for pie," Heath said.

The waitress looked relieved. "We have apple, peach, French silk, and lemon crème," she said, leading them to a booth.

As they sat down, Heath asked Candace if she knew what she wanted. "A cup of decaf," she said to Kerri, "and a piece of French silk." She could use a good dose of chocolate tonight.

Heath ordered the peach and a glass of water. As Kerri walked away, Candace asked Heath what he thought of the meeting.

"I think we'll have to wait and see," Heath said.

"Do you think your friend will have some ideas?" Candace slipped out of her coat.

Heath shrugged. "We just reconnected online last month. I'll send him a message tonight and see if we can chat."

Heath seemed so casual about contacting the man that he hardly seemed serious, or hopeful, about it.

"I can't imagine what will happen if the hospital closes," Candace said.

Kerri arrived with the water and coffee and then quickly left.

"Try not to visit Worryland," Heath said.

"Worryland—is that like Candyland?" Candace tried to smile.

"The opposite," Heath said. "Believe me you don't want to go there." He wrapped his hand around his water glass. "We have to take this a step at a time."

"What will you do if the hospital closes?" she asked.

Heath shrugged. "I have no idea."

"You haven't even thought about it?"

He scooted his glass on the table, staring at the trail of condensation it left behind, and then looked Candace in the eye and said, "Sure, I've thought of it a little. I'll apply for other jobs around here. If I don't get one, I'll apply in Princeton. If I don't get one there, I'll have to think about moving."

"We'd have to put our houses on the market. Who would buy them?" Candace shuddered. "Who would want to move to a town with no hospital?"

Heath held up both hands. "I refuse to think that far. It doesn't do any good."

"But there's no point denying things might get desperate."

"I agree," Heath said, as Kerri approached with the pie. Both Candace and Heath turned their attention toward her.

"Enjoy," the waitress said, her ash blonde ponytail bobbing around her head as she set the plates in front of the two.

Heath took a bite of pie and then continued. "But there's no use speculating that the worst is going to happen. We have to take it a day at a time." He held his pie in midair and spoke quietly, "Live by faith."

Candace nodded in agreement and took a bite of pie. Heath didn't talk a lot about his faith, but she knew it was there as a steady foundation for the way he lived.

If she lost her job and had to move, would her mother come with her or move in with Susan? Her mother loved Deerford. It would be so hard for her to relocate. And Brooke, at thirteen, was at a bad age to move too.

"Candace?" Heath's blue eyes searched her face. "Where'd you go?"

She put her fork on the edge of the plate and picked up her coffee. "Nowhere."

"Worryland?"

She nodded and then took a sip of the decaf, aware of how difficult it was for her to keep her mind off the issues at work.

"Stick with me, okay?" His gaze was intense. "We'll get through this, I promise."

We'll get through this. Her heart jumped at the realization that they had become a *we*.

Elena stood in the doorway of Izzy's room and stared at her granddaughter by the glow of the Little Pony night-light beside her bed. Three Madeline books were on the bed beside Izzy. She'd probably read them to herself before she went to sleep. Now she was clutching her stuffed pig, Oinky; his snout was smashed against her neck in an endless embrace. Elena bent to kiss her granddaughter's forehead. The swelling of her lip was nearly gone and the bruising was much lighter. Elena squinted in the dim light. The wound was healing nicely, and she was grateful she wouldn't have to suffer through having stitches removed.

Elena yawned—it was ten o'clock and definitely time for bed—and closed Izzy's door behind her. She would tell Rafael good night and then join Cesar in bed.

Her son had his math book for his class at the community college spread out on the kitchen table, but he was texting on his phone.

"Did you talk with Izzy's teacher?" Elena asked.

He closed his phone, put it on the table, and picked up his pencil. "I left her a message but she didn't call back."

"Did you find anything online?" Elena nodded toward his laptop on the far edge of the table.

"A few things. I was going to look more tonight." Rafael's voice sounded tired.

"Have you talked to Sarah about all of this?"

Rafael started to erase something on the paper in front of him. "No. And I don't plan to."

"What if there's a history of reading problems in her family?"

Rafael turned his head toward her. "Is it hereditary?"

"It could be . . ." Elena's voice trailed off.

Rafael sighed loudly. "I have a test tomorrow. I'll think about talking with Sarah after that."

Elena told him good night and headed down the hall. She understood that Rafael felt a little overwhelmed. It was a lot to deal with right now and navigating his relationship with Sarah was tricky. For all these years, he was solely responsible for Izzy. And legally he still was. Sarah had given up her parental rights. But Elena knew that now the young woman sincerely—and lovingly—cared about her daughter. And that was a good thing for Izzy.

As she neared the bedroom door, Elena could hear Cesar's soft snore. She'd been hoping to talk with him about Hope Haven tonight, but obviously she'd missed her chance.

Chapter Ten

ANABELLE SAT AT THE COMPUTER IN THE nurses' station tightening the schedule for the upcoming week when Leila Hargrave approached the desk. Anabelle peered over her reading glasses at her supervisor.

"I bet you hate to see me coming." Leila wore a skirt and blouse that did nothing to hide her plump figure. "Can we talk?"

"Sure." Anabelle stood, her heart thumping. "Let's go into the break room."

Leila followed her, and Anabelle shut the door behind them. The two stood facing each other.

"You need to let a nurse go," Leila said. "I wanted to tell you in person."

"Any chance I could ask two to go to part-time?"

Leila shook her head. "They'd have to agree to go part-time with no benefits. That's what's killing us. Even if we end up paying overtime—occasionally—we save by not having to pay another employee benefits."

"When?"

"Today."

Anabelle didn't respond.

Leila sighed. "As soon as possible."

"The nurse I need to let go is off today. Can it wait until tomorrow?"

"You won't be doing her a favor."

Anabelle nodded. She knew that. But she would be giving herself time to think things through.

"That's fine," Leila said. "Just do it as soon as possible. We have a severance package. I'm doing all that I can."

"I know," Anabelle responded. "It can't be fun for you either."

Leila was not usually a warm person—she did what she had to do—so Anabelle was surprised when her eyes teared up a little. Leila swiped at them quickly.

"What other departments have to cut back?" Anabelle asked, her voice kind.

Leila quickly regained her composure. "I can't say." She was all businesslike again. "Report back to me, please."

Anabelle nodded and the two walked out of the room. Leila took off toward the elevators while Anabelle counted the hours until she could go home. But there would be no escaping Marie's dilemma. What would the young mother do to support her children?

As James parked his van in the driveway of the Morris home, the physical therapist started out the front door. She'd come early today because that worked the best with her schedule.

James jumped down to the cement and called out a greeting.

She looked up, her face red and her blonde hair falling over one eye. She had a chart in one hand but the other flew into the air. "I can't work with that kid," she stormed. James forced himself not to smile. She couldn't be more than a few years older than Joel. "He's so belligerent."

"What happened?" James stepped toward her.

She blushed further. "I don't want to talk about it."

James didn't ask if she'd be back. He figured if he asked that question now, the answer would be no. With no more explanation, Polly climbed into her little commuter car and drove off. James prepared himself for a rough few hours and stepped up on the porch.

Melanie opened the door, wearing a coat, and waved him inside. "I have an appointment in town," she said.

James nodded. He'd be here for four hours. That should give her plenty of time. "So PT didn't go too well this morning," he ventured, slipping out of his jacket.

"I don't think she has much experience working with patients with injuries like Joel's." Her voice was low.

James didn't answer. Chances were Polly had worked with stroke victims and others with injuries that left them less in control of their words and actions. And James wasn't sure whether Joel's acting out was due to his injuries or his bottled-up anger.

Melanie grabbed her purse from the table near the door and hurried out, calling out a good-bye—which James assumed was intended for Joel—over her shoulder.

Joel feigned sleep when James approached him. "Time to get moving," he said.

Joel didn't respond.

"What'd you do to scare Polly off?"

Joel opened one eye and said groggily, "No one told me I was scheduled to be tortured first thing this morning."

"Sure they did. It was on the calendar."

Joel closed his eye.

"Did you forget?" James pushed the button to raise the bed.

"Must have," Joel muttered.

"Guess I'll have to be the taskmaster today," James said.

"You?"

"What? Would you rather fall behind on your recovery? Delay your start in rehab?"

Joel didn't answer and didn't open his eyes but muttered, "I'm still tired. Really tired."

James lowered the bed back down, partway. He'd let Joel rest awhile longer. Maybe he'd had a hard night. As James picked up the PT binder that Polly had left, Joel's breathing changed. By the time he sat down in the straight-backed chair and began leafing through the notebook, it was obvious the young man had fallen back to sleep. James kept reading and studying the exercise diagrams.

It wasn't long until Joel began to stir though. A second later he began to thrash around and James put the binder down and stepped toward the bed. Joel's eyes flew open, wide and scared.

"You okay, bud?" James put a hand on Joel's good arm.

The young man jerked away and his eyes darted around the room. Then he froze.

"Everything's all right," James said, his voice low and steady.

Joel let out a sigh. "I'm home, right?"

"Yep. Safe and sound."

"I had a dream."

James waited for him to say more, but he didn't. "Do you have them often?"

Joel shook his head and then pursed his lips. "Actually, I do have them a lot."

"Are you back in Iraq?"

"Maybe." Joel inhaled and turned his head toward James. "It's morning, right?"

James nodded and looked at his watch. "It's nine twenty. I'm here with you. Your mom isn't here right now; she has an appointment in town."

Joel snorted. "You mean my dad has an appointment."

James raised the bed again, sensing Joel was ready for the day now. "What's going on?"

Joel's eyes darkened and then he shook his head. "Hey," he said, "that PT chick doesn't have a sense of humor. If she'd stuck around for a few more minutes, I would have done my exercises. But she got all offended and left in a huff."

"She has a specific job to do. If you're not going to cooperate, she's not going to stick around."

Joel was sitting up now. He opened his mouth as if to say something and then closed it quickly.

"She's a professional," James said. "You need to treat her that way." He was beginning to wonder if Joel had a problem with respect. He wasn't behaving like a good soldier.

When Joel still didn't respond, James said, "I'm going to finish up the exercises." He reached for the notebook.

Joel closed his eyes. "I'm tired."

"Nope. I already gave you a break. Do you need a pit stop?"

"How about a bedpan?"

"That's a joke, right?"

Joel shrugged.

James said, "You're past that. And you're not going to get one in rehab." Then he paused for a moment. "You didn't throw one this morning? At Polly?"

A sheepish look spread across Joel's face and then he muttered, "I shouldn't have."

"Don't tell me," James said. "Tell her."

Joel nodded and then changed the subject as his attention fell on his wheelchair. "I hate that thing."

James ignored him and positioned the chair for the transfer.

An hour later, as James finished the last of the exercises, Melanie returned home. She stood in the doorway to the living room and watched as James lowered Joel's leg back down to the bed.

"How was the appointment?" Joel didn't look at his mother as he spoke, and James detected sarcasm in the young man's voice.

"There wasn't an appointment. Your dad didn't show up."

"Figures," Joel said.

"I'm going to go rest for a few minutes." Melanie turned on her heel before James could say good-bye.

When James was ready to leave a few hours later, after giving Joel lunch and getting him settled back in the hospital bed, he stood for a moment at the end of the hall. Melanie hadn't been out of her room since she'd returned home. He decided to go ahead and leave. If Joel needed her, she would hear him.

He quietly slipped out the front door. He had no idea what the family's problems were but obviously more was going on than Joel's injuries.

Elena pushed through the doors of Rishell Elementary just as the dismissal bell rang. Every couple of days, she liked to pick Izzy up straight from the classroom to see her new artwork and say hello to the teacher. She was determined that every person involved in her granddaughter's life know how much the little girl was loved. Just because she lived with her daddy and grandparents, and not her mother, she didn't want anyone to assume Izzy wasn't well cared for.

As the heels of her boots clicked along the linoleum, Elena looked straight ahead to the kindergarten classrooms in case Izzy slipped out to the hall and toward the other exit. As she neared the room, Elena heard Mrs. Allison ordering the children to be quiet. "You need to follow my instructions," she was saying, an element of exasperation in her voice. "Give the flier about the fund-raiser to your moms as soon as you get home."

Elena winced as she stopped in the doorway. It probably didn't bother Izzy that everyone assumed all kids lived with a mother, but it bothered Elena.

"Now line up at the door," Mrs. Allison said.

Izzy waved the flier at Elena from the back of the room, and her gray eyes lit up in a smile. She wore her hair in pigtails, each still in the perfect corkscrew curl they had been in that morning, and they bounced against her arms.

Mrs. Allison turned abruptly and startled when she saw Elena. "Oh," she said.

"Hello." Elena hadn't meant to surprise the woman.

"Could you wait for a moment—until I get back from walking the students to the exit?"

Elena nodded.

"I need to talk with you." Mrs. Allison then snapped her fingers and the last of the children fell into line. In no time they had all filed out of the room.

"Buela!" Izzy wrapped her arms around her grandmother's middle, her backpack bumping against Elena's legs.

"How was your day?" Elena pulled back and looked down at Izzy.

"Great!"

"Any new artwork?"

Elena was praising the near perfect symmetry of Izzy's purple and blue butterfly when Mrs. Allison came back into the classroom.

"What a day!" She stopped at her desk. "Two students went home sick, plus we had an unexpected fire alarm and a downpour during recess."

Izzy looked up at Elena. "It was so much fun! The raindrops were as big as cookies, and we all started running toward the building."

Mrs. Allison laughed. "Isn't it great to see things through the eyes of a child?"

Elena nodded and put her hands on her granddaughter's shoulders.

"Isabel," Mrs. Allison said, "I need a note delivered to the office. Could you do that for me?"

"Of course." Izzy's voice sounded like a professional's. She took a slip of paper from her teacher and then, looking at Elena, said, "I'll be right back."

"I had a phone message from Isabel's father, from yesterday," Mrs. Allison said as soon as Izzy was out of earshot.

"Good," Elena said.

The teacher frowned and then said, "I'm afraid he isn't taking Isabel's reading problem seriously."

"I think he's a little confused about it. She's reading really well at home."

"And it seemed she was starting to read here at school too, but now she only recognizes a few of the letters on handouts. I thought she knew the ones above the chalkboards earlier in the year, but now I'm thinking she memorized them." Mrs. Allison pointed to the letters crowning the room. "And when I give her a worksheet she won't do it."

"Won't?"

"She stuffs it in her desk and says she's lost it."

"She reads to us at home. . . ." Suddenly Elena felt unsure.

"She probably has those books memorized too. There's no doubt she's smart, but her pre-reading skills are lacking. In fact, it seems like they're getting worse. I don't remember her acting this way at the beginning of the year."

Elena paused and then asked, "What do you recommend that we do?"

"Work with her more. Read to her every night."

"We do," Elena said.

"Flash cards."

"Is there someone here who can test to see if she has a learning disability?"

"Not without her father's cooperation."

"I know Rafael would cooperate. He wants what's best for Izzy." Elena heard her granddaughter's footsteps in the hall. "We'll figure this out."

Mrs. Allison seemed relieved. As Elena and her granddaughter left the building it began to rain again. Izzy squealed as she rushed toward Elena's Jeep Liberty. Elena remembered Izzy's pointing out letters in the hospital room. She knew her granddaughter knew the letters of the alphabet. Why would she pretend she didn't?

Candace turned on the projector in the hospital conference room and inserted her USB flash drive into the computer and checked to see that her PowerPoint presentation uploaded properly. It was the first session of her spring birthing class, but tonight she wanted nothing more than to be at home, curled up on the couch with Heath.

Six expectant mothers, all first timers, had signed up for the class, five with their husbands and one with her sister. She'd had as many as ten moms and their labor partners at a time, but six was a good number. Any fewer than that, and it tended to make the participants a little more self-conscious.

At five minutes to seven, her students began to arrive, coming in with their pillows and their questions. Candace had arranged the chairs in a circle in front of the table.

Just after seven, two of the couples still hadn't arrived. Her students were usually very punctual, but Candace decided to wait a few more minutes. At ten after, as the chitchat grew thinner, she decided to go ahead and start the class, giving her introduction spiel. The first class would cover an overview of pregnancy, the development of the baby, and basic nutrition. Later classes would cover the stages of labor and delivery.

She started by introducing herself and citing her years of experience as an obstetrics nurse, ten at Hope Haven, and adding that she was a certified childbirth instructor. Then she had the couples go around and introduce themselves. The mother-to-be and her sister hadn't arrived yet, so all of the couples were women and their husbands. Their ages ranged, Candace guessed, from twenty-two to thirty-seven, and they were all in their third trimester.

She smiled as she looked around the room at the four bulging bellies. For the first time in four years she surprised herself by thinking that perhaps she still might have another baby. She was thirty-nine, probably a little older than the oldest mother in attendance.

After the introductions, she started the presentation that showed the development of the fetus. There was nothing more spectacular or amazing. At four weeks, the baby's brain and spinal cord had begun to develop, along with the baby's heart and the buds that were the beginnings of arms and legs, even though the embryo was only four to six millimeters long. As Candace spoke, she glanced at the door occasionally, expecting the other two couples to arrive.

By eight weeks, fingers and toes had formed and all of the internal organs were developing. Candace was pretty sure all of the mothers in the group had read enough about their developing babies to already know the information she was sharing, but from experience she knew that many of their partners hadn't educated themselves about the growing fetus. The presentation emphasized the humanity of the baby from the beginning and what a miracle the entire process was. No matter how many times she taught a birthing class or how many babies she helped deliver, she was wowed every time by the miracle of pregnancy.

She continued with the slide show. By twelve weeks the baby's nerves and muscles were working together and he or she could make a fist. By twenty weeks, the gender of the baby could be identified. "How many of you know whether you're having a girl or a boy?" Candace asked.

Three of the mothers raised their hands.

"We don't want to know," the fourth mother said. She was the oldest in the class.

Candace affirmed the responses. "We didn't want to know with my first, but we found out ahead of time with our second," she added, noting that she'd used plural pronouns. *We*. Candace and Dean. Actually he was the one who had really wanted to know whether they were having a boy or a girl when she was pregnant with Howie.

Candace gave up on the other two couples' arriving. She couldn't help but be curious as to why they hadn't, though. She'd confirmed all six of the couples earlier in the week. Usually a mother-to-be would call the hospital at the last minute if she couldn't come.

When she reached the description of the baby at thirty-two weeks, she began wondering if the rumors around town about the hospital cutbacks had discouraged the two couples from attending.

After the slide show, Candace passed out information about nutrition, emphasizing that the third trimester was when the baby began storing iron and calcium and it was as important as ever for the mother to eat an extra healthy diet.

Next Candace talked about exercise. "Labor and delivery are physical events," she said. Several of her students laughed. "Of course we don't want you running a marathon, but stretching exercises, walking, swimming, and light aerobics will make the end of your pregnancy more comfortable and keep you strong for the work ahead of you."

She ended the class with the couples getting down on the floor on mats to practice relaxing techniques. She emphasized relaxation in each of the classes, hoping that by the time labor began the couple was proficient at working together.

It was eight forty-five by the time the last couple left the conference room. Candace wondered if it was too late to call the couples who didn't attend and then decided to anyway.

The first call went into voice mail, and Candace left a message, saying she was wondering if the couple planned to attend the remaining classes.

A woman answered the second call after the fourth ring. "Oh, I should have let you know," she said, her voice cheery. "We decided not to attend—my sister and I. My husband travels a lot."

"Do you mind if I ask why?"

"My aunt is Emmaline Palmer, a board member at Hope Haven. She said they might shut down the Birthing Unit, so I've decided to deliver at the Princeton hospital."

"Those rumors are unfounded. . . ." Candace's voice trailed off.

"She *is* a board member," the woman responded.

Candace knew exactly who Emmaline was. She leaned against the conference room table, dumbfounded. "Well, good luck," she said.

"Thanks." The woman's voice was still cheery. "To you too."

Looks like I'm going to need it, Candace thought as she hung up the phone.

Chapter Eleven

THURSDAY MORNING ANABELLE CHECKED THE staffing schedule before report and found a note that Marie had called in ill because she was home with a sick child. Anabelle was sorry the child was sick but thankful she could put off letting the woman go a little longer, unless Leila pushed her to call and do it over the phone. She really hated dealing with people that way, though.

With the increased workload, Anabelle's day passed more quickly than usual, and in no time, it was the end of the shift. She scrambled to reconcile the meds and give report. Before she left, she remembered Leila had asked her to check in, so she hurried down to HR—only to find Leila gone. She left a note on the woman's desk that she'd stopped by.

By the time she left Hope Haven she was worn out, but she'd told Cameron she'd pick up milk and bread on her way home. In the middle of the grocery store parking lot, someone called her name. She turned around and moving toward her two rows over was Donald Armstrong, his John Deere baseball cap securely on his head.

"Anabelle," the mayor of Deerford called out again, "how are you?" He joined her, chatting about the sunshine they'd had all day and how it was too bad the clouds had rolled in during the last hour.

"I've been at work all day, so I didn't realize I'd missed such a fine spring day." She mustered up a smile for the mayor.

His voice lowered and he leaned closer. "How's the advisory committee coming along?"

Anabelle shrugged. "It's slow going, but I hope that will change. We meet again tonight."

He glanced around, looking as if he expected someone to be spying. "Could I buy you a cup of coffee?"

"Sure, but I have a few groceries to pick up."

"Can you meet me at the Parlor?" he asked.

"I'll see you soon," Anabelle said. The Parlor was farther from the hospital than Cuppa Coffee or the Diner on the Corner, so it made a good place to meet if the man wanted to talk about Hope Haven. If he had questions for her, he was going to be disappointed, because she didn't have any answers.

As it turned out, Donald didn't expect any. His objective was to relay information, and he wanted Anabelle to share what he had to say with the advisory committee. "I already called Albert Varner about it," he said, his hand on the bill of his hat that rested on the tabletop. "But . . . well, he didn't seem very sympathetic."

"He's overwhelmed," Anabelle said.

"That's a nice way of putting it," Donald said. He wrapped his hands around his coffee cup and glanced around the restaurant. It was practically empty. "This is strictly confidential," he said, "except I do want you to share it with the committee." He went on to say that a small manufacturing company had been looking at Deerford as a place to open an operation that would employ thirty people. "Not a huge deal but definitely significant."

Anabelle nodded. It felt like a huge deal to her. Thirty new employees could mean over a hundred new people in Deerford when family members were counted. That was definitely significant.

"But," Donald continued, "the company's worried about the hospital here. They've heard the rumors about cutbacks and maybe a possible closure. They can't open up a shop in a place with inadequate health care. If they do, their insurance premiums will go up and they won't be able to afford to expand. Plus employees don't want to transfer to a town without a hospital."

Anabelle flinched. Of course, people wouldn't want to move to Deerford if the hospital closed. If Hope Haven hadn't been in Deerford when Kirstie had been hit by the car fifteen years ago, her daughter would have died. And how many residents would have succumbed to heart attacks if the hospital hadn't been around? And how many motorists would have died in accidents on the highway if the EMTs hadn't been able to transfer them to Hope Haven within minutes of the accident?

"I can certainly see that traveling farther means greater risks when it comes to health care." Anabelle looked Donald straight in the eyes.

He nodded. "This is affecting the whole town," he said. "Something has to be done. Please tell the advisory committee that all of Deerford is depending on them."

"You push me, Buela." Izzy swung high, her long curly hair rising up behind her and then falling gracefully as she pumped her legs, back and forth.

Elena stepped behind the swing and gave Izzy a push and then another.

Sarah stood on the other side of the swing set, smiling. Elena knew she was enjoying the little girl. She'd been working a lot, including Sundays, and Izzy had commented on it, so Elena had called Sarah to see if she could meet them in the park. It was good for Izzy to see her mother and good for all of them to be outside with the spring sun shining down on them. It was a treat, with the days growing longer, to go to the park after school and work, even though it was still chilly.

Elena pushed Izzy a few more times, but then the little girl was ready to stop. She slowed herself and then leaped to the ground, making Elena gasp. She didn't want another trip to the ER, but Izzy landed on her feet and bounded over to the slide.

Elena and Sarah followed her.

"Rafael called the other day," Sarah said. "About Izzy's reading."

"Oh?" Elena hadn't been sure whether her son had followed through with calling Sarah.

"I told him to take it seriously." Sarah exhaled slowly. "I had a hard time reading. It wasn't until the third grade that I really got it, and by then the other kids—and most of the teachers—thought I was stupid." She paused and then said, "I don't want Izzy to go through what I did."

"What was the problem?" Elena felt compassion for the young woman.

Sarah shrugged. "No one knew. All of a sudden it just started making sense, but no one at home read to me or worked with me the way you do with Izzy."

Elena didn't respond.

"Thanks," Sarah whispered.

"For?"

"Being such a wonderful grandmother. I wish I'd had someone like you."

Elena put her arm around the young woman and squeezed her shoulder. "I'm not sure what to think of Izzy's reading. She keeps getting flustered and upset when I try to see how she's doing with her letters and all."

"That's what Rafael said."

"I'm thinking we should have an evaluation done."

"Rafael thinks she's too young," Sarah said. "That kindergarten is for having fun. He says he wants to wait until next year to deal with all of this."

Elena wasn't surprised.

"All I know," Sarah said, "is that by the end of first grade, I was already feeling stupid."

They were interrupted by Izzy at the top of the slide. "Look at me!" she yelled.

Both women waved to her and then Elena gave her a thumbs-up. She turned her attention back to Sarah.

"It wasn't just school that the reading problem affected," she said. "Pretty soon I didn't feel like I could do anything right."

"Yippee!" Izzy yelled as she zipped down the slide.

"I don't want that to happen to her." Sarah had tears in her eyes.

"Neither do I," Elena answered and gave Sarah another hug, wishing the young woman had had someone who believed in her twenty years ago.

Chapter Twelve

IN THE LATE AFTERNOON, POLLY ARRIVED AS JAMES wheeled Joel into the living room from the bathroom. He'd agreed to work late to accommodate the woman's schedule. After greeting the two, she said Joel should stay in his chair. "I have a stand in my truck I'm going to bring in," she said. "We'll start today's session working with that."

"I'll go get it," James said, starting toward the door.

"No thanks." Polly slipped ahead of him. "I can do it." She returned hauling in a chest-high contraption of PVC pipes. "It's sturdier than it looks," she said. "And easy to move."

She maneuvered Joel's chair away from the bed and into an open area of the living room and then positioned the stand in front of him. "I need your help," she said to James. "Hold this side firmly."

James followed her instructions.

Next she showed Joel how to grab on to the bars of the stand and pull himself up out of the chair. He complied. "Now sit down and do it again," she said, her voice firm.

"What's the point?" Joel shot her a dirty look.

"To build up strength so you can transfer yourself—and walk again."

He plopped down into the chair and then pulled himself up again. James steadied the stand as he did.

"Do it ten more times." Polly stepped away from the two of them and opened up the PT notebook. James was pretty sure she was ignoring Joel on purpose because she thought he would do better without her constant attention. She didn't want to give him a reason to lash out at her again.

By the time Joel had done six up-and-downs, he was sweating. By the time he'd done eight he couldn't get back out of his chair. He sat for a moment and then tried again, pulling hard with his good arm to get himself to a standing position. Finally he made it but fell back hard, making the chair bounce a little.

"Rest for a minute and then do the last two," Polly said, not looking up. James was surprised that she had been keeping track.

Joel waited a couple of minutes and then pulled himself up and lowered himself slowly. After another long wait, he pulled himself up a final time and then plopped back down. As he did he whispered, "Sorry."

"Pardon?" Polly turned toward him.

"Sorry for how horrible I've been to you."

"Really?" Her hands were on her hips. "Does that mean no more bad language?"

He nodded.

"Or flying bedpans?"

He nodded again.

"Then, thank you. I accept your apology," Polly said. "Back to bed for your stretching exercises." James helped Joel with his transfer, aware that the muscles in the young man's legs were still shaking from exertion and stress. James guessed it hadn't been easy for him to apologize.

He was getting a good workout. According to his chart, the doctors had said there was no doubt that Joel would walk again, but his muscles and nerves needed to be rehabilitated, and he needed to regain his strength.

As Polly lifted and lowered Joel's right leg, she told him he needed to start doing the exercises twice a day. Once with help and once on his own. "It's part of your taking responsibility for your recovery," she said.

He groaned.

James turned his attention to his paperwork, but it wasn't long before Polly asked for his help again. She had him hold Joel's right leg at a forty-five-degree angle while she lifted his left leg. Joel closed his eyes, and James asked Polly how long she'd worked as a physical therapist. "Two years," she answered. "I got my degree at the university in Peoria."

"Master's?" James asked.

"Doctorate," she answered.

He was impressed. She was young to have completed so much schooling. She must have gone straight through.

"It's a great career," she said. "There are lots of job openings, especially for those of us who specialize in working with people with disabilities."

James enjoyed helping her and intended to help Fern do some of the exercises, thinking they would help her strength and flexibility too.

"Go ahead and put his leg down," Polly said.

As James finished his charting, Joel's mother stepped into the living room.

"I need to go into town," she said.

James stood. "Do you want me to stay until you get back?"

"No," she said. "I've called a neighbor to come sit with Joel. She'll be here before Polly leaves."

After Melanie left, Polly told James he should go ahead and go. She nodded toward Joel, who still had his eyes closed. "I think I wore him out. I'm about done."

James gathered his things and headed out the front door just as his cell phone rang. It wasn't Fern. The number looked like a Hope Haven number. He answered it quickly. It was Leila Hargrave.

James's heart pounded faster. "Hi, Leila."

"I'm filling in for the nurse supervisor who does the scheduling for Med/Surg," she said, referencing his former department. "Would you like to pick up a short shift this evening? We're shorthanded, and you know that floor better than anyone. Seven to eleven at the most. You may be sent home earlier if we have a couple of discharges."

"Sure," James answered. He wasn't going to pass up work, that was for sure. As he drove toward Deerford, a flock of starlings turned upward and then swooped toward a red barn in the distance, heading for home. James couldn't help but wonder what it would be like at the hospital. He hoped he wouldn't feel too uncomfortable. At least it was the evening shift, and the administrators would soon be headed for home.

Not too long after he arrived, signed in, and changed into hospital-provided scrubs, word got out that James was picking up a shift. Face after friendly face stopped by Med/Surg to greet him.

"I don't have anyone to banter with anymore," Elena complained.

"What?" James retorted. "No one is as clever as I?"

Elena slapped her hand toward his shoulder, brushing his sleeve. "Now don't go putting words in my mouth. I didn't say that."

Anabelle stopped by to say hello and so did Candace. Even Leila Hargrave sashayed through the Med/Surg and talked with him for a moment.

"Anabelle Scott told me this afternoon that you've taken a home health position. From the way she put it, sounds like you're enjoying it."

"It's work; it's keeping me busy. It's temporary though," he said.

"So you're still hoping to come back to Hope Haven?"

"Definitely, yes," James answered.

He was assigned seven patients, all listed by first name on the whiteboard at the nurses' station. He made his way from patient to patient, checking in with each one. Five were postsurgery, one had pneumonia, and the last one, a man named Gary, had alcohol poisoning. He was shocked to enter the man's room and find Gary Morris huddled in the bed, sound asleep.

James opened his chart on the computer. He'd been found at eleven in the morning, passed out in Deerford Park. Detective Cesar Rodriguez had called an ambulance, and the ER team had pumped his stomach. He'd been dehydrated and suffering from hypothermia, which explained both the fluid bag on the IV pole and the mountain of blankets piled high on top of the man.

There was no indication of how long he had been at the park. Neither Joel nor Melanie had said anything about Gary's being gone all night—not that they would have. James looked around for any sign of Melanie—a purse, a book, or a sweater—but there was none. He checked the fluid bag on the IV pole and noted it was half empty. He'd be surprised if Gary spent the night, but he might, depending on his fluid levels and temperature. James decided to check on his other patients and then come back to Gary, hoping the man woke up in the next hour or so.

Two hours later, when James poked his head in the room for the sixth time, Gary's eyes were open.

"How's it going?" James stepped into the room.

Gary struggled to sit.

James showed him the button on the railing to raise the bed and Gary pressed it, turning his face toward James. "Have we met?" he asked.

James nodded. "I'm Joel's home health nurse."

Gary groaned. "Lucky me."

"No worries," James said. "How are you doing?"

Gary closed his eyes. "I don't want to talk about it, okay? And I don't want Melanie or Joel knowing about this either."

James didn't respond as he reached for the thermometer. He wondered if Melanie already knew—if that was why she'd come into town. Perhaps she was out in the waiting room, trying to decide what to do about her husband.

James took Gary's temperature—it was up to ninety-seven—removed the stack of covers, and put a fresh blanket from the warmer over him and then layered three more over that. "Are you warm enough?" James asked.

Gary nodded.

"Hungry?"

The man shook his head.

James checked his blood pressure. It was still low—90/60. Of course, alcohol was a depressant, so his blood pressure would stay low until it was out of his system.

"I'll be back shortly," James said after he recorded Gary's vitals in his chart.

"Just do what you have to do, and leave me alone as much as possible," the man responded, his voice low.

A half hour later, James was on his way to the Med/Surg nurses' station when he saw Cesar at the desk.

"How's it going?" Cesar shook James's hand and gave him a hearty pat on the back.

"Good."

"Heard you've got my guy tonight. How's he doing?"

"Better. I'm guessing he'll be discharged in a few hours."

"Where's he going to go?"

James had the feeling Cesar knew more about what was going on than he did. "Home?"

Cesar shook his head. "Not according to his wife. She said she's done."

James's eyes popped wide. Poor Melanie. She had enough to deal with as it was.

"Mind if I go chat with him?" Cesar took a step.

"Are there legal ramifications for overdosing on alcohol?"

Cesar pulled out his notebook. "Probably not. He wasn't driving, but I need to question him now that he's conscious."

James led the way down the hall and motioned to Gary's room. He entered after Cesar.

"Do I need a lawyer?" Gary struggled for a moment to pull his hand out from under the layers of blankets to push the button and raise the bed to a sitting position.

"It's up to you," Cesar said. "You've been down this road before."

"I wasn't driving. And I'm past my parole on my violation from five years ago. I stayed sober, honest. It's just been a couple of times, all in the last month, that I've fallen off the wagon."

"What's your plan now?" Cesar asked.

Gary turned his eyes toward the windows.

"Rehab? AA? Both?" Cesar sounded like he was talking to a delinquent.

"I'm not sure," Gary said, his voice still low. "It's not like I have a full-blown problem. Just a relapse."

Cesar's eyebrows shot up. "What does your wife say?"

"That's just it. I'm not sure if I heard her right."

"I think you did," Cesar answered.

Gary looked straight at the officer. "She's not going to give me a second chance?"

"She already did," Cesar said. "You might not remember it, but I'm the one who hauled your sorry self into the ER two weeks ago too. If you can't get yourself into rehab, then I'll bring charges and the court will mandate it." With that, Cesar nodded his head brusquely and said good-bye. He shook James's hand on the way out.

James stepped forward to check Gary's vitals. As he worked, he prayed for the man, for Melanie, and for Joel.

Gary's temperature and blood pressure had improved, but James knew he was a sick, sick man. After he'd charted the new information he turned back to Gary. "Do you have any questions?"

The man shook his head, barely. He wasn't as tall as his son, and in the hospital bed covered in a pile of blankets, he looked a little shrunken, as if he were sinking into himself.

"Do you want to talk?" James asked.

Gary shook his head again, but his eyes grew watery. "Just leave," he said. "Please leave."

Chapter Thirteen

ELENA FLIPPED THE SWITCH ON HER COFFEE machine and immediately the rich scent of decaf brewing filled the kitchen. She had made a cobbler from berries in her freezer for the evening, hoping some refreshments would make the advisory committee more bearable—that, and holding the gathering in her house instead of in the sterile meeting room at the hospital. Maybe a change of scenery would finally get things moving for the group. It was the least she could do, considering Dr. Hamilton had asked everyone to meet later than usual, at eight o'clock in the evening, to accommodate his schedule.

She turned toward the back door, thinking she'd heard a car. Cesar's face appeared in the window. She met him at the door.

"Long day," she said and then kissed him.

"It's good to be home." He started down the hallway. She knew he was heading straight to his safe to lock up his pistol, just like he did when he arrived home after every shift he ever worked. She appreciated that he always put Izzy's safety first.

"Your dinner's in the oven," she called after him. "Do you remember I have a meeting here tonight?"

He groaned in response. She'd had the feeling he would forget.

She pulled the pan of ziti from the oven and busied herself dishing up a plate for Cesar, adding salad, green beans, and a slice of sourdough bread. He appeared a few minutes later wearing sweatpants and a long-sleeved T-shirt. "Where is everyone?"

"Rafael has class and Izzy's putting on her pajamas. Can you put her to bed during my meeting?" She handed him his plate.

"Sure."

She let him eat in silence, pulling the cobbler from the oven and putting the ice cream out to soften. The committee members would be arriving soon.

"I hauled the same guy into Hope Haven again," Cesar finally said.

"What guy?" Elena had no idea what he was talking about.

"Remember the one with alcohol poisoning a couple of weeks ago?"

Elena sat down across from her husband. She vaguely remembered.

"He was at the park, passed out, before noon."

"Oh dear," Elena said.

"He has a son who was injured in Iraq."

Elena put her hand over her heart. "Does he have a wife?"

Cesar nodded as he swallowed. "Says she doesn't want him to come back home. She's done with him."

"Oh dear," Elena said again.

Cesar met her eyes. "Why do people risk so much? What makes it worth it?"

"Addictions make people do all sorts of things they wouldn't otherwise."

"Why would he risk his marriage?" Cesar wiped his mouth with his napkin.

Elena shrugged. Cesar knew as much about human nature as she did—probably more. "Could be his pain is greater than his logic right now," she answered just as the doorbell rang.

Cesar went back to eating his dinner.

Elena opened the front door and ushered Anabelle in. Anabelle had just stepped into the living room as Izzy came running in, her long, curly hair free around her shoulders, bouncing against the soft cotton of her pajamas.

"Aunt Anabelle!"

Anabelle scooped her up into a hug.

"Will you read to me?" the little girl asked, pointing to the stack of books on the coffee table.

Anabelle quickly agreed, and as the two settled in, Elena hurried back to the kitchen to gather up bowls and napkins. While she arranged everything, she kept an ear on Anabelle and Izzy.

"How about if you read to me now?" Anabelle asked.

"Okay," Izzy said. "How about this book?"

As Izzy began to read, Elena recognized the story of *The Runaway Bunny*. She hadn't read it to Izzy for months, but it seems the little girl was reading it word for word, at least from what Elena remembered.

Anabelle looked longingly at Izzy's stack of books on Elena's coffee table as Dr. Hamilton called the meeting to order. If only she could have read to Izzy all evening instead of having to deal with the advisory committee. Everyone seemed as tense as ever, regardless of Elena's hospitality.

Varner asked if he could have the floor first and Dr. Hamilton nodded. "The newspaper is looking to do another story. Has a reporter contacted any of you?"

All of the members responded that they hadn't been approached.

"Does anyone know if James Bell's been contacted?"

Everyone shook his or her head again.

"He hasn't or no one knows?" Varner's voice was full of frustration.

Everyone indicated they didn't know, all at once.

"Why do you ask?" Anabelle opened her notebook.

"The reporter who called me had a lot of questions about James. I think she wants to do a human interest story on him."

"Cool," Elena said.

Varner bristled. "Not cool. There's no way the piece would be sympathetic toward the hospital. It would only stir up more trouble."

"James wouldn't speak against Hope Haven," Anabelle said, digging in her purse.

Elena opened the drawer of the end table next to her, pulled out a pen, and tossed it to her friend.

"Thanks," Anabelle mouthed.

"If any of you hear from James, please let me know." Varner leaned back in the wingback chair.

Anabelle wanted to roll her eyes. Now they were being treated like a spy ring.

"Since we're supposed to be an advisory committee," Dr. Hamilton said, taking back control of the meeting. "I would like each member to go around the room and report to Albert and then offer him their advice."

Varner frowned.

"Starting with you, Anabelle."

"I have a couple of things." She told the committee about having coffee with the mayor and what he said about the manufacturing company who wanted to open a shop in town and their hesitation to do so. "This isn't just affecting us. It's going to affect the economy of the whole town."

Varner looked uncomfortable.

"Maybe we could approach the company. Maybe they and other businesses in town could contribute to a 'Keep Hope Haven Open' fund," Anabelle said.

"Unless they have a billionaire backing them, it wouldn't be enough," Varner said.

Anabelle wished McGarry had attended the meeting. He seemed to at least have a measure of optimism compared to Varner's dour attitude.

Next Anabelle shared about Marie and how she needed to lay her off but the single mom had been out yesterday and today with her sick child. "She's used up all of her sick days and her vacation time," Anabelle said. "And when she comes in, I'm going to have to tell her she doesn't have a job."

"Why have you waited?" Varner was sitting up straight in his chair. "You should have called her."

Everyone in the room was silent for a moment and then Dr. Hamilton said, "That's a hard phone call to make. I agree with Anabelle that it's something easier to communicate in person."

"Then go to her house," Varner said.

House? Anabelle picked up her pen. *Try apartment.*

"Anything else, Anabelle?" Dr. Hamilton's gray eyes were gentle.

She shook her head, afraid that if she spoke she might start crying.

Candace quickly reported that two couples in her labor and delivery class had opted out because of rumors that the Birthing Unit at Hope Haven was going to close.

"Did you actually talk to these people?" Varner asked.

"I spoke with one of the moms, and the other left a message. Both cited the same reason."

Varner crossed his arms. "We have not decided to close the obstetrics wing."

Candace's voice was firm. "One of the mothers is the niece of a board member. She told her the Birthing Unit might close, so obviously the board has talked about it."

"They've talked about a lot of things," Varner answered.

Dr. Hamilton nodded toward Elena.

"I have nothing to report," she said, "except there's more cobbler, ice cream, and decaf. How about a little break?"

No one actually took seconds, except coffee, but everyone was relieved to get up and move around for a few minutes. Except for Varner; he stayed glued to his chair, poking away at his smartphone.

When they gathered again, Dr. Hamilton asked for a report from Heath.

"I heard back from my buddy," he said.

"You didn't tell me that," Candace chimed in, visibly surprised.

"He called after work." Heath blushed a little, looking as if he were aware of his faux pas in not telling Candace his information first. "Anyway," he said, "it turns out that he has a heart for nonprofits. On the side, he offers consulting services on grant writing to struggling organizations."

"How much does he charge?" Varner grumbled.

"You won't believe this," Heath said. "He only asks for expenses."

"Wow." Candace looked appreciatively at Heath. "He's a nice guy, isn't he?"

Heath agreed and then said, "But it gets better. He'd like to visit Deerford and give us some ideas as far as grants, but—and this is the unbelievable part—by the time we'd talked he'd already done some research on Hope Haven. It seems like he might be interested in the CIO position. He's been looking for a small town to relocate his family to."

Varner winced. "Who said we have a CIO position? It's not in the budget."

"I told him that. He said he'd still like to take a look at the town and hospital. And at the informatics programs we have in place so he can advise us about writing grants."

"He's from California, right?" Varner clutched the arm of the chair.

"He's been living there. He's from a small town in Washington originally."

Varner leaned forward. "And he works for an e-charting company?"

Heath nodded.

"There's no way he'd be interested in coming here."

Heath shrugged. "Like I said, he usually asks for his expenses to be paid to consult with nonprofits, but he's paying for his way out, so we have nothing to lose."

Varner crossed his arms. "But why would he be interested in Deerford at all?"

Heath smiled. "His wife grew up in the Midwest. She wants their kids raised in the same environment she was."

There were soft murmurs around the room, and Candace smiled.

"What's the guy's name?" Varner asked, pulling out his smart-phone. Anabelle wondered if he planned to do an Internet search on the spot.

"Skip Mullen," Heath replied and then paused for a beat. "Lloyd Mullen. But everyone calls him Skip."

Anabelle wrote down Heath's words, verbatim. For a moment, she felt optimistic—until she remembered she needed to let Marie go tomorrow, one way or the other.

Candace had gone for a walk before the meeting, trying to squeeze in a little exercise and ended at Elena's house. Afterward Heath insisted on giving her a ride home, even though it was only five blocks away.

"That was the best of our meetings yet," Heath said.

"It was still stressful," Candace said. If Varner wouldn't come to the meetings, they might be able to accomplish something, but he was a dark cloud, threatening doom and gloom.

Heath didn't respond and they drove in silence for a moment as Candace wondered if perhaps he was growing tired of her pessimism. Finally she said, "It's easier for you. You don't have to worry about how you'll feed your family."

Heath shot her a quick glance and then said, "Ouch."

"I just don't think you're taking the Hope Haven dilemma seriously."

"Candace." Heath turned onto her street. "Your worries are my worries, honestly."

Candace crossed her arms. "Do you think your friend will be able to help?"

"I don't have any idea." Heath parked his Jeep along the curb in front of Candace's house.

The living room light was on and so was Brooke's bedroom lamp. Her curtain fluttered a little. Candace turned her attention back to Heath. "Are you annoyed with me for worrying?" She reached for the door handle.

"No. Not at all."

"But you were so quiet there for a while. I thought..."

Heath tapped the side of his head. "I was thinking about something else. I need to talk with you—that's all." His forehead wrinkled and he looked as if he was at a loss for words.

Candace's heart rate quickened, and the door handle, which had felt cool to her touch a moment ago, was suddenly warm.

His voice was a little shaky. "I was wondering"—he took a deep breath—"if..."

Candace couldn't speak to help him out because she had no idea what he was trying to say.

"It just seems that so much of our energy is going into the hospital." Heath stopped. "And not as much into our relationship lately."

A rush of realization overcame Candace. He was right.

"It's not that Hope Haven isn't important—because it is. But I think our relationship is more important. I don't think we should hit Pause because of all this." He was looking at her now, his blue eyes intense and serious.

"I'm sorry." Candace reached out and took his hand.

"No, you don't have anything to be sorry about."

"No, I tend to focus on one thing. I've been obsessing about what's going to happen with Hope Haven. Dwelling on it relentlessly. Trying to figure out what I'll do if it closes."

Heath put his arm around her, drawing her close. "I'm here for you. And the kids."

She brushed at a tear that escaped from her eyes. And then another. It had been so long since she had someone to rely on, that she almost couldn't remember how to do it.

Heath lifted her chin and met her gaze. He smiled a little, showing his dimples. Then he kissed her. A sweet, lingering kiss. She clung to him.

"It's going to be okay," he said.

She nodded, her head tucked against his neck.

"I love you."

Candace's heart lifted at his sweet words. "I love you too," she responded. She felt his love for her and hers for him. It was a joy that gave her new hope.

As Heath walked her to her front door, the curtain in Brooke's window fluttered; a moment later, her light flickered off.

Candace wondered what Brooke could see from her room. After one last hug and quick kiss, Candace told Heath good-bye and slipped through the front door, locking it safely behind her. Inside, her hand still on the knob of the door that she'd just pushed closed, she leaned her forehead against the wood. A moment later she heard Heath's Jeep start. She listened as the sound of it faded away.

Her joy faded into loneliness as she started up the stairway to her room.

Chapter Fourteen

*J*AMES SAT AT THE KITCHEN TABLE NEXT TO Gideon. It was eleven thirty, and Fern had been asleep for hours. He yawned. James was looking forward to his turn.

"It's so late," he said to his oldest son. "Can't this wait?"

"I just have a few more questions," Gideon said. "I don't get the differentiation functions."

James was pretty sure he didn't either, especially this late at night. He scooted closer to his son and tried to concentrate on the open textbook between them. "Do you have your list of trig derivatives?" James asked.

Gideon pulled a sheet of paper from his notebook.

"Which one do you need to plug into the first problem?"

Gideon hesitated and then said, "Number four?"

"I think that's right." James realized he wasn't sure.

Gideon groaned. "Think? Dad, you took this stuff in school."

"College trig was eons ago," he said. "Do what you can tonight and then go in early tomorrow and check in with your teacher." James stood.

"Dad." Gideon's eyes were soft and vulnerable. "Are we doing okay?"

James sat back down. "What do you mean?"

"Mom was paying the bills this afternoon when I got home from school, and she seemed stressed."

She was probably wondering where the money to pay next month's bills was going to come from. He hadn't been paid from the home health agency yet, and his partial unemployment benefits hadn't come through either. Once he accepted the part-time job, he'd had to refile his claim. It would be another week or so before it was processed.

"We're doing okay." James patted Gideon's shoulder. "We're trusting God, step-by-step."

"I've started a list of colleges I want to apply to."

"Good."

"But I'm wondering if I shouldn't bother with the more expensive ones."

"You'll have your Junior ROTC scholarship."

"I know."

"Make your list and apply where you want. We'll know what our long-term financial picture is by the time you need to accept. Don't worry." James stood. "If I've learned one thing in my fifty-plus years, it's that things work out."

Gideon closed his book. "I'm going to get up early in the morning and work on this. Then I'll check in with my teacher." He started to slip his laptop into his backpack.

"Mind if I use your computer?" James asked. Gideon's was faster than the desktop in the office.

"Sure." He handed the computer to James and slung his backpack over his shoulder as he left the kitchen.

James sat back down and opened the laptop. He hadn't told the boys that if Cody could find another buyer for the house before James had a full-time job again, they would lose it. Even if they couldn't keep the house, he didn't see the family moving from Deerford. He'd considered that a couple of years ago and decided not to. They had way too much invested to leave now. But if he couldn't find decent work as a nurse maybe he should consider another field of medical work. He clicked onto the Internet and searched for the physical therapist programs in Peoria. He enjoyed working with Polly and was pretty sure a career in physical therapy would fit with his skills, plus there seemed to be ample jobs in the field. If classes were one or two nights a week he might be able to make it work.

As the listings popped up, he sighed. Who was he kidding? He was fifty-four. It would be ridiculous to go back to school at his age. Nevertheless, he clicked onto the first listing. The doctorate in physical therapy was at Bradley University, a private school, which would mean even higher tuition, and he and Gideon would be in college at the same time, which would actually mean financial aid would be better for both of them. He read about the program for a few more minutes and then clicked off the site and onto the Illinois State unemployment page and the job listings. He wasn't surprised that no nursing jobs were listed in Deerford or in Princeton. There were several in Peoria—a couple in skilled nursing facilities and a supervisor job in a hospital. He scanned down the listings. There were more physical therapist positions posted than RN jobs. He went back to the listings in Princeton. Two physical therapist positions were posted there.

Maybe he should go back to school.

Health care was still one of the most secure fields to be in; in another year or two jobs would be plentiful again, but not in Deerford if Hope Haven closed. Nearly every nurse in town would be moving somewhere else or retiring. The thought made him grimace. He couldn't even think about retiring, not that he wanted to. He still had years of work left in him. He loved what he did; he had no desire to stop.

He clicked back to the physical therapy program site and stared at the screen. "Lord," he prayed out loud, "what do You want me to do?"

He didn't hear an answer, not that he expected an audible voice. But he didn't feel a peace either, like he usually did when he prayed. It was easy for him to tell Gideon they needed to take it a step at a time, but he was growing impatient with no hope of a full-time, permanent job in Deerford anytime soon.

He closed the laptop with a sigh and trudged down the hall to bed. By morning, he needed to find his optimistic place again. He didn't want Fern to see him this discouraged.

On her short drive to Hope Haven, Anabelle prayed that Marie would be at work. Talking to her in person would be much easier than calling her on the phone. But when she arrived in the

Cardiac Care Unit, the first thing she did was check in with the night-shift nurse supervisor. Marie had called in sick again to stay home with her son. Anabelle knew the woman was now out of leave days and wouldn't be paid for missing this shift at all. She made a mental note to check in with Rev. Tom Wiltshire about the situation. Maybe there was some sort of benevolent fund that could help the young mother.

After report, Anabelle busied herself with the two patients she'd assigned herself. She hadn't replaced Marie. All of the other nurses absorbed what would have been her patients. Anabelle knew, with the extra workload, that the day would speed by.

It was eight thirty before she had a moment at the nurses' station to make the phone call. She looked up Marie's number on the computer and then dialed, pushing back in her chair away from the other nurses.

The phone rang and rang and then finally went into voice mail. She left a brief message, asking Marie to call her as soon as possible and then hung up the phone.

Anabelle stood, stretched, and headed back down the hall, rolling her shoulders as she walked, trying to get rid of the tension in her back. Sunday would be Lindsay Belle's first birthday, and she and Cameron were going to the party. Anabelle had bought the little girl a new outfit—a hot-pink striped dress and pale pink leggings—and a purple tricycle with a push handle. The image made her smile. She needed to think about good things for the rest of the week—about her granddaughter and her children and her husband. She sighed. Work was definitely getting to her.

She turned into room 5. An eighty-year-old man who'd had a heart attack was waiting for an angio. He'd told her earlier in the morning that he'd been retired for twenty years and it had been the best two decades of his life. What was holding Anabelle back from making the same decision? It could be a win-win situation for more people than just her.

James didn't feel any more optimistic Friday morning, but he hid it from Fern. She didn't mention their finances, and he didn't mention the lack of any jobs to apply for in Deerford. When he kissed her good-bye at the kitchen table and told her he'd be back in time for lunch, she reached for his hand and held it to her face.

"I'm worried about you," she said.

Her skin was cool and smooth against his palm. "Why?"

"I just think this is harder on you than you're letting on."

"I'm fine." He turned his hand until it was holding hers and squeezed gently.

"I don't want you pretending," she said. "Protecting me. I want you to be able to be honest." Her brown eyes were full of sincerity.

"Thanks," he said. He hadn't told her there were absolutely no jobs to apply for in Deerford or Princeton. And he wasn't going to mention going back to college yet, not until he'd done more research. The truth was that he didn't want to worry her.

James mulled things over as he backed out of the driveway and then drove out of their subdivision, past the outcropping of trees, headed for the Morris home.

What he really needed was a permanent job in Deerford, and soon. God was bigger than the hiring freeze. God was bigger than Hope Haven's financial problems. James accelerated as he turned onto the highway.

The morning was bright and clear. A farmer drove his tractor in a plowed field, pulling a seeder over the furrows of soil. The bushes along the highway were leafing out, and a flock of geese flew north in the distance. As he pulled into the Morrises' driveway, he noted the tulips and the sound of birds chirping in the row of poplar trees that served as a windbreak along the property. He scanned Melanie's flower beds. Weeds poked up, along with the flowers. Nelson's troop was planning to come out tomorrow to spruce up the yard.

He stepped toward the house and caught a glimpse of Gary's SUV through the window of the garage. James stopped a moment, wondering if that meant Melanie had allowed Gary to return home. Or maybe his license had been suspended and he was storing the rig. He proceeded toward the house and rang the bell.

"Come in!" It was Joel's voice.

James opened the door and stepped inside.

"I'm in here," Joel shouted, his words coming through loud and clear.

James took off his jacket and placed it on the straight-backed chair near Joel's bed and then headed toward the kitchen.

"Mom went into town. I'm getting breakfast." Joel sat in his wheelchair beside the cabinet on one side of the kitchen, a cereal bowl on the pull-out breadboard that was a couple of inches below the height of the counter. His hand shook only a little as he poured his cereal. "Could you get the milk out for me?"

James opened the fridge, pleased that the young man was taking the initiative to serve himself. "Anyone else here?"

"Would that be anyone functional?"

"Functional. Nonfunctional. Just wondering." James handed Joel the half-gallon milk jug, wondering if Melanie had bought the smaller container on purpose. It looked like Joel could handle it.

"Dad's in Mom's room," Joel said.

James thought that was a funny way of referring to his parents' bedroom. Regardless, it looked like Melanie had allowed Gary to come back home.

Joel took the milk and began to pour it, but it sloshed over the edge of the bowl. He redirected it and finished successfully and then put the cap back on. James put it back in the fridge.

Joel had an I-did-it expression on his face . . . until he spooned up his first bite. On the way to his mouth, half of the milk and cereal fell to his lap. He tried it again and the same thing happened a second time. Then a third. His hand shook uncontrollably. James wasn't sure if it was the angle—the board was higher than a table would be—or his medication that was making him tremor.

Joel looked at his lap, turned slightly in his chair, and then heaved the spoon toward the window.

"All done?" James kept his tone matter-of-fact.

"Actually, no." Joel grabbed the bowl and heaved it too but it fell short of the window and fell into the sink with a crash, breaking into pieces, splattering milk and cereal on the stainless steel and up onto the tile splashboard.

James stepped out of the room and crossed his arms, not wanting to give Joel an audience. Another crash came and then another and then steps pounded up the hall toward them.

"What's going on?" Gary appeared, barefoot and wearing jeans and T-shirt. "Joel! What are you doing?" The man stopped when he saw James.

There was another crash from the kitchen.

"Aren't you going to stop him?" Gary grabbed James's arm.

James held up his hand, imploring Gary to wait and be quiet, but the man barged into the kitchen. "What in the—"

"Get out of here!" Joel shouted. "I don't want to see your alkie face."

James expected Gary to shout back, but he didn't. James stepped into the doorway. Gary held Joel's good arm with one hand and had his other arm around his son's shoulder.

Joel sobbed, "Let me go."

Gary released him.

Joel began rolling his chair with his good hand in a jerky motion. "Get out of here," he snapped at his father.

"Joel!"

"I don't have any respect for you." The young man's eyes were red and piercing. "My life got messed up by an IED. What's your excuse?"

James stepped away from the door and a moment later Joel banged into the molding around it and then repositioned himself and made it through.

"Ready for a shower?" James asked in a detached voice.

"As ready as I've ever been," Joel barked, still shaking. James wheeled him down the hall to the sound of Gary banging around in the kitchen. James assumed he was cleaning up the mess.

An hour later, as James helped transfer him to his bed, Joel said he hadn't heard from his chaplain for two days. "They were going to be shipped home soon," he explained. "But I don't know if they already have or if something happened. He hasn't e-mailed me."

"Did you check this morning?"

Joel shook his head. The family didn't have a laptop, only a desktop that Melanie had moved out to the living room so it would be more accessible for Joel. "You know, everyone worries the most when it's almost time to come home." He exhaled slowly. "I hadn't started worrying yet when it happened to me."

"Let's check when you wake up."

"Isn't Polly coming?" He almost sounded like he was looking forward to seeing her.

"Not until this afternoon."

Joel nodded his head. Breakfast, his rampage, and the encounter with his dad had worn him out.

After Joel fell asleep, James decided to inventory the soldier's prescriptions to see if any needed to be filled. He also wanted to make sure none of the pills were missing. Gary obviously had a drinking problem; it might be that he would abuse prescription pills too, and Joel was on some pretty heavy-duty meds.

James sorted out the bottles and compared them with the prescriptions in Joel's chart. All were accounted for. He made a note of the two that would run out by the middle of next week. According to the doctor's notes, Joel was due for an appointment next at the veterans' clinic in Springfield for a head injury assessment. He would check with Melanie about that.

When he finished, James decided to call her. He wasn't paid to babysit—but he felt uncomfortable leaving Gary and Joel alone in the house. She picked up on the third ring, and she was obviously on speakerphone. "I'm just a couple of minutes from the house," she said. "Can you stay until then?"

James assured her that he could. As he waited, Gary appeared in a dress shirt and slacks. "I have a couple of business calls," he said. He started toward the kitchen and then turned back. "Mel decided to offer me another chance. Said she couldn't handle Joel right now on her own. As you can see, he's still a handful."

"What are you going to do to make sure you can make good on her offer?"

"Not drink." A defensive look passed over the man's face.

"What else?"

"Look." Gary's eyes flashed. "I went through rehab several years ago. I know how to handle this."

"Several years ago you didn't have a son who was almost killed in Iraq. This is a lot of stress. AA would be a big—"

"I've got to go," Gary said, turning away abruptly. As he opened the door to the garage, James heard a vehicle pull into the driveway. He stood at the living room window and watched Melanie climb from her car.

Gary backed his SUV out of the garage, rolled down his window, and gave her a terse nod. Melanie scurried toward the house. James thought she might open up about what was going on, but she didn't. He told her what happened in the kitchen, and she winced but didn't respond.

"I'll be out tomorrow with the Boy Scouts," James said.

"It's tomorrow?"

James nodded.

"I'd lost track," she said.

James thought she might ask to postpone, but she didn't.

"See you then," she said.

James brought up the doctor's appointment, and she said it was on her to-do list to schedule an appointment. He hoped she'd do it soon.

James left her at the foot of Joel's bed, staring at her sleeping son. His head was turned so his scar wasn't visible, and he had a peaceful, almost angelic, look on his face.

Chapter Fifteen

ELENA OPENED THE BACK DOOR TO THE HOUSE and Izzy scampered in ahead of her shouting, "Daddy!"

Rafael was supposed to be in class on Friday afternoons, but his van was in the driveway.

"Daddy!" came Izzy's voice from down the hall.

Elena hung her jacket on the hook by the back door and then followed her granddaughter to put her purse in her room. Rafael came toward her, dressed in his work uniform, with Izzy in his arms.

Between work and school, Elena hadn't seen her son since Wednesday.

"My class got canceled and the prep chef at Baldomero called in sick. I told Grandma I'd go in and help out for a few hours."

Elena smiled, thankful Rafael was willing to help her mother out and take on extra responsibility at the restaurant. "What about dinner? Remember Sarah is coming."

"Can we eat around eight? I'll be back by then."

Elena nodded. "I'll let Sarah know."

Rafael walked down the hall as he talked and Elena followed him. "I had another call from Izzy's teacher."

"From Mrs. Allison?" Izzy wrinkled her nose. "Why?"

"Grown-up stuff," Elena interjected before Rafael could answer.

"She said you talked with her the other day," he said. "When were you going to tell me?"

"When I saw you next," Elena answered.

"Hey, mi bonita," Rafael said to his daughter, lowering her to the carpet. "Would you go check my van for my phone? I'm hoping I left it in there."

She nodded and left a little reluctantly.

Elena waited until the carport door banged closed behind her granddaughter. "Mrs. Allison says that Izzy's inconsistent. Sometimes she can identify letters, and sometimes she can't. She's afraid she's memorized the big letters above the blackboard."

"But she's reading already," Rafael countered.

"Or memorizing."

"No one could memorize that well." He crossed his arms over his white smock with BALDOMERO, the name of Elena's mother's restaurant, embroidered over the pocket.

Elena wasn't so sure. She was beginning to think that, maybe, Izzy was bright enough to memorize whole books. "This is about figuring out Izzy's problem and then meeting her needs," Elena said.

Rafael took a deep breath and exhaled slowly.

"What is it?" Elena reached for his hand.

Rafael's dark eyes were full of sadness. "How can such a perfect little girl have any problems?"

Elena choked on a laugh. "Rafael, everyone has problems."

"But she has everything going for her—"

The carport door banged again. "I found it!" Izzy's footsteps could be heard across the kitchen linoleum, and then she appeared, skipping toward them.

"I've got to go to work," Rafael said. He bent down to Izzy. "We'll have tomorrow, okay? Just you and me." He kissed her forehead.

She nodded and threw her arms around her daddy's neck, giving him a kiss on his stubbly cheek. "Just you and me," she repeated.

Rafael looked up to Elena as if to say, *See? I told you she was perfect.*

She smiled at her son and whispered, "We'll talk more later." He needed to know he was in denial. No child was perfect. The sooner he realized that, the better parent he would be.

He nodded. "And I'll do more research later tonight, after dinner."

After he left, Elena sent Izzy to her room to play while she bustled around the kitchen pulling together everything she'd need to fix supper. She called Sarah and let her know of the change of plan.

Around seven thirty, the doorbell rang.

"Mommy!" Izzy's voice and the sound of running feet echoed from the hall. Elena met her at the door, but let her open it. Sarah dropped to one knee to scoop her daughter into a bear hug.

"Come on into the kitchen." Elena closed the door behind Sarah after she disentangled herself from Izzy and stood.

"Buela, can I bring coloring books in and color with Mommy?" Izzy leaned against Sarah's leg.

"I'm sure Sarah would enjoy that." Elena led the way back to the kitchen while Izzy ran back to her room.

Half an hour later, Elena turned the pork loin steaks under the broiler. Sarah sat at the kitchen table and colored with Izzy. When mother and daughter were together, Elena was reminded of just how young Sarah was. Only twenty-six. She'd been twenty when Izzy was born; the same age Elena had been when she gave birth to Rafael. But Elena hadn't had a troubled childhood and a drug problem that left her unable to cope with motherhood. Sarah was doing the best she could now and was winning Izzy's trust—and Elena's.

"Oh, I like this color," Sarah said, holding up a shade of blue from the set of 128 crayons. "Periwinkle."

"Periwinkle," Izzy repeated.

"See." Sarah held the crayon in front of Izzy. "P-E-R-I-W—"

"Those letters are too little," Izzy said. "I can't read them."

Elena pushed in the oven rack, closed the door, and stepped toward the table. "Are you sure?" She put a hand on her granddaughter's shoulder.

Izzy giggled. "Just kidding," she said, taking the crayon and reading, "P-E-R-I-W—" She giggled again.

Rafael had arrived ten minutes earlier and had gone back to his room to change clothes and, Elena assumed, to do some quick research about six-year-olds and reading. Elena was more convinced than ever that something strange was going on.

"We'll be ready to eat in five minutes," Elena said to her granddaughter and to Sarah. "I need help setting the table."

Izzy quickly put the crayons away while Sarah closed the coloring books. The two of them set the table together, counting out the cutlery, putting the forks on the left and the knives and spoons on the right, just as Elena had taught Izzy.

It was 8:20 PM by the time dinner was on the table, which was much later than they usually ate. It wouldn't give Izzy much time before she needed to go to bed—but at least it was Friday night and she could sleep late tomorrow. Elena and Cesar sat at their usual spots, at the ends of the table. Izzy scooted up on to the chair on one side of the table, leaving the two side-by-side chairs for her parents. Elena smiled as she placed her napkin in her lap.

A blush spread over Sarah's fair complexion as she sat down. As everyone settled into his or her chair, Izzy announced she would pray. She extended her hands toward Elena and Cesar who took them and, in return, extended their hands toward Sarah and Rafael. Everyone paused for a long moment as Rafael took Sarah's hand.

"Look we're a circle," Izzy said, giggling a little, and then she said very seriously, "Let us pray."

Elena braced herself for what Izzy might say, but the prayer was a simple blessing on the food and evening. Elena couldn't help stealing a glance at Rafael and Sarah. Both seemed reasonably relaxed. She closed her eyes tightly as Izzy said, "Amen," and then whispered an amen in response as everyone opened their eyes.

Rafael was polite to Sarah as he passed her the pork first. Izzy caught his eye and beamed. He smiled back, a glimmer—of what, Elena wasn't sure—in his eyes. The conversation covered Rafael's work, school, the band, Sarah's position in the hospital cafeteria, and the rumors of cuts at the hospital.

"Every day some new rumor is going around," Sarah said, scooping a forkful of peas. "Not that any of us working in the cafeteria really know what's going on. I just know I don't want to lose my job."

"I'm feeling more optimistic," Elena said, purposefully not sharing any information about Heath's friend. It was too soon to say anything, and she didn't want to be responsible for another round of rumors.

After dinner as they sat in the living room, Rafael asked Cesar if he would mind putting Izzy to bed. The little girl began to pout. "I want to stay with you and Mommy," she said to Rafael.

"I know," he responded gently. "But it's far past your bedtime, and there are some things we need to talk about with Buela."

Cesar got down on all fours. "Want a ride?"

Izzy's face lit up, but then she turned toward her parents and said, "God's going to give me the desire of my heart."

Rafael frowned for just a moment and then recovered, giving his daughter a hug and a kiss. Izzy hugged her mother too and then climbed on her grandfather's back. She gave them one last look and then stated emphatically, "And don't forget, Sunday's coming!" With that, the little girl jumped on her grandfather's back and yelled, "Go, Tito!"

"What was that all about?" Rafael asked as his daughter squealed in delight on her way down the hall.

"I'm not sure," Elena said. But she could certainly guess—at least about the desire of Izzy's heart. She wasn't sure about the reference to Sunday.

Rafael said he'd been doing some research and wanted the three of them to come up with a plan to address Izzy's reading. He glanced at Sarah. "You're right, I should have taken this more seriously from the beginning. I just couldn't jive what the teacher was saying with what Izzy was doing, but I think that was my own denial." He sighed. "I found a few things online about reading and six-year-olds," Rafael said. "Everything from 'don't worry about it if they're not ready' to 'have them tested for dyslexia.'"

"Do you think she has dyslexia?" Sarah's voice was full of concern.

"From what I've read, no." Rafael looked troubled. "But what do I know? Maybe we should get her tested."

Elena leaned forward in her chair. "Something interesting happened this evening. Izzy said she couldn't read the letters on the crayon—but then she did. Except . . . " Elena looked at Sarah.

"She only repeated the ones I'd said." Sarah had noticed too.

Elena nodded. "She's quite the clever girl." She turned to Rafael. "Did she have her eyes checked at her five-year appointment?"

He nodded.

"Did they check her for being farsighted?"

He had a puzzled look on his face.

"Did they hold a chart close to her eyes?"

He shook his head. "No, they just did the big chart on the wall. It had a picture of a dog and cat. And a boat. Things like that."

"I think you should get her eyes checked," Elena said.

"What should I tell her teacher?"

"You could call and tell her you'll be in touch with her as soon as you find out what the results of the eye exam are." Being farsighted could explain the headaches, the being able to identify the letters far away but not up close, and Izzy's determination to memorize stories so it would appear she was reading. The little girl was clearly motivated. She was probably embarrassed not to be able to do what others in her class could.

"What do you think, Sarah?" Rafael asked, his voice tender.

"Sounds like a good plan," she said, glancing at Elena. "I hope it's simple enough that a pair of glasses will fix it." Sarah had a faraway look in her eyes, and Elena was sure she was thinking about her own hard childhood.

None of them could completely protect Izzy. Already she was dealing with unwed parents and the consequences of having been abandoned by her mother, only to have her resurface in her life again—but they could all work together to nurture, protect, and meet her needs now.

Chapter Sixteen

ATURDAY MORNING, JAMES DROVE NELSON AND four other Boy Scouts from his troop out to the Morris home. Gary's SUV was in the driveway, and James wondered if Melanie remembered to tell him about the yard cleanup crew that was coming out to help.

The boys piled out the side doors, and James opened the back of the van and began handing them gloves, rakes, shovels, and hoes. The front door of the house opened, and Gary appeared, a cup of coffee warming his hands.

"James," he called out, as if they were the best of friends. "How nice to see you." He fixed his gaze on the boys. "And Scouts, I can't thank you enough for coming out to help us."

Melanie, wearing a brown quilted jacket and a bright blue bandanna tied around her head, stepped out of the house behind him. She didn't look nearly as enthusiastic as her husband. In fact her face was pale and pinched, but then she smiled at the boys and once again James admired her grace. He introduced each of the boys.

"Let's hope the rain will hold off." Gary turned his head upward toward the dark clouds.

"We brought raincoats," Nelson said. "We'll be fine."

"Then you're true Scouts," Gary answered.

James suggested they split into two groups, one for the front yard and one for the back. Melanie said she would work with the first group, but James quickly said it wasn't necessary, that they didn't expect the Morrises to work with them; they wanted to serve the family.

"Nonsense," Melanie said. "This is just what we needed to get us out of the house. It will do us good."

James conceded and said he would float back and forth, starting in the backyard. He and Gary began working on the flower bed to the right of the patio while three of the Scouts began in the flower bed to the left. First they all gathered the small branches and twigs that had blown down during the winter storms.

Gary breathed in deeply and let out a satisfying sigh as he worked. "Boy, it's great to be outside," he said. "Even though it's chilly."

James agreed. It had been a long winter.

"Although I'm sure once I'm in Texas, I'll be wishing for cooler weather." Gary dropped an armful of twigs on the grass.

"I thought Melanie would go with Joel," James said. It only made sense since she was the one who had taken a leave of absence from her job.

"We had a change of plans, just yesterday," Gary said. "Melanie's going back to work, and I'll go with Joel."

James had a hard time imagining Melanie going along with the arrangement. Last he'd heard, she was ready to dump Gary. And now she was trusting him to go to Texas and manage Joel's care? What if the stress was too much for him?

James worked quietly, thinking about Joel. It was ten o'clock. He probably was sleeping. His heart warmed at the thought of the young man. It wasn't that he felt fatherly toward him, but he definitely felt protective. Joel was a fellow soldier. James would do anything he could for him.

He dumped a load of small branches on the pile Gary had started and then began weeding, stealing a glance at the Scouts every once in a while. They were working hard and had piled their coats on the patio. In less than ten years, they would be Joel's age. Surely the country wouldn't still be at war then. Who knew, maybe by then a new war would have started. James swallowed hard. He hoped not, in a way only a veteran could. Those who hadn't been to war sometimes glorified it. But not a vet.

His biggest concern was Gideon. If he stayed with ROTC in college, when he graduated he'd go into the army as an officer, which was a safer place to be than enlisted. That was six years from now. Still, it was a risk. He sighed, thinking about how his parents must have felt when he joined the service.

And it had been a good decision for him, as it would be for Gideon if that was what he pursued. He would be proud of Gideon if he served.

He could convince himself of that until he stopped and thought of Joel. What if one of his sons was injured like that—or worse? Because, in the long run, Joel was going to be one of the lucky ones.

But what if something like that happened in his family? How would he be able to take care of Fern and an injured grown child?

He sighed. It was ridiculous to think like that. Anyone of them could get injured in a car accident. Or have a stroke. Or heart attack. Or come down with MS. He knew nothing in life was certain.

"How's the job hunt coming for you?" Gary asked.

"Pardon?" The man's question caught James off guard.

"Melanie said you'd lost your job at Hope Haven. That's why you're doing the home health thing. Changing bedpans and all that."

James grimaced. He'd heard that from people before when they found out he was a nurse. People didn't seem to realize all that nurses did. They seemed to think the education for the position was a piece of cake and that once a nurse got a job the hardest thing he or she did was feed people and empty bedpans. "I'm hopeful I'll get something soon," James said.

"I heard the hospital is closing," Gary said.

"Really?" James responded. "I hadn't heard that." He was thinking it was time to go check on the crew in the front yard, thankful that's where Nelson was and not in the back listening to Gary.

"Oh, come on," the man said. "That's all the town is talking about."

James gave him a blank stare.

"At the grocery store. The bank. The Chamber of Commerce meeting at the beginning of the week. It's going to ruin the town."

James picked up a hoe and began chipping away at the weeds.

Gary grabbed a rake and began raking up the leaves that had accumulated against the foundation of the house. "I take it you don't want to talk about it."

James shrugged. "Not really. Like everyone else, I'm waiting to see how things work out."

Gary snorted. "When I get back from Texas, I'm out of Deerford. There's nothing to keep me in this town."

"What about your job?" James asked, before he realized Gary had said *me* and not *us*.

His voice was low as he said, "I lost it yesterday afternoon. Had a meeting with my boss—he canned me."

James stood up straight and leaned against the hoe. "I'm sorry." No wonder the man planned to go to Texas with Joel. He didn't have anything else to do—except look for another job.

Gary shrugged. "It was bound to happen sooner or later."

He couldn't imagine an employer being so coldhearted as to fire the father of an injured vet, but James realized he might not have the whole story. James wanted to commend Gary for not going out drinking after such hard news, but he was uncomfortable saying anything. They worked for a few more minutes in silence, and then James headed to the front yard to check on the boys.

He heard Melanie laughing before he rounded the corner of the garage. It was the first time he'd detected anything close to joy coming from her. "Nelson," she said, "you must not take after your dad." She was bending over a dead crow, trying to scoop it up with a shovel. Nelson stood away from the group with his hand over his mouth, shaking his head, his bony elbow bouncing around as he did.

James smiled. "Want some help?"

Melanie stood up straight. "Sure," she said, handing him the shovel. "The bird must have hit the window."

"It's probably been dead a few days," James said, slipping the shovel underneath it. "If it'd been dead longer, it wouldn't smell so bad." As he stood he saw Joel through the window, staring at him. But when James locked eyes with the young man, he jerked his head away. "Joel's awake," he said to Melanie.

"Do we get to meet him?" Nelson asked, speaking through his hand.

"I hope so," Melanie said, her voice still bright. As James headed toward the garbage can, she apologized to Nelson for laughing.

"No worries," he said. "You're right. I don't take after my dad. I'm more like my mom." It was true that Nelson looked more like Fern and had her small bones and build. But it looked like he might get James's height. He'd grown lanky over the last few months.

"Oh, you do take after your dad," she said. "In other ways . . ."

When James returned, the boys were back at work weeding out the beds.

"I'm going to go check on Joel," Melanie said. "I'll be back in a few minutes."

James went back and forth between the front and backyards, but Melanie didn't return, so he decided to stay in the front. He peered into the window a couple of times but didn't see Melanie or Joel. Perhaps she was helping him in the bathroom. James didn't understand why, if Gary was going to accompany him to Texas, he wasn't more involved in his son's care now.

The boys had all packed lunches, and at noon, they all gathered on the patio to eat. Gary invited them inside, but James insisted they stay in the backyard. He didn't want to leave a mess behind. The boys ate quickly and then ran down to the creek. In no time they were climbing the willow trees and James was so involved in watching them that he wasn't aware that the patio door had opened until he heard Joel's voice behind him. Melanie was maneuvering the wheelchair over the ramp.

"Hey," James said, turning around. "Good to see you."

Joel wore a baseball cap, a green fleece jacket, and jeans. He squinted into the sun that had poked through the clouds, making a brief appearance.

Melanie and Gary glanced at each other but didn't speak.

"I'm going to go get some coffee," Gary said, rubbing his hands together and darting through the open door.

Joel focused on the boys in the distance. "Which one is yours?" he asked.

"The thin kid in the gray sweatshirt." It was an old one of James's with the word ARMY across it in bold, block letters.

"Indoctrinating him early, huh?" Joel's tone was matter-of-fact.

"Not this one. It's my oldest that's in Junior ROTC."

"I'm enjoying having the boys around," Melanie interjected. "It makes me think of Joel and his friends at that age. We had a houseful every Friday night and Saturday."

Joel didn't reply. James wondered where the friends were now and why none of them came around but then decided he couldn't know for sure. Maybe they came in the late afternoon or evening. Maybe it just seemed like Joel didn't have any friends.

The boys started playing tag, running around the willow trees. Nelson disappeared down the bank and a second later there was a yell. He scrambled back into view, his legs muddy up to his knees.

"Good thing Nelson isn't cleaning your house," James mused.

"Dad would have killed me for that." Joel's voice was bitter.

"Don't exaggerate," Melanie said.

Joel pushed back in the chair a little. "I want to go inside," he said.

"But it's so nice. Don't you want to enjoy the sun while it's still out?" Melanie's voice sounded disappointed.

"What sun?" Joel tilted his head around.

"Take off your cap," his mom said.

"And show off my scar? No thanks."

"The boys would like to meet you," James said.

"Really? 'Cause it looks to me like they want to run around on their perfectly good legs and have some fun."

"Joel . . ." Melanie put her hand on her son's shoulder, but he jerked away.

"Maybe some other time," James said, staring straight ahead.

"Yeah, like in another life when I'm not . . ."

James wanted to say, *Feeling sorry for yourself*, but bit his tongue.

". . . ruining everyone's life."

James swallowed hard as Melanie began to wheel Joel back into the house. Was he blaming himself for his father's problems?

"See you Monday," James called out but Joel didn't answer.

Chapter Seventeen

ELENA SCOOPED POTTING MIX OUT OF THE BAG with her trowel and spread it around the geraniums in the terra cotta flower box that sat on her gardening bench. She would have Cesar place it on the rack just below the kitchen window when he got home.

She'd been gardening ever since Rafael had taken Izzy to get her eyes checked. He'd decided to take her to the eye doctor at a department store in Princeton. Elena had done her best not to say anything against this plan, thinking he should look for a doctor who specialized in children, but she was afraid he would take her advice as criticism. She also knew it was important for him to pay for the appointment and that he could afford that eye doctor better than a specialist.

She moved on to another pot, adding soil and placing another geranium in it. Next she dug little holes for the blue lobelia, planted them, and watered all of the flowers. She usually planted pink and white petunias but wanted a look with more contrast this year.

When she heard a car turn into the driveway, she peeled off her gloves and rounded the corner of the house. Rafael was lifting Izzy from her car seat in his van as Elena approached.

"Wait right there and close your eyes!" Izzy commanded. "I have a surprise for you."

Elena stopped in her tracks and put her hands over her face.

"Are you peeking?" Izzy demanded.

Elena shook her head vigorously, wanting desperately to cheat. There was no way, if Izzy did need glasses, that she would have gotten a pair so soon.

"Okay, you can look now," Izzy said.

Elena dropped her hands and squealed. Izzy stood before her with a pair of old lady readers on—red glasses with rhinestones on the corners. "Oh my," Elena said, glancing from Izzy to Rafael and back to Izzy.

Izzy giggled. "They're just like Aunt Anabelle's."

Elena began to laugh. "These are a joke, right?"

Rafael's eyes twinkled and Izzy grinned from ear to ear.

"Actually, these almost work for her," Rafael said, "and only cost a dollar."

"But they're just until the ones my size come in," Izzy explained.

"We figured you'd be ready for these in a year or two," Rafael said, swatting at his mom's arm as he walked by.

"Ha-ha," Elena retorted.

Rafael led the way into the kitchen from the carport. "You were right, Mama. Izzy's farsighted. The doctor said glasses should do the trick."

Elena sighed with relief, thankful that Rafael had acted quickly once he'd gained some clarity on the situation. Rafael said he had to hurry to finish an assignment before getting ready for work and gave Izzy a hug, telling her she'd been a trouper.

"Do you like them?" Izzy looked up at her grandmother as her father hurried into the house, her eyes sparkling as bright as the rhinestones on the glasses, her gap-toothed smile as cute as it could be.

"I love them." Elena bent down and kissed her granddaughter on the cheek. "Want to help me finish up with planting flowers? Then we can go read."

Izzy nodded and carefully took the glasses from her face and put them in a case. "Daddy said to always take good care of my glasses and to only use them for reading and schoolwork. 'Cause that's what the doctor said."

A half hour later, Elena and Izzy washed up, then picked out several books and took them into the living room. Rafael, dressed in his white work smock again, joined Elena and Izzy on the couch. The little girl carefully took out her glasses from their case and put them on her face again. Elena had to concentrate on not laughing. Her granddaughter looked cuter than ever.

"What book would you like to start with?" Rafael asked.

"*Goodnight Moon!*" Izzy grabbed it from the top of the stack. It had been a favorite of hers from when she was tiny. Elena knew she had it memorized.

"I want you to read it," Rafael said. "Not recite it."

Izzy looked up at Elena with a confused look on her face.

"Let's look at some of the letters first," Elena said, purposefully not looking at her son. "What's the first letter?"

"I," Izzy said. "Like in my name." She bent down closer to the book. "And then an *n*."

"Good!" Elena put her arm around her granddaughter and squeezed.

"What does it spell?" Rafael asked.

Izzy paused for a moment and then asked. "In?"

"Great!" Elena squeezed her again.

"What does the next word say?" Rafael had a demanding tone to his voice.

Izzy cuddled against Elena.

"Come on, it's a really easy word." Now Rafael sounded a little impatient.

"Why is Daddy mad at me?" Izzy whispered to Elena, low enough that Rafael couldn't hear. Before Elena could answer, Izzy said loudly, rubbing her temples, "My head hurts." The readers wiggled up and down on her face.

"So much for the glasses." Rafael stood.

Izzy rubbed her temples again and then scampered off the couch and hugged him good-bye. "Tomorrow's Sunday," she said.

Rafael nodded.

"Will you go to church with me?" She looked straight up at him, her arms still around his legs, her glasses halfway down her nose.

"We'll see," he answered. "But I'll probably be pretty tired. It's my only day to sleep in."

"Please?" She pushed the glasses up with her index finger.

"Maybe," Rafael said.

"Mommy's going to be there. Right, Buela?"

Elena nodded.

Rafael bent down and gave his daughter another hug.

After he left, Izzy scampered back onto the couch. "I'll read to you, Buela." With that she opened the book again and off she went, saying, "'In the great green room there was a . . .'" Elena didn't interrupt to ask her about individual words. Izzy turned the pages at exactly the right times and didn't miss a word, straight through to the very last, "Good night noises everywhere."

Candace stood in the open doorway of her house, watching Howie shoot the basketball. It bounced off the rim, but he snatched up the rebound and shot it again, this time swooshing it through the hoop.

"Good job!" she called out, clapping her hands. "Now it's time to come in and finish cleaning your room."

"But, Mommy," he wailed.

"No buts." She put her hands on her hips. "That was our deal."

He grabbed the ball and headed toward the house. She stepped aside and ushered him in.

"Mother!" Brooke's voice came from the family room. "Your cell phone is ringing."

"Answer it please." Candace shut the door and pointed to the sports equipment bin, motioning for Howie to put the ball there, not on the floor. He complied.

"It's Heath!" Brooke yelled.

Candace hadn't heard from him all day, and they'd only said hello in passing at the hospital yesterday. His high school friend had flown into Peoria that morning and was going to check out Deerford today and tomorrow and then meet with Varner and McGarry on Monday. She was trying her hardest not to worry about her job, but it was easier when she was with Heath than when she wasn't.

"Hey." Heath's voice was cheery. "Would you and the kids want to come over for a barbecue?"

"I told Mom I'd barbecue here tonight."

"Invite her too," Heath said. "Dad will be here." The two enjoyed each other's company.

"Let me ask her and I'll call you back," Candace said.

"Candace . . ."

"Uh-huh." She started down the hall toward her bedroom. Maybe he did want to talk about the other night, and she didn't want the kids listening in.

"How are you doing?" he paused.

"Okay—trying not to worry."

"I've been pretty busy the last couple of days, getting ready for Skip and all that. But I miss you."

She took a deep breath. "I miss you too," she said. The loneliness that had started the other night had persisted. She headed down the hall and up the stairs to her bedroom, wanting some privacy as they spoke to each other.

"It would be really nice to see you tonight," Heath said.

"I'll talk to Mom and get back to you." She stood beside her bed now, staring at the photo of her and Dean. He would understand her loneliness. He would understand that she'd grown to love Heath. She was sure of it.

"Okay," Heath said. "Call me back as soon as you talk to your mom."

Candace stood for a moment longer, staring at her wedding picture, after she and Heath said good-bye. She knew she loved Heath. She wanted to marry him, truly. If anyone could complete her life—and handle her kids—it was Heath. She was surprised at how much she longed for him. How much she felt the way she had when she and Dean first fell in love, even though she was nearly twenty years older now.

She sighed. Love was ageless. And timeless. She was relieved to know she could feel it again.

"Candace," Janet's voice came down the hall.

"In here." She stepped out of her doorway.

"Would you mind terribly if I didn't stick around for dinner? One of the women from the senior center asked if I'd go to a movie with her, and I was thinking it would be good for me to get out."

"I was just going to ask if you wanted to go to dinner at Heath's." Candace clutched her phone in her hand.

"That's tempting." Janet tilted her head. "But I'm going to choose the movie."

Candace eased her grip on her phone. She would call Heath right back. There was nothing she wanted more than to spend the evening with him, his father, his friend, and her children.

Heath was thrilled and told her to come over anytime. Candace peeked into Howie's room where he carefully returned a book to its shelf. He'd managed to clear a path from door to bed to closet. That was progress.

She stepped back out into the hallway. "Brooke, Howie, get shoes and jackets on. We're going to Heath's for supper."

The children's cheers were echoed by Candace's heart.

After a filling meal of grilled chicken, Candace relaxed against the back of the rattan chair on Heath's deck as he and his buddy bantered back and forth. The day had grown progressively warmer and the predicted rain never materialized.

"Come on!" Skip was practically out of his chair. "You're the one who stole Mr. Austin's globe and suspended it in the middle of the gym like a disco ball."

Heath's dad put his hand to the side of his head and rubbed his temple as if developing a headache. "There are some things I don't want to know."

"Oh, believe me," Skip boomed, "it gets a lot worse."

"Did you really do that?" Howie's eyes were nearly as big as his plate.

"Yes. *Um*, no." Heath shot Candace a look. "I had help."

Candace laughed, sure Howie had no idea what a disco ball was. "This is what people Mommy's age do when they get together—embellish the past." She took his plate.

"Huh?" Howie's head was tilted.

"They're joking," Candace said and then muttered, "Mostly."

"Sorry." Skip looked demurely at Candace. "So, tell me about Deerford. What are the schools like?"

"Great!" Howie chirped. "Except my class doesn't have a globe—"

"They're good," Candace said. "The class sizes are small. There's a good gifted and talented program." Brooke had been part of that since she started school. "And lots of parental involvement."

Skip looked pleased. "My wife is from a small town in Indiana. She's tired of the city and wants the kids to grow up in more of a community."

"That's Deerford to a tee," Heath said.

"Margie also wants me to stop traveling so much." Skip sighed. "It's taking its toll."

"What exactly is it that you do?" Candace pushed the stack of plates she'd collected to the center of the table, and Heath jumped up and took them into the kitchen as Skip answered.

"I've been with e-Char from the start-up and travel around to hospitals all over the world, implementing the system."

"Wow." Candace was impressed that he was one of the founders of an international company. Albert Varner was right. There's no way a person with his experience would lower himself to work at humble Hope Haven.

"The government's higher standards on charting have done wonders for our business," Skip said, "and we already were doing quite well." He took a drink of iced tea and then said, as Heath rejoined them, "Enough about me. Margie gave me a whole list of things to ask about." He tapped the side of his head. "Oh yeah. How about churches?"

Howie began kicking the table leg as Candace launched into a description of their church. She told Howie to stop. When he started again, Heath's dad quietly invited the little boy to go on a walk with him.

"Why don't you go along too?" Candace whispered to Brooke, who seemed a little miffed to leave the adult conversation—she was probably hoping for more high school prank stories—but followed Heath's dad and Howie down the steps to the yard. Candace was afraid that if Howie ran ahead, Daniel wouldn't be able to keep up with him, but Brooke would.

The conversation between Candace, Heath, and Skip continued. Skip said he planned to drive around the next day and look at houses for sale in both Deerford and Princeton, because the Realtor he talked with had said there was a bigger selection in the larger town. That sounded serious to Candace. Still, she couldn't believe he would really be interested in the Hope Haven job, no matter whether he decided to live in Deerford or Princeton.

After a while, Skip looked at his watch and excused himself, saying he'd promised Margie he would call. Candace and Heath cleared the rest of the table, going back and forth to the kitchen. When all the food was put away, Candace said she'd load the dishwasher.

"I'll do that later," Heath said. "I was hoping we could spend some time together." He grinned. "But not in the kitchen." He led the way out to the front porch.

They sat side by side on the wooden swing. Heath took her hand and entwined his fingers in hers. "After we said good-bye the other night, I wasn't sure if I'd communicated what I was thinking very well," he said.

"Oh?" Candace sat up a little straighter and turned toward him.

"It's not just that I think, in the long run, that our relationship is more important than what's going on at work. It's that I want to invest as much time into us as possible." He chuckled. "Even though I won't have much extra time in the next few days. But I feel we're headed somewhere, and I don't want to get off track."

"Somewhere?" Candace nearly whispered the word.

Heath scooted a little closer until the sides of their legs touched. "Yeah. Like in the future. It hit me the other day that when we're seventy neither one of us will be working at Hope Haven. But I hope we're—"

"Mommy!" Howie ran up the walkway toward them with something in his hand. "I found a cocoon!"

Candace leaned back against the swing, a little exasperated, but Heath, laughing, leaped to his feet. "Cool!"

Candace sat for a moment longer and then stood too. In a second all of them, including Skip who came out with his cell phone still in his hand, gathered around Howie, who had his hand extended, the inch-long silk case resting on his palm.

"I told him to leave it alone," Brooke said. "He shouldn't have disturbed it."

"Let's put it in a jar," Heath said. "Then we'll let it go after the chrysalis's pupation period ends and it emerges."

"Do you think it's a butterfly?" Howie asked. "Like a monarch?"

"Could be. But my guess is it's a moth." Heath patted Howie's head. "I have an empty jar inside."

Candace appreciated Heath's enthusiasm and energy. It was definitely what Howie needed. Her son couldn't even remember his father. Tears sprang to her eyes. She was sure that was what

Heath was getting at. That someday they'd be retired, together, swinging on a front porch.

Later, as she stared at her wedding photo again before turning out the light, Dean felt farther away than ever. A twinge of sadness passed through her, but only for a moment. Her last thought before falling asleep was that she should think about moving the photograph. Not tonight but sometime soon . . .

Chapter Eighteen

After church on Sunday, the Scotts and the Giffens gathered at Ainslee and Doug's house for lunch, though no one seemed much interested in the coriander-spiced baked chicken or tomato and fennel salad Anabelle knew Ainslee had gone to great pains to prepare.

As soon as the lunch dishes were cleared, the birthday party started. Anabelle took in the scene. Lindsay Belle held the place of honor in her high chair at the head of the table, a bouquet of bright balloons floating above her head. The little darling wore her hair in two little pigtails, sticking straight out from her head.

Ainslee was on her right, putting a single candle shaped like a 1 in the middle of the organic carrot cake, Doug capturing every second on video. Doug's mother Louise, Cameron, Kirstie, and even Evan snapped photo after photo, while Doug's father George made faces at the one-year-old, trying to get her to smile.

Lindsay Belle was totally unaware of the paparazzi in front of her as she chewed on the wooden spoon Ainslee had given her to keep her occupied. She was also unaware of the pile of presents in the living room awaiting her. She'd been eight months old at Christmas and not old enough to be interested in gifts. It was amazing what a difference of four months could make in the life of a baby.

Anabelle felt the joy of the day as she watched her granddaughter's eyes grow large as Ainslee put the cake in front of her with the one fat candle burning. Doug, looking extra sporty with his baseball cap on backward, started singing, "Happy birthday to you . . ." and everyone joined in. Lindsay Belle startled for just a moment, and then a smile spread across her face, showing her two bottom teeth, and she dropped the wooden spoon and began to clap.

When the song ended, Ainslee said, "Blow out the candle."

Lindsay Belle looked around confused but then Ainslee pursed her lips and began to blow and Lindsay Belle copied her. Together they blew it out and everyone clapped, including Lindsay Belle, her dimpled hands flying back and forth through the air.

Anabelle considered again how much the little girl had changed since Christmas. It would only continue, exponentially, for the next few years. In no time she would be as big as Isabel. If Anabelle retired, she could watch her a couple of times a week. Then when another baby came, she would be available to help Ainslee even more.

She never thought she would be a grandmother who provided child care, but that was before Lindsay Belle was born. It had been a year since that marvelous night, yet it seemed like only a month ago. Cameron turned the camera on her and snapped it.

"Oh you," she said, waving him off. He came toward her, the camera away from his face, and stood with his hand on Anabelle's shoulder. She reached up and squeezed it, and he kissed the top of her head. Being a grandmother was more exhilarating than she'd ever dreamed it would be, and she knew Cameron felt the same way about being a grand-father. It was amazing how this little girl had drawn them even closer together. When their children were little, they sel-dom had the time to step back and just enjoy them. But with Lindsay Belle, that was the norm. She squeezed Cameron's hand again.

Ainslee served a tiny sliver of cake onto a pink paper plate and put it on Lindsay Belle's high chair tray. The little girl poked her finger in the middle and then stuck it in her mouth. "Yum-yum," she said, and then startled when everyone broke out laughing.

"Eat it," Doug said, the video camera glued on Lindsay Belle.

"O-tay, Dadda," she said, and poked her finger into the icing. As she tasted it, a big smile spread across her face and she ran her finger through the icing again. As far as Anabelle knew, it was the first time Lindsay Belle had tasted sugar.

"Oh, isn't she precious?" Doug's mom said, leaning toward Anabelle.

Anabelle agreed as Ainslee asked her to pass out the plates of cake. Anabelle jumped to her feet, realizing she'd been in a Lindsay Belle–induced fog. They all were, except for Ainslee who was doing all the work. As she put cake at everyone's places, they reluctantly abandoned their cameras for dessert.

"Don't you wish you could spend every day with her?" Louise said, her eyes still on Lindsay Belle.

Anabelle nodded but didn't point out that if she did, it would probably strain her relationship with Ainslee. A couple of more times a week would be wonderful though.

If she retired, she could quilt more too. She was looking forward to when she could teach Lindsay Belle to quilt. That would definitely be a highlight as far as being a grandmother.

"What are you thinking about?" Kirstie asked.

Anabelle turned toward her younger daughter and wondered how long she'd been staring at Lindsay Belle. "About teaching Lindsay Belle to quilt."

Kirstie rolled her eyes. "Good grief," she said. "Let her be a little girl first."

Cam laughed. "What do you think about teaching her?" he asked Kirstie.

"How to annoy Ainslee," Kirstie teased.

"Lucky girl," Anabelle chimed in, "to have so many people who want to teach her things."

They all laughed. Lindsay Belle began to fuss, and Ainslee said they'd better move on to the presents because it was nearly nap time. It was only one fifteen, but Anabelle remembered how things could quickly fall apart for a tired—and sugared up—baby.

Ainslee took the video camera when they moved into the living room, and Doug sat on the white carpet with Lindsay Belle, away from the coffee table that no longer had a towel clipped to it, and handed her the first gift. It was the outfit from Anabelle and Cameron in a flowery gift bag with tissue paper and ribbon.

Lindsay Belle pulled on the ribbon and let go of it. She frowned as it sprang back toward the bag.

"Let's take it out," Doug said. He thrust Lindsay Belle's hand into the bag and she pulled out the outfit with a smile. In a second she had the dress on top of her head.

It took twenty minutes to get through the rest of the presents. Lindsay Belle held up well, entertaining everyone with her responses. When the last gift in the pile had been opened, Ainslee turned off the video camera and said, "Nap time."

"Wait." Anabelle stood. "There's one more. We left it on the porch."

"Mother." Ainslee's old tone was back. "It's not a pony, is it?"

Cameron laughed. "We wouldn't do that to you."

Doug had Lindsay Belle on her feet and was holding her hand, helping her toward the front door. Anabelle followed. She could imagine maneuvering Lindsay Belle through the neighborhood with the push handle on the tricycle after she retired, not straining her back because she wouldn't have to bend over as often.

Doug opened the door and Ainslee filmed.

"Cool," Doug said, helping Lindsay Belle onto it.

She grinned and gripped the handles.

Cameron snapped her photo.

Ainslee lowered the video camera from her face. "Mother," she said, "this is too much. Our neighbors have one they're going to loan to us."

"But this one is new," Doug said, looking up.

"Doug's right," Cam interjected before Ainslee could get her dander up. "We bought this for Lindsay Belle because we wanted to. And now you don't have to worry about any damage that might happen to someone else's property." He crouched down beside his granddaughter, who turned the handlebar back and forth, and he tickled her neck under her chin.

Ainslee still looked uncertain. "If you insist. But I still worry about your spending so much money on her when there's a perfectly good tricycle we can borrow for free. After all, you'll both be retired soon."

Anabelle opened her mouth to assure her daughter she had no plans of retiring anytime soon, but the expression on Cam's face quelled her response . . . and any Ainslee might have had.

The party ended after that. Ainslee whisked Lindsay Belle off for a nap and Doug thanked all of the guests and told them good-bye, insisting he didn't need any help cleaning up. He'd be done in no time.

On the way home, Anabelle sighed deeply.

"It's all right," Cameron said. "They kept it."

"Oh, it's not that. Well it kind of is." She stopped, not quite sure how to say it, but she realized that one of the things she liked about work was how affirming it was. There was a protocol to follow. She was able to do things right. People appreciated her and valued her. Sure, Cameron was affirming, but without work, would she feel competent and validated? If she watched Lindsay Belle a couple of times a week would she end up feeling like a failure that many times a week too? Because a couple of times a month were hard enough as it was.

"If they decide they don't want it, we can keep the tricycle at our house," Cameron said.

Anabelle nodded. That was a perfect solution. And maybe someday Ainslee would trust her enough to let Lindsay Belle come over by herself.

James sat on the bed beside Fern Sunday evening. "I have some new flexibility exercises I want you to try," he said. "They should help your balance and coordination." He'd spent the afternoon researching exercises for Fern and had found a plethora of information. She'd incorporated yoga into her routine and had worked with a physical therapist off and on through the last couple of years, but he decided he should take a more active role. He was the only one who could work with her daily.

She wore sweatpants, a long-sleeved shirt, and warm, fuzzy socks on her feet.

"We'll start with the leg stretches," he said, grasping her ankle. As he lifted and lowered her leg, he began telling her about the doctorate program in Peoria. He'd done more research and found they had a two-night-a-week program. It would take longer, but it would be doable for him and still allow them to live in Deerford. She seemed to be listening intently but didn't respond.

"What do you think?" James asked, lifting her other leg, just as the phone rang. James lowered her leg and answered the phone. It was the evening shift supervisor from Med/Surg at Hope Haven, asking if he could come in for the night shift. He covered the mouthpiece, told Fern, and she nodded. He told the nurse supervisor he'd be more than happy to fill in.

After he hung up the phone, he returned to the side of the bed.

"You should get some sleep before you go in," Fern said, looking at the clock.

She was right, of course. "Let's finish the exercises first," he said.

Fern sat up on the bed. "We can do them tomorrow. Your rest is more important. You're not thirty anymore," she teased as she reached for her walker.

"That's for sure." He looked at the clock too. He had three hours before he needed to leave for the hospital. That much sleep would make a big difference when it came to making it through a night shift. Just before he drifted off, he realized Fern hadn't responded to his query about what she thought about the PT program.

At 2:00 AM, James was transferred down to ER. "They have a patient coming in," the Med/Surge night-shift nurse supervisor said, "and since things are fairly calm here, I said I'd send you down."

It wasn't that the ER was busy, it was just understaffed, and it made more sense to redirect him than call someone else in and pay them overtime, and it meant he wasn't going to get sent home only three hours into an eight-hour shift.

James met the ambulance outside in the bay. It was freezing cold, literally, and he rubbed his arms, trying to keep warm, his frosty breath a cloud in front of his face. As he waited for the EMTs to open the back doors of the ambulance, James was surprised to see Cesar striding across the parking lot. When he spotted James, he detoured toward him.

"Picking up a shift?" Cesar extended his hand.

James nodded, and they shook hands. "What brings you out tonight?"

"I was following a late-night lead—which didn't pan out. But I came across something else." He nodded toward the ambulance. "Any guesses?"

A sick feeling swept through James. "Gary?"

Cesar nodded. "Found him in his SUV in the parking lot behind the post office. Passed out. Empty bottle beside him."

James groaned.

"He's out cold," Cesar said.

"One stomach pump coming up." James stepped closer. It was Gary all right. His face was ashen gray and there was vomit on the front of his jacket.

Cesar slapped James on the back. "Have fun."

"What's next for him?" James asked.

"I'm going to book him this time on public intoxication. I should have done that the very first time—and would have if he'd been driving, but since driving wasn't involved in any of these incidences..." His voice trailed off. "Still, I feel like a fool for giving him two chances. Guess the third time isn't quite so charming in this situation." Cesar glanced at his watch and then at James again. "I have another lead to follow. I'll be back in a couple of hours. He should be conscious by then, right?"

James nodded, wondering what toll the detective position was taking on Cesar—and on Elena. It had to be a stressful job. He turned his attention back to Gary, wondering if the man could comprehend how lucky he was not to be dead.

Gary didn't come to until after they finished emptying his stomach with the gastric lavage. With the tube still down his throat he couldn't speak, but his eyes said it all. He was clearly surprised that James was caring for him—again.

James didn't say anything as he removed the tube and got Gary out of his clothes, cleaned up, and into a hospital gown.

As he covered Gary with a warm blanket and then piled more on top, the man curled up into a fetal position and closed his eyes. James patted his shoulder and left the room to find a plastic bag for his clothes.

An ER nurse motioned him to the nurses' station. She tipped her head toward the curtain that hid Gary and said, "His wife called looking for him. Of course I couldn't tell her that he was here, but she guessed."

"Is she coming in?" James asked.

The nurse shook her head. "She said he could figure things out on his own this time."

James wanted to say good, but refrained.

"Is he going to be all right?" the young woman asked.

James nodded. "In the short run, yes." Who could know about the long run? That was up to Gary.

Checking the IV, hooking up another bag of fluids, charting what he'd done, and checking Gary's blood pressure, temperature, and pulse regularly kept James busy over the next couple of hours. In no time, Cesar was back, pulling open the curtain.

"Can I take him to the courthouse?" he asked.

"You've got to ask the doc," James said. "I don't make those decisions."

An annoyed look settled on Cesar's face and he walked away. He came back a few minutes later with Dr. Weller in tow.

"Well, well." It was the doctor's on-call night, and he'd been summoned for another case an hour before. "How's our repeat patient doing? Is he as bad as last time?"

"No," James answered. "His temperature and pulse are normal, and his blood pressure is up to 120/90."

"You must have gotten him in sooner," the doctor said to Cesar.

"I do my best, sir," the police officer stated, his voice thick with sarcasm.

Gary opened his eyes and groaned.

"He's all yours," Dr. Weller said.

"I'll get the discharge paperwork started." James moved so the young ER doctor could move past him out of the room.

Cesar stepped closer to the bed and clasped his hands behind his back. "You have the right to remain—"

Gary held up his hand. "Please—"

"—silent." Cesar continued.

James pulled the bag of Gary's dirty clothes out from the cupboard, then stopped. He couldn't bear to take them out of the bag, but he wasn't about to call Melanie and ask her to bring a clean pair into town. Maybe Gary could wear a pair of scrubs to the courthouse.

Cesar finished reading the man his rights.

"I need to talk to my lawyer." The man lifted his head.

"Fine," Cesar said. "You can call him from the jail after you've seen the night-court judge."

James slipped past the curtain on his way to the nurses' station for the discharge paperwork, but the sight of Rev. Wiltshire stopped him. The chaplain had a pair of scrubs in his hands. "Dr. Weller called me," he said.

Relief washed over James. "Could you talk to Mr. Morris?"

The pastor said he'd hoped to and followed James down the hall.

Cesar said he'd get a cup of coffee and be back in ten minutes. James handed Gary the scrubs and then finished the discharge papers while the man changed. As soon as he was done, Rev. Wiltshire came into the room.

"I didn't get a chance to meet you last week," he said.

"But you heard about me?" Gary slipped his feet into his shoes.

Rev. Wiltshire nodded.

"Yep." Gary sat up. "I'm the mess-up with the kid injured in Iraq. I'm the jerk that can't seem to stop drinking."

"That's not what I heard," the pastor said. He smiled. "Not the 'mess-up' part. Nor the 'jerk' part. I heard about your boy—and that you're a guy with a lot going for him."

"Oh yeah. Well, that wouldn't be me. Lost my job. Lost the son I used to know. Most likely lost my wife with this latest binge." He snorted and then rubbed his neck. "No, I'm the guy without a thing going for him. I'm the guy who's ruined everything."

Rev. Wiltshire pulled a chair nearer the bed and sat down. "I agree, you have messed up. But you still have a lot going for you, so let's talk about what you're going to do next."

"Get booked and then talk to my lawyer."

"Sounds like a start. And then?"

"Look for a job . . ."

"What about your wife?"

Gary shook his head as tears filled his eyes. "She'd be stupid to stay with me."

The pastor nodded his head. "I agree."

James looked up from the computer in time to catch Gary's look of surprise.

"So what are you going to do?"

"I went through rehab a few years ago."

"And how did that work for you?"

"Good."

Rev. Wiltshire's voice rose. "Then why are you here?"

"Well, it worked until Joel got injured. Then things went downhill."

"So you need something more local."

"Oh, I see what you're getting at: AA."

"And Al-Anon for your wife."

Gary turned his head toward James. "That's what this guy recommended."

"It's what the judge will recommend too." The pastor drew closer to Gary. "Could I pray for you? Ask God to give you wisdom and help you break your addiction?"

The man nodded, just slightly, but he bowed his head as Rev. Wiltshire said, "Dear Lord, I lift up Gary to You . . ."

James slipped away and almost bumped into Cesar on the other side of the curtain. The detective put his finger to his lips and both men stood still until the chaplain finished his prayer.

"I almost hate to arrest him now," Cesar whispered, clearly touched.

"It's the best thing for him," James responded.

Cesar nodded. He knew that, of course. James went to find Dr. Weller to sign the discharge paperwork and found him in a darkened equipment storage room about to fall asleep on the cot set up for the nighttime on-call attending physician. James hated to disturb him and slipped out quickly after obtaining the signature.

When he returned to the curtained area, Cesar finished off his coffee and dropped the paper cup into the garbage. "Let's go," he said to Gary, his voice rough and tough again.

James watched as the two men shuffled through the double glass doors and headed toward the unmarked police car, and he was surprised to see the brightness of the morning sky. He looked at his watch—almost seven o'clock, meaning his shift was about over.

After James finished cleaning up Gary's room, he headed out the back way to the staff parking lot. As he reached his van, Anabelle's Ford Fusion pulled up beside him, and she swung open her door.

"James!" she stood quickly. "Did you get hired back?"

"Nope. Just helping out in the ER."

"Are you still doing your home health stint?"

James opened the door to his van. "For a week or so more."

"Then what?" Anabelle pushed the door to her car shut.

He shrugged. "I'll see what God provides."

"Candace, Elena, and I are going to get together this afternoon and pray. We're meeting by the Wall of Hope." She looked skyward, and then added, "Weather permitting." Then she turned back to James. "We'd love to have you join us. It would be just like old times."

James felt a woeful smile cross his lips, but he was too tired to stop it. "I'd like that," he said.

"We'll be meeting as soon as day shift ends."

He thanked her, said good-bye, and climbed into the driver's seat, feeling ancient. He was getting too old for night-shift work. He was glad he'd left a message for Melanie last night, saying he'd be at their house around noon. He'd be able to get a few hours of sleep.

It was probably crazy to tell Anabelle he'd come back to Hope Haven to pray, but he needed that too. Maybe more than anything.

Chapter Nineteen

NABELLE SAT AT THE END OF THE TABLE during report, listening to Debbie Vaughn, who was giving the shift change report, and stealing glances at Marie. She looked tired and absolutely wrung out.

"That's all," Debbie said. "Hope everyone has a great day." Then she muttered, "Hope the rest of us have a great sleep." She would be the most likely to take Anabelle's job. It had been obvious for quite some time that Debbie was tired of night shift. Anabelle couldn't remember how many years the woman had been working that shift, but probably close to ten by now.

"How's your son doing?" Debbie asked Marie.

"Better. We had quite the week but he's finally responding to his treatments. I hated to miss work last week, but I didn't have any other choice." Marie stood, a pained look on her face.

Anabelle, her heart racing, followed the woman out to the hall, wondering if it would be better to break the news at the beginning of the shift or at the end. She decided on the end.

She could start by asking if Marie had gotten her message. The woman hadn't called her back.

Marie turned around. "Thank you for telling Rev. Wiltshire about my situation," she said quietly and sincerely. "He brought a box of food by on Friday and had some ideas for me as far as resources to tap in to. And,"—her eyes swam—"he prayed with me and my kids. I felt a peace I haven't experienced in weeks."

Anabelle impulsively hugged Marie, and the younger woman melted into her arms. She wanted to tell her everything would be all right—and it would be, someday. But how could she tell her that now, and then tell her she didn't have a job later in the day?

Marie pulled away and swiped at her eyes with her forearm. "I can't tell you how much this job means to me. And this hospital. I've never worked anywhere like Hope Haven."

Anabelle nodded. "I agree. It's a pretty special place." She was unprepared for the tears that suddenly filled her own eyes and the sinking feeling in her stomach.

"Are you okay?" Marie reached for her hand.

"Just feeling emotional, that's all." Anabelle pulled a tissue from her pocket. She'd wait until the end of the shift to give Marie the bad news. "Let's get to work."

The women parted, and Anabelle stepped behind the nurses' station, feigning the need to look something up on the computer. She dropped down into the chair and stared off into space. If she retired and Debbie took her job, who would take Debbie's job? If it was someone from night or evening shift, Marie would have to take their job and she wouldn't be working days anyway. It was an absolute fluke she was working days as it was. Right now, the evening- and night-shift nurses, except Debbie, preferred those shifts for one reason or another: they coincided with their husbands' shifts, or didn't and therefore met their child care needs, or they wanted the extra pay for shift differential or they preferred working shifts that were more low-key. There were a multitude of reasons—all reasons that wouldn't work for Marie.

Anabelle crossed paths with Marie several times during the shift, and each time the young woman met her with a grateful smile. By quitting time, Anabelle had decided to retire for sure. She and Cameron could get by without the extra income. Sure, it would mean not buying as many things for Lindsay Belle—and also not being reprimanded by Ainslee every time they did—but that wasn't an issue at all compared to Marie's not being able to provide basic needs for her children.

After report, before heading out to the Wall of Hope to pray, Anabelle slipped down the back stairs to the first floor, to the HR department, but Leila Hargrave wasn't in.

"What do you need?" Penny Risser, who'd been leaning over looking at something on the HR administrator's computer, asked.

Anabelle stepped away from the nursing administrator's desk. "To talk to Leila."

"She's in a meeting." Penny nodded toward the wall that connected HR to the CEO's offices. "With the administrators and a guy from California."

Anabelle stepped toward the administrator's desk. "Is it Heath Carlson's friend?" She'd heard he was in town.

Penny shrugged. "All I know is that the man is 'gathering information.' Whatever that means."

Anabelle thought for a moment and then turned back to Penny. "I'll talk to Leila tomorrow." She felt a twinge of guilt for not letting Marie go yet. She'd definitely disobeyed orders, something she couldn't recall ever doing before as a supervisor. "Thanks," she said to Penny and then headed down the hall toward the Wall of Hope.

"Joel, I've got to go. I told you I have a meeting in town." James was out of patience. The young man had been demanding and out of sorts all afternoon. James had asked him several times if there was something bothering him, but Joel had insisted there wasn't. Without Joel's bringing up his dad, there was nothing James could say.

Joel's lower lip actually jutted out. For a moment, James wanted to laugh but knew that wouldn't do any good. "I'll see you tomorrow," he said. "In the morning. Polly will be here too."

Joel adjusted the hospital-style bed so he was sitting up straighter. "Wait. There's something I need to ask you."

James turned around.

"Mom made an appointment with the doc I'm supposed to see. Can you take me?"

"I thought one of your parents was going to."

"Dad was." Joel turned toward the window and his voice grew quieter. "But I would rather you did."

James rubbed the back of his neck. "I'll check with your parents and my supervisor. I'm not sure what the protocol is on this sort of thing."

Joel turned his head back toward James. "Thanks," he said. "I appreciate it. See you tomorrow."

Exhaustion crept up on James as he drove into town. His phone rang and, thinking it was Fern, he flipped it open to speakerphone.

It was Cody. "I have someone who's interested in looking at the house, this afternoon or tomorrow morning." Her voice sounded apologetic. She explained the person who wanted to see it was from out of town and in Deerford on business. He was trying to see as many houses as possible in a short time, both in town and in Princeton. She had no idea what would come of it—but she felt she had to show the house. She was sorry.

James tried to soothe her feelings, telling her he understood. And he did. "Tomorrow morning would work best," he said.

He closed the phone as he reached the city limits and gripped the steering wheel even tighter, feeling utter despair for the first time.

Candace stepped out into the courtyard, relieved to find the space warmed by the afternoon sun. The morning had been cold, but the day had grown progressively warmer. She turned toward the picnic table by the wall and called out a hello to Anabelle.

The older woman looked up from her knitting and smiled. "I was beginning to wonder if anyone else was going to show up."

"I had a patient who just delivered," Candace explained. "And Elena had to go pick up Izzy. She'll be right back." She brushed a leaf off the bench across from Anabelle and sat down. "Have you heard from James?"

Anabelle shook her head.

"What are you knitting?" Candace settled down onto the bench opposite her friend.

"A cap for Lindsay Belle. For next winter." She held the lime-green creation and the skein of yarn bounced off the table into her lap.

As they chatted, James hurried into the courtyard. "I thought I was late," he said, "really late."

"You are," Anabelle chided. "It's just that Elena's later."

They all laughed, mostly because Elena was never late. When James explained he'd come from his home health job, Anabelle chastised him for working too much.

"Isn't that ironic?" he said. "I'm unemployed—and working too much." He smiled, and Candace was relieved to see the grin that she'd missed so much.

"I admire how you're trusting God," she told him. "You put me to shame. I've really been struggling with the threat of the hospital reducing staff and maybe even closing."

"You don't know of what you speak," he said, and then smiled again. "Actually, I need to be reminded to trust. I'm feeling pretty desperate."

Candace couldn't imagine James needing a reminder, not with how he'd trusted God through Fern's illness, the demands of raising teenagers, having to move out of their old house because of mold, and waiting for it to sell.

Elena arrived a moment later with Izzy in tow. As they sat down at the table, the girl whispered something to her grandmother and Elena said, "That's okay, they'll be safe in the car. You can show Aunt Anabelle later."

Anabelle perked up. "What do you want to show me, Izzy?"

"Long story," Elena interjected. "I'll tell you later. We've held everyone up enough."

Izzy looked disappointed but began coloring, a little outside the lines, in her book.

Anabelle started the meeting, listing things to pray about. The hospital. The upcoming advisory meeting. A job for James. Provision for all of them.

"Skip Mullen," Candace added.

"Skip who?" James asked.

"He's Heath's friend, from California. I met him over the weekend. He's a really nice guy and seems to have a handle on what's going on. He's an expert on e-charting and informatics and grant writing. All of that. Of course, he's used to making way more money than Hope Haven could pay."

Everyone nodded in agreement. James's gaze fell on the Wall of Hope and then he refocused, asking Candace if there was a chance Skip was looking at houses.

Candace nodded. "Yes, here and in Princeton."

James groaned. "Maybe you could pray he finds one in Princeton. It sounds like he might be looking at the rental we're in tomorrow morning."

Candace's stomach fell.

"Oh, James." Elena's voice broke. "I thought you'd already bought that house."

"The process stopped when I was laid off."

Candace felt sick. The house was perfect for the Bell family. As much as she'd wanted Skip and Margie to move to Deerford, she was suddenly hoping they'd find a house for sale in Princeton too.

James said, "Just pray; we'll trust God with it."

As everyone talked, Izzy began to hum a tune. It took Candace a few bars to realize the song was familiar, and it appeared that it registered with James at the same time because, in unison, they blurted out, "Trust and Obey."

Izzy smiled. "I learned it in Sunday school yesterday." She resumed humming.

"Could we sing it together?" Candace asked. "Before we pray?"

All agreed and with Izzy leading them, the four friends sang, "'Trust and obey, for there's no other way, to be happy in Jesus, but to trust and obey.'"

Anabelle began her prayer by asking that all of them would trust God with Hope Haven and with their own needs too, including any hard decisions each might be faced with. She mentioned James and all the things that were out of his control: a job, the house, Fern's health. Candace prayed along silently, adding that she would trust God with her relationship with Heath and their future too.

After the prayer meeting ended, the women said good-bye and left in a hurry to run errands and head home to start dinner for their families. James lingered for a moment, staring at the Wall of Hope again. Finally he stood, stepping toward it, squatting down to read the names of the donors engraved on the waist-high bricks that formed the planter. Above his head the tulips growing in the box were starting to fade, their white, yellow, red, and pink petals hanging loosely from the stems. He leaned his forehead against the bricks. It had been good to pray with his friends, but he still didn't feel peace.

Lord, he silently cried out, *what do You have for me?* He waited a moment. *Should I go back to school? Should I change careers?* Still he felt no peace. The bricks were cool against his forehead and he started to get up, when a feeling swept over him.

Lean on Me.

They weren't audible words—but a feeling. The feeling swept through him again.

Lean on Me.

James rested his head against the cool bricks again. *Is there something else I should be doing? Pursuing?* he prayed.

The feeling swept over him a third time. *Lean on Me.*

Okay. He stood. *I will. Help me to trust You. Help me to remember, every minute of every day, to lean on You.* Peace finally swept over him. He wouldn't pursue the PT program. Even two nights a week would be a stress on his family. He would wait—and lean.

Chapter Twenty

ANDACE PULLED INTO THE PARKING LOT OF THE mall, close to the shoe store, and glanced at Brooke. "One pair of Vans, right?"

Her daughter crossed her arms. "Could I get two?"

"Two aren't in the budget, sweetie," Candace answered pulling into a parking space. One pair wasn't in the budget either, but it seemed like overnight Brooke's feet had outgrown all of her school shoes. Her PE shoes were getting tight and would need to be replaced soon too. By summer, she would need new sandals . . . and new clothes. Candace sighed as she climbed from her Honda CRV.

Brooke walked a couple of steps ahead of her on the way to the entrance. Her long blonde curls bounced against her back, and even though she was still short for her age, her legs seemed to have grown a few inches in the last month. And that, combined with her thin build, gave her the look of a model.

She turned and stopped, waiting for Candace to catch up. As Candace reached her daughter, Brooke took her mother's hand and swung it back and forth. Even though her daughter was officially a teen, she was still a little girl—at least some of the time.

It felt like it took Brooke forever to decide which pair of shoes to buy. She tried on a pair of neon green and then pink. When the salesclerk left to help someone else, Candace suggested Brooke try the black shoes, thinking they would go with everything.

"I'll give them a try." But Brooke sighed loudly as she looked in the mirror. Next she tried on a purple pair and then a pair that were forest green.

When the salesperson—who had a tattoo of a rose on her bicep—returned, she told Brooke she couldn't go wrong with black. "It looks bad with everything," she said.

Brooke nodded, her face thoughtful. "Yeah," she responded, "I was thinking the same thing."

After Candace had paid and they were leaving the store with the black Vans on Brooke's feet, she whispered, "*Bad* actually means *good*."

"I figured," Candace whispered, putting her arm around her daughter. "How about a smoothie to celebrate a successful shopping trip?" she asked in a normal tone. She could squeeze that much out of the budget.

"Sounds good!"

"Or would that be *bad*?" They both laughed as they quickened their steps.

Ten minutes later as they sat at a table in the food court, Brooke pointed across the way, to the jewelry store. "Mom, isn't that Skip?"

Candace squinted. It sure looked like him.

"And I think that's Heath." Brooke was halfway out of her chair.

Candace almost stood too but then sat back down. Heath and Skip were walking out of the jewelry store. She felt her face redden and hoped Brooke didn't notice.

She didn't. She was waving her hand. "Hey, Heath! Skip!" she called out. "Over here!" And then Brooke started walking toward the men, with Candace a few steps behind her.

Heath and Skip exchanged looks and what Candace was sure were sly smiles and then headed their way. "What are you two doing here?" Heath asked.

Brooke raised her foot. "Shoes." And then her half-full cup. "Smoothie." She grinned at both men. "How about you guys?"

"*Um.*" Skip shot a look at Heath. "I was shopping for my wife."

"But Heath's the one with the bag." Brooke's voice was incredulous, but she didn't go so far as to exclaim, "Awkward!" Instead Candace just thought the word.

"He's holding the bag for me," Skip said, extending his hand.

"Yeah. Why am I carrying this?" Heath swung the bag toward Skip. "Carry your own gift."

The two men laughed, and Candace felt her face grow warmer. Maybe her suspicions were wrong.

"We were just going to go grab some dinner," Skip said. "Care to join us? My treat."

Brooke looked at Candace in anticipation, but Candace shook her head. "We already ate, and I need to get home and get Howie to bed."

"Aw, Mom," Brooke said.

"Next time," Skip said.

They chatted for another few minutes. Heath seemed as cool and calm as could be, and pretty soon Candace convinced herself that the gift really was for Skip's wife. Heath had probably grabbed it off the counter as a joke.

"Well, we'd better get going," Candace said. As they said their good-byes, Heath gave her a hug, and then Skip winked at her and once again she felt flustered as they turned to leave.

"What do you think Skip bought his wife?" Brooke pushed open the mall exit door and Candace followed her outside, dropping her smoothie cup in the garbage can to her right.

"I have no idea," Candace said. "But probably something really nice."

"I hope I have a husband someday who buys me jewelry. . . ." Brooke's voice trailed off as they reached the car. Candace sighed, inwardly grateful her daughter was clueless as to what she had thought that Heath might have been up to.

After Brooke and Howie were settled down for the evening, Candace made herself a cup of peppermint tea and sat on the other end of the couch from Janet, who was working on the crossword puzzle in the *Deerford Dispatch*.

Janet looked up. "I need a word for *idea*. Six letters."

"You know I've never been good at—wait." Candace counted the letters on her hand. "How about *notion?*"

"Oh, you're right." Janet looked at Candace, a pleased expression on her face. "Thanks." She wrote the letters down and then another word. Finally she turned her attention toward Candace. "Did you want to talk, dear?"

"No," Candace said.

"Then why are you sitting down?"

"What do you mean?"

"You're always busy. Always on your feet. If you take the time to sit down, you have a reason."

Candace put her mug on the coffee table. "I was just wondering, generally, what you think of a widow remarrying."

Janet pushed her reading glasses to the top of her head. "Is there something you need to tell me?"

Candace shook her head. She'd definitely made up her mind, but she wanted to be prepared for what others might think, such as her mother and sister. She continued, "You know, is it possible to honor one's first husband and remarry? That sort of thing."

Janet turned sideways and tucked her legs beneath her. "Has Heath proposed?"

"Mom." Candace's face grew warm.

"Has he?"

"No."

"But you think he's going to?"

"I'm not sure," Candace answered.

"Well . . ." Janet leaned against the arm of the couch. "I think only you can decide what's best for your kids and how to honor Dean—all of that. But,"—her eyes twinkled—"I think you and

Heath are really good together. And I think he would be a wonderful father to both children. Plus I think it would be a compliment to Dean for you to marry again. You know, you two had such a good marriage. You can be hopeful about another good one because of it."

Candace took a deep breath. That wasn't something she'd thought of before.

"Now go get some rest," Janet said. "You've had way too much on your plate for the last few weeks."

Candace stood and took a step toward her mother quickly, kissing her on the forehead. "Thank you," she said.

Janet grabbed her hand and squeezed it. "Say your prayers and get some sleep. You'll see. Everything will work out for the best."

Chapter Twenty-One

THE NEXT MORNING AFTER REPORT, ANABELLE called Leila's office to see if she was available to talk for a moment. Leila said she could come up to the CCU, but Anabelle insisted on running down to her office. She didn't tell Leila, but she didn't want any of the other nurses to overhear their conversation.

"How did things go with Marie?" Leila asked as soon as Anabelle hurried into her office. "She hasn't checked in with me yet."

"That's because I haven't spoken with her," Anabelle answered, sitting down.

Leila cocked her head to the side, and Anabelle hurried on, speaking rapidly. "I've decided to go ahead and retire. That will open up another slot on the floor. I've been thinking that Debbie Vaughn would probably apply for my job, and chances are another nurse might be interested in her job. That wouldn't mean that Marie or James—"

"Whoa!" Leila placed her hands in a time-out position. "You've lost me."

"I want to retire."

"So you don't have to lay off Marie?"

Anabelle nodded her head and then shook it. "Not entirely. It's just that—"

"You don't want Marie to lose her job?"

"Her husband left and her youngest has asthma—a really bad case. She had to take all of last week off, and she's out of sick time and vacation leave. And besides, James really needs a job too."

"Anabelle, you know you can't take responsibility for other people's lives."

"But I don't need this job. We can make it without my income. . . ." Her voice trailed off.

"But you're the best CCU supervisor I've had and—I'd bet a million bucks on this—you're not ready to retire."

Anabelle sat up straight. "And Marie isn't ready to get laid off. And James wasn't ready to be let go either."

Leila exhaled slowly. "I admire your loyalty—and your concern. But you can't make such a rash decision—"

"No, I've thought about this. Really."

"—so soon."

They stared at each other for a moment. Finally Leila said, "Wait a week, please."

For a moment Anabelle thought her supervisor was going to say more but when it was clear she wasn't, she asked, "What about Marie?"

Leila sighed and then said, "I've stalled so long on her position it won't hurt to wait a few more days. Actually, I think it's dropped from Varner's radar for the moment." The woman swiped the back of her hand over her brow. "Just between you and me, this has been the most stressful few weeks of my career."

Anabelle could only imagine.

"We need to hang tight," Leila said. "Things are either going to get better soon—or a whole lot worse."

James arrived at the Morris home feeling much better than he had the day before. But he braced himself as he walked toward the front door, wondering if Gary would be back at the house and what kind of mood Joel would be in.

Lean on Me, he chanted silently.

Melanie met him at the door, her eyes cold. "You knew."

"Pardon?" James said, taking a step backward.

"You knew Gary went on another binge when you were here yesterday. He said you took care of him at the hospital."

James nodded.

"Why didn't you tell me?"

"I couldn't. Confidentiality."

Her shoulders slumped and she shook her head. "And here I was pretending everything was all right."

He wanted to tell her that she wasn't very good at pretending but refrained. "Is he here?" James asked.

"He went to an AA meeting this morning. He should be back anytime."

James said that was good to hear.

"And I'm going to an Al-Anon meeting this afternoon," Melanie said. "My third."

"That should help you as you move forward," he said. He wanted to add that it should help her deal with Joel too, not rushing to meet his every need, especially the ones he could take care of himself. But that was probably something that would be better absorbed if Melanie learned it on her own. Funny how addictions and injuries and illnesses could all play out in similar ways. A person's best intentions were sometimes harmful.

"I wasn't going to let Gary come home," she said, "but the women at the meeting yesterday listened as I talked through everything. None of them gave me any advice, but by the end of the meeting, as I listened to the other stories, I decided if he agreed to go to AA meetings and therapy, I would give him more time."

James knew it was important for both of them to be supported—they were going to need a lot to get through these hard times.

An hour later, as James helped Joel finish dressing, Gary arrived, humming a tune as he came through the door. When he saw James he stopped.

"How's it going?" James's voice was casual.

"Fine." Gary turned and headed toward the kitchen.

"Whatever," Joel said.

James put Joel's shoes on the floor beside his chair, intending to respond, but then he said, "I've come to the conclusion in life that most people do the best they can with what they have."

Joel snorted.

"The thing is, they usually need additional resources to do better. More support. Or education. Or a new system to be able to cope."

Joel didn't respond.

"Want to go outside until Polly arrives?" James asked. "It's warm already."

"Sure," Joel answered, "as long as there aren't any fourteen-year-olds running around and having fun."

James ignored the comment and rolled him toward the patio doors. Gary was pouring himself a cup of coffee in the kitchen. Neither father nor son spoke.

James wheeled Joel onto the little ramp and then onto the concrete slab patio. The planters now had petunias growing in them, which Melanie must have added, and a bird feeder hung from the eaves.

"Mom spruced things up a little after you and the Scouts left." Joel rested his good hand on the arm of the chair, and turned his face toward James. "Did you ask about taking me to my appointment?"

James squinted a little as he spoke. "It turns out I can, if no one else is able." The sun was warm against his face.

"My parents have been fighting over who should go with me to Texas."

Gary obviously shouldn't go, thought James. *The man isn't dealing with the stress he's already been handed. What would he do with the stress of Joel's rehabilitation? And what good would he be to Joel if he went on a binge? Melanie's the only viable choice.*

"The thing is, I don't want either of them to go. Dad for the obvious reasons. Mom because she babies me."

James could see that. Sometimes mothers had a hard time letting their sons be the men they needed to be.

"I think I'll do better on my own."

"Ask the doctor at the VA clinic what he thinks," James said. "He'll be able to tell you what your needs are going to be."

Joel nodded. "That's what I was thinking too."

James pulled up a plastic chair and sat beside Joel as they gazed beyond the willow trees and the creek to a hawk soaring over the next field.

"This is really the pits," Joel muttered.

James nodded but didn't say anything.

Joel's voice sounded far away when he started speaking again. "I never expected this. I thought I might die, but I never thought I'd get so messed up." He pressed his good hand against the arm of his wheelchair. "But then I feel so guilty for being such a whiner. There are so many other soldiers worse off than I am," he said. "They say I'll walk again. Do you think that's true?"

"Based on what's in your chart, I'd say so," James answered, wondering if Joel had been believing, all along, that he wouldn't. "Plus you're making good progress in PT."

Joel winced. "I've been a real jerk to Polly."

"Yep." James kept his gaze on the hawk. "You did apologize."

"And to you."

James turned his head toward Joel and smiled.

"I'm sorry."

"Apology accepted," James said and patted the young man's shoulder. "Now, just don't get off on the wrong foot in Texas, okay? Be cooperative from the beginning."

Joel frowned. After a while, he said, "My parents need to focus on themselves. Not even their marriage—just themselves. I'm not blaming my injuries— because obviously they had a lot of stuff going on before—but this sure has brought out the worst in them."

James didn't respond.

"When I was in high school, my dad started going on binges. Before that, my friends hung out here all the time, but then Dad started coming home drunk on Friday nights, and it was so embarrassing that I stopped inviting my friends over and ended up being pretty mean to most of them to get them off my back. Then Dad got a couple of DUIs—and he went into rehab. By then I was pretty angry. I graduated and kept on going. Joined the army. Didn't look back." Joel was quiet for a moment.

"And your dad stopped drinking?" James finally asked.

"Yep. Seems so—as far as Mom knows. If he didn't, he hid it." Joel snickered. "I guess one thing he did learn was not to drink and drive—seems he was more into drinking and passing out in random places this time."

James didn't say anything.

"Guess he couldn't take my injuries." Joel stared off into the distance. "Guess it makes it all my fault."

"Is that what you think?" James put his arm around the young man.

"I don't know what to think." Joel's voice was barely audible.

James took a deep breath but didn't respond. It would be better if Joel could talk himself through this one.

"Come on," Joel finally said. "Where's your pithy advice?"

James cringed, but something he'd read several years ago came back to him. "Someone said once that ten percent of life is circumstances and ninety percent is how we react to those circumstances."

Joel hooted. "Boy, I sure got a packed ten percent."

James nodded. "You did."

"But," Joel said, "I take it your point is I can choose to react the way my parents have, or I can choose a different way."

"Something like that," James said.

"How about you? Mom said you'd been laid off from the hospital. How are you reacting?"

James heard a car in the driveway and assumed it was Polly's. He stood. "Have you ever heard of the song 'Lean on Me'?"

"You're kidding?" Joel laughed. "Remember me telling you about my chaplain? He used to sing that song to us. It was a hit by some guy named Bill, right? Like a hundred years ago or something."

"Bill Withers. And it was only about forty years ago." James smiled and started singing, raising his voice when he got to the chorus. He stood and grabbed the back of Joel's chair as he sang about being a friend who could help someone carry on when they couldn't do it under their own strength.

He waited for a moment, looking out over the creek and then said, "I can't be that friend to you. Neither can your mom or dad. All of us are going to let you down. Only God can help you carry on."

"That's what my chaplain told me too." Joel's voice was barely audible again.

"Have you heard from him?" James asked, as he turned the chair around toward the door.

Joel shook his head. "I e-mailed my buddies in the platoon and haven't heard from any of them."

"If something had happened to any of them it would have been in the news." James pushed Joel into the house. "They're probably holed up at a staging area, waiting for a plane home," James said as the doorbell rang. With the army it was always hurry up and wait, but maybe the chaplain didn't have access to e-mail while he was waiting.

"I'll get it," Joel said, placing his good hand on the wheelchair and lurching it forward a jerk at a time. The bell rang again and James was afraid Polly might open the door herself, but she waited. Joel pulled it open, a smile on his face.

As Polly made her way through the door, pushing the PVC-pipe structure ahead of her, James hummed the last stanza of the song a couple of times as a reminder to himself. Cody was showing the house this morning. Fern's mom and dad were going to take her out for coffee so she wouldn't be home.

Cody had said she'd call as soon as possible with any information. James patted his pocket to make sure his cell phone was still there. So far no one had called. As he watched Joel tease Polly, a sparkle in his eye, James began to hum the song again.

Candace found herself smiling as she went about her work even though two nurses had been sent home since they didn't have anything to do. She had one patient in early labor, relaxing in the whirlpool, and another who was seven centimeters dilated. As she rounded the corner to the nurses' station, she nearly bumped into Heath.

"Hey, you," she said. "What brings you up my way?"

His blue eyes lit up. "You. Can you get away for lunch?"

"Twenty minutes, maybe. Max."

"Let's go then," he said.

Candace checked in at the nurses' station and told them to page her if she was needed sooner before heading down the hall with Heath.

She hurried through the salad bar, knowing that would be quicker, while he ordered a sandwich. She'd already started eating by the time he arrived at the booth in the back of the cafeteria that she'd chosen hoping for some privacy. Her patient who was at seven centimeters might take all afternoon—or fifteen minutes.

Heath slid into the booth beside her instead of across the table. They talked about work for a little bit and then Heath said, "It was fun to see you and Brooke at the mall last night."

"It looked like you and Skip were doing some male bonding."

Heath laughed. "It's been fun to have him around. He's a good guy."

Candace agreed.

"And a good example to me," Heath added.

"How so?" Candace put down her fork, picked up her napkin, and wiped her mouth.

"He's ambitious but is doing his best to put his family first. He's willing to take risks."

"And you're not?" Candace asked.

"Oh sure, if it's to track down a gray kingbird."

Candace knew that they were rare in the area and that Heath had never seen one.

"I want to get better at taking risks."

Empathy swept over Candace, and she had the sudden urge to kiss him. Maybe he was having a hard time working up the nerve to propose—not that she wanted him to right now. She knew he would make sure the time was right. His gaze intensified as he watched her, and she couldn't help herself; she leaned forward and met his lips with hers. He kissed her back and then grinned as they pulled away.

Suddenly self-conscious, Candace looked around, but they were alone in the back of the cafeteria. No one had seen them. He took her hand and held it for a moment, and the look on his face was priceless.

Just as Candace was about to ask what was next for them, her pager went off. "I've got to go," she said.

"Leave your tray." Heath scooted out of the bench and she followed. "I'll get it." That was another thing she loved about him. He noticed the little things that made her feel cared for.

"Thanks," she said, blowing him a kiss as she hurried away. They still hadn't had time to finish their conversation, but right now a new life was coming into the world and that was where her focus had to be.

James sat down beside Fern on the couch and put his arm around her.

"How was work?" she asked.

"Good." Home health care was different from working in the hospital. There, he would care for the same patient for a few days in a row and get to know the family to some extent on the med floor. When he was working surgery he didn't have much of an opportunity to get to know the patient or family. He realized, working with Joel, how much he enjoyed interacting with people on an emotional level. He'd never come to care about a patient the way he cared about Joel. And now the young man would be leaving in a week, Lord willing.

"And how are you feeling about things?" Fern's eyes were full of concern.

"Okay."

"James?"

"Honestly?" He smiled. When the boys were little, he and Fern used to have "couch time" when they got home from work before they started cooking dinner. The boys would spend the time in their room, playing, while Fern and James talked about their days and planned out the evening and the next day. If either had a grievance with the other, they would voice it. If either was unsettled about something, they would talk it through. At first, the boys would fight and try to get their attention, but they'd stood firm. They needed a little time each day to open up and talk. They both credited that time together as the foundation of their marriage.

"James?" Fern prodded.

But for the last few years, since Fern had been diagnosed, James had shared less and less about how he felt, not wanting to burden her.

"How are you *really* doing?" she asked.

James smiled a little and then began to talk. "I won't even have a part-time job in another week, probably. I haven't heard from Cody yet about the house, and I'm afraid even if it doesn't sell right now, we still won't be able to buy it and we'll have to move again sometime. I worry about college for Gideon."

Fern reached for his hand and stroked his long fingers, one at a time as he spoke.

"But." He paused, not sure how to explain. He forged on. "I feel peace, like God wants me to trust Him with this, to lean on Him."

Fern nodded and then said, "I feel so bad that all of this falls on you."

James wrapped his hand around hers. "There are times when I let it all fall on me, and that's wrong because I couldn't do this without your support and without the help of the boys. And I'd be a mess if I didn't know God was with us each step of the way." He thought of Gary Morris. It really didn't take much for a person to end up in a personal hell on earth.

James rested his head against the back of the couch and closed his eyes. He still hadn't recovered from picking up the night shift Sunday.

"What's going on this evening?" Fern asked.

"Scouts," James muttered. "The meeting should have been last night, but we rescheduled because the church needed the meeting space. But maybe I won't go. I'll get one of the other dads to cover for me."

"Nelson said there was going to be a surprise."

James opened his eyes and lifted his head. "I haven't heard anything about that."

Fern's eyes twinkled. "If you're at all up to it, I think you should go. More than one young man will be disappointed if you don't."

Elena waited until Izzy had changed into her play clothes to tell her she'd picked up her glasses earlier in the afternoon. She pulled the case from her purse and handed it to her granddaughter. "Can you tell me what we said about you taking good care of your glasses?"

Izzy held the case in her open palm. "Always put them in the case when I'm not wearing them. Always put the case in my backpack so I can take the glasses back and forth to school with me. And..." She thought for a moment and then continued, "don't ever put the glasses' lenses down on my desk or a table at school or home."

"Good," Elena said. "Let's go into the living room, and you can put them on and read to me."

Izzy smiled and took the glasses out of the case, which she slipped into her backpack. "May I put them on now?" she asked.

Elena said yes, and Izzy carefully slipped the mauve plastic frames onto her face, grinning as she did so.

"They look marvelous," Elena said. "You did such a good job choosing them."

"Daddy helped me," Izzy said. "They're not as fancy as my dollar glasses or as Aunt Anabelle's, but I like them." She took off skipping into the living room, and Elena decided she would take a photo of Izzy in both pairs of glasses to show Anabelle. Her friend would get a kick out of Izzy's stylish ways.

They settled down together on the couch and Izzy picked up *Goodnight Moon* again, turning to the first page. "In the"—she began sounding out each letter—"g-r-e-a-t. Great." She turned her head up to Elena and grinned.

"Great reading!" Elena said, squeezing Izzy's shoulder.

"Green...room..." She didn't know every word but she figured out most of them as she made her way through the book. After the last page, she said, "The glasses make the letters stay still. They were all swimmy before, even with the red pair."

Elena leaned back against the couch, relieved, as Izzy reached for a Madeline book.

"One more, and then I need to start dinner," Elena said. And then go to the advisory committee meeting. She took out her phone. "Let me take a photo of you before you start—and one with your other glasses too."

"For Mommy?"

"You bet."

"And Aunt Anabelle too?"

Elena nodded and then clicked the photo. Maybe it would help lighten up the meeting.

Chapter Twenty-Two

ANABELLE LAUGHED AT THE PHOTOS ON ELENA'S smartphone as the advisory committee members gathered in the hospital boardroom. "Izzy certainly is a little girl with style," Anabelle said, removing her own glasses, "and personality."

Elena slipped her phone back into her purse, and Anabelle sat down at the other side of the table and pulled her notebook from her purse. Heath, Candace, and another man, whom she assumed to be Skip Mullen, came in the back of the room laughing. The man was tall and solid, had a head full of sandy hair, and blue eyes. He had an open face and an easy smile.

Albert Varner followed the trio, his face still pinched and worried.

Skip approached the table and introduced himself to Anabelle and Elena. His handshake was firm and pleasant. When he found out they were both nurses, he said, "My mom was a nurse. I always admired her work as a child, but it wasn't until

I got into this business that I realized all she did. You are my heroes."

Anabelle couldn't help but smile. From some men, the comment might sound like flattery, but from Skip Mullen it sounded sincere. He had a natural charisma, but it seemed genuine and down-to-earth. He took a chair beside Elena, and Heath and Candace sat down across the table. Varner and McGarry sat at one end of the table and Dr. Hamilton sat at the other. The good doctor had obviously met Skip earlier in the day, when the two had discussed the hospital and Dr. Hamilton's concerns.

"I've asked Skip to tell us, as a group, what his priorities would be as CIO of Hope Haven," Varner said.

Anabelle focused on the man, wondering how he could possibly consider taking the CIO position at Hope Haven when the pay would have to be minimal—if the board would even approve the position at all. He was Heath's age—in his late thirties. He wasn't ready to be put out to pasture. *How can Hope Haven possibly compare with his previous work experiences?* she thought.

Skip looked around the table as he greeted the group, making eye contact with each individual. Anabelle remembered she needed to be taking notes and turned her attention back to writing as Skip spoke.

"First, it's essential to tap into government grants for funding. What you have has worked for the last few years, but as a nation we need..." He spent a few minutes talking about national e-charting requirements. Obviously, he knew what he was talking about and had advised other small hospitals on how to obtain funding. "The government wants small hospitals to survive. They are essential to the economy of small-town America. We can't afford to let them die." He recited a few statistics about hospitals that had obtained government grants, instigated new informatics programs, and then turned their finances around.

He paused for a moment and then spoke slowly, saying the money in the grants he was certain he could secure would more than cover not only his salary, but the needed changes to the electronic charting, and would help supplement other programs.

McGarry leaned forward in his chair and said to Skip, "We can't begin to match your current salary, not even by a fraction."

"And you would be foolish to," Skip answered. "Your money is better spent on other things."

"Just how much salary would you be expecting?" McGarry gripped his pen tightly in his hand.

"I've seen your administrator's pay scale," Skip answered, "and I can live with that."

"Surely it wouldn't support the lifestyle you and your family are used to," Varner interjected.

Skip looked offended for half a second and then explained, "We're actually quite frugal. My wife and I are determined to raise our children in a simple environment where they'll learn the value of hard work. Plus, I'll be honest, I've invested through the years, and our financial future is secure."

When no one responded to his comment, he cleared his throat and said, "Let's get back to discussing what's most impor-tant here. The future of Hope Haven. It's essential to maintain all the departments the hospital already has. Hope Haven must keep a strong and vital obstetrics program. The Holistic Cardiac Program needs to be continued. With an aging population, it will bring in more money than it will lose, if we take a look past the five-year mark."

Anabelle glanced up, but Varner was poker-faced, and Dr. Hamilton was busy taking his own notes. Skip shared a few more of his ideas and then asked if anyone had questions. The discussion continued for another half hour, and then Dr. Hamilton thanked Skip for all of the information and his time.

Skip offered his thanks to the entire group.

Varner took out his smartphone. "Zane and I will talk some more and then meet with the board next Tuesday evening, a week from tonight. We'll give you a call after that."

Skip nodded. "I'll look forward to it."

Anabelle jotted down the exchange between the two men, and then Dr. Hamilton asked if anyone else had anything they wanted to discuss. No one did, and he adjourned the meeting at eight thirty, the earliest any of the advisory committee meetings had ended so far.

After all of the other members had left, Candace, Heath, and Skip talked for a few more minutes in the parking lot of Hope Haven. The night was clear and warm. "Tell Margie it's always this nice here," Heath joked. "No rain. No wind. No cold. No snow."

"Oh, she's looking forward to the snow," Skip interjected.

"Remember, she's from Indiana," Candace added. "Winters might be a shock after living in California for years though."

"How has the house-hunt gone?" Candace asked, wondering if he'd actually seen the Bells' house that morning as planned.

"There's a house here that might work. And a couple of places in Princeton. The commute would be a fraction of what I do in LA." It was only seven miles—and had hardly any traffic.

Skip said good-bye and hugged Heath with a good old-fashioned bear hug, then gave Candace a tender hug, and thanked them both. "I'll be in touch soon," he said, adding, "I can't wait to see what God has planned for all of us."

As Heath gave Candace a ride home, she hoped Skip Mullen would take the job at Hope Haven, whether he and his family decided to live in Princeton or Deerford—though she prayed James and Fern got to keep their house too. She couldn't imagine anyone in a better position to help the hospital move forward and reach financial stability than Skip.

When they arrived at her house, Candace invited Heath in for a cup of coffee. He readily agreed. With mugs of decaf in hand, they sat on the couch talking over the events of the last few days. Janet had already put Howie to bed by the time they arrived, and Brooke was supposed to be doing her homework in her bedroom.

She appeared in the doorway to the living room. "Have you seen the colored pencils?" She had a large sheet of white paper in her hand for her science assignment.

"Did you check the desk drawer?" Candace responded.

"Oh yeah," Brooke said, as if she suddenly remembered that was where they'd been kept for the last five years.

Brooke took off up the stairs, and Howie appeared wearing his Buzz Lightyear pajamas. "I'm thirsty," he said, his eyes dancing.

Candace told him to go get a drink of water and go back to bed. He knew he would be allowed only one. As he headed back past the living room, he dawdled in the doorway, smiling.

"Howie," Candace said. "I'll come check on you before I go to bed, but Grammy already tucked you in. Don't come out again."

He kept smiling, his face toward them, as he ambled on toward the staircase.

Before Candace could say another word to Heath, Brooke was back, asking for an explanation of photosynthesis. As Heath finished answering her question, Howie began yelling from his bedroom.

Heath began to laugh. "I think I should get going," he said.

Candace shook her head. "They're not usually this busy at bedtime."

"They're probably curious, wondering what we're up to." He winked as he stood.

Candace walked Heath out to his Jeep. He put his hands on either side of her face and kissed her tenderly and then said good night. As she turned to walk back to the house, the curtain in Brooke's window fluttered, and Candace was pretty sure she saw two faces behind it. She smiled as she hurried on toward the front door.

James yawned and glanced at his watch. It was almost nine o'clock, and as Nelson wrapped up the meeting, James wondered why Fern had encouraged him to come. The boys had planned another service project, talked about a camping trip in the summer, played a game of sardines, ate a bag of chips, and passed around a two-liter bottle of cola that one of the boys happened to have in his backpack.

James was about to encourage Nelson to wrap things up when he heard someone at the door to the foyer of the church. He stood, assuming it was one of the dads arriving to take his son home—probably just what was needed to break the meeting up. He peered into the darkness on the other side of the glass door, not recognizing the person at first.

Suddenly it registered. Gary—and with him was Joel, sitting patiently in his wheelchair.

James pushed the door open and welcomed them in, confused as to why they were at the church.

"Nelson invited us to come so the Scouts could all meet Joel," Gary explained.

"Sorry we're late," Joel said, as Gary wheeled him through the door. "I started to chicken out, but Dad said I needed to face my fears."

James turned his attention to the father, and Gary shrugged his shoulders. "I figured if I'm trying to face mine, he should face his."

James reached out and shook Gary's hand and then Joel's. "Thank you for coming, both of you. This is going to mean a lot to the boys. And it means a lot to me," he said, thankful Fern had talked him into coming to the meeting. "An awful lot."

As James led the way down the hall, Nelson came out of the meeting room. "Joel," he said, quickening his steps. "Thanks so much for coming. I was beginning to think—"

"That I wouldn't show? No way. I need to make up for hiding the day your troop came out to help my folks." Joel extended his right hand and Nelson shook it and then everyone followed the boy back into the meeting.

"We have a special visitor," Nelson said, as everyone filed into the room. "Joel Morris. He's going to talk with us about his experience in the army."

James and Gary sat down in the last row of chairs as the boys milled around Joel.

"Why'd you join up?" Shane asked.

Joel began telling them his story, starting with deciding to enlist his senior year of high school. The boys listened intently. It was the same story Joel had told James in bits and pieces over the last few weeks, but with more humility and less anger. The boys all listened eagerly, soaking in every word. There was nothing like a true story to make war real.

Afterward, as the boys gathered around Joel, Gary turned toward James. "Joel and I talked things through. Both Melanie and I are going to take him to his doctor's appointment."

James nodded.

"But thank you for being willing to take him. Thanks for being a friend to him and to all of us." As Gary spoke, his eyes were on his son as the young man showed the Scouts the scars on his arm.

Chapter Twenty-Three

ON FRIDAY MORNING, JAMES FOUND HIMSELF singing "Trust and Obey" as he drove to the Morris home. It had been a good week so far for the Morris family. Joel had been much more settled, cooperating with both James and Polly. His parents, who were each attending support meetings every day, were more peaceful too.

Yesterday, both of Joel's parents had taken him to Springfield for his doctor's appointment, and James was looking forward to finding out what they had learned.

He parked behind Gary's SUV, and he heard music playing as he approached the house. He couldn't remember ever hearing any tunes in the home. When he'd asked Joel if he could turn some music on several different times, the young man had emphatically declined.

Gary opened the door for James and then turned the music down. "Can't stand this stuff," the man said, shooting a playful look at Joel, who had his feet over the edge of the hospital bed, ready to get going for the day.

Joel smiled and said, "You won't have to listen to it for long."

Gary headed into the kitchen and James positioned Joel's wheelchair, asking, "How did the doctor's appointment go?"

"He said I'm good to go for rehab."

"That's great," James said, and he meant it, even though it meant he was out of a job.

"And he said I won't need anyone with me in Texas, so neither Mom nor Dad is going. They can stay home and work on their own stuff."

James didn't comment, but silently he agreed that that was probably best for all of them, including Joel.

"But," Joel said, as James helped him transfer into the chair, "the biggest news is that Brooke Army Medical Center has an opening for me on Monday."

"Wow." James nearly stumbled as he stepped behind the wheelchair. *I'm out of a job beginning today.* "How are you going to get down there?"

Joel grinned. "I had an e-mail from my chaplain; he's back in the States. He has a month off before he reports back to the unit." Joel maneuvered his chair a short distance and then let James take over. "Anyway, he wants to go down with me. Mom and Dad will take me to Chicago on Saturday, and then we'll fly to Texas on Sunday. I booked our tickets online last night."

James leaned forward, over the chair, in awe of everything that had fallen into place for Joel.

"The doctor said my arm's looking better, and he thinks I'll regain full use of it. So, I've been thinking maybe I can go into computer programming or something like that. The doc said to talk with the occupational therapist in Texas."

"How about your legs?" James asked.

Joel sighed. "It could be worse. He said I have permanent nerve damage, but with therapy and exercise, in time I should be able to walk with braces. Like I said, I know I'm lucky . . ."

"It's still a loss," James said. "A big loss."

As James turned on the shower he thought of being out of a job so soon. He would need to reapply for unemployment, back to full time. He still hadn't received his first part-time check; he hoped this wouldn't delay everything again. He reminded himself that his friends had told him not to give up hope about a job at the hospital because Heath's friend might be hired for a CIO position. Ironically, if the man was hired and decided to buy their house, they'd have to move anyway. Cody said the guy wasn't going to make a decision until he knew if he had a job or not. So maybe it wouldn't happen. Maybe the guy would choose one of the places in Princeton, but James couldn't put his hope in what *might* be. He needed to put his hope in God and then move forward with what was prudent.

While Polly worked with Joel one last time, James chatted with Gary in the kitchen for a moment.

"Melanie's going back to work, and I have a couple of leads on jobs," Gary said. "And I have an AA sponsor."

James patted the man's back. "Sounds great."

Gary sighed. "I have no idea whether I can save my marriage. In fact, I know I can't,"—he grimaced—"because I'm realizing just how powerless I am. But I'm going to do what I can and pray I can stay sober." He crossed his arms. "I have to learn to let Melanie go and allow her to make her own decisions. Same with Joel."

James tilted his head.

"Joel's injuries really shook me up. It scared me to see how little I could do to help him or ease Melanie's worries. I couldn't take the uncertainty of everything any longer."

James wasn't sure if that was an excuse or the truth, but figured Gary's sponsor and his AA group would help him set his thinking straight if it was off target.

"It was nice to visit your church the other night, for the Scout meeting," Gary said.

"It was really good to have you and Joel join us. It meant a lot to the boys—and to me."

"It's been a long time since I've been inside a church," Gary said. "Since I was a kid. But it's something Melanie's been asking for. Anyway, visiting a few churches is something we would like to do."

James smiled. "I know any of the congregations in Deerford would love to have you."

Two hours later, James told Joel good-bye and wished him well. Then he bade Gary farewell and asked him to pass on his best wishes to Melanie too. James felt sad as he walked out to his car. And tired. He pulled onto the highway and accelerated, thinking about what he really wanted to do. He hadn't worked in the new heart-surgery program long enough to know how much he would have liked it in the long run, but chances were he would have missed his Med/Surg job. With the cardiac-program job, he wouldn't have a lot of contact with patients—and he really liked patient care. Sure, Med/Surg wasn't the same as home health, but it did give him day-after-day involvement with the same patients and their families.

The tune to "Trust and Obey" filled his head again as drops from a spring rain began to splatter his windshield. He was reminded of the prayers he'd said for Joel and his family and the prayers he'd said for himself in dealing with them. "Thank You, Lord," he whispered.

Anxiety percolated inside of him when he thought of his job situation, the house, and college looming for Gideon. Maybe the idea of going back to school captured his interest because it would give his life purpose. He had to remind himself over and over that just because he didn't have steady work, his life didn't lack purpose.

Chapter Twenty-Four

ELENA FELT AS IF SHE WERE HOLDING HER BREATH over the future of Hope Haven. Skip Mullen seemed like a formidable force and someone who could turn things around, but none of them was convinced that the executives and the board would agree to hire him.

Her worries eased a little on Saturday, mostly because Izzy was a great distraction. She wanted to read to Elena every minute, and since Rafael was working all day and a spring storm had swept into the region, curling up on the couch with her granddaughter was the perfect thing to do.

Sunday morning dawned bright and beautiful. The sunshine awakened Izzy before Elena had a chance to, and the little girl was in her father's room before Elena could stop her. Rafael's gig had lasted late into the night, after he'd already put in ten hours at the restaurant.

Elena stood in the doorway to his room and heard Izzy say, "Sunday's here again! Will you come to church with me today?"

Rafael groaned and muttered something, but Elena couldn't hear exactly what.

Izzy patted his bare shoulder and then said, "That's okay. You can sleep."

But as Elena plopped a waffle onto Izzy's plate, Rafael stumbled into the kitchen, his eyes bleary and his hair sticking out in fifty-five different directions. "Mi bonita invited me to church." He patted Izzy's head as he spoke. "So what's the deal? Will Mommy be there?"

Elena nodded. "I think she's helping with Sunday school." Last she'd heard, Sarah finally had a Sunday off.

Rafael yawned. "What time is church?"

"Eleven."

"I'll see you then," Rafael said and padded back down the hall as Izzy began to clap.

"Yay," she said. "Mommy and Daddy are both going to go to church."

Elena poured more batter in the waffle iron. "Maybe," she said. "But don't be surprised if he goes back to sleep. He's really tired."

Izzy stopped clapping. "But he said he'd be there."

"I know." Elena bit her lower lip. She just didn't want Izzy to be disappointed.

"Do you think he'll meet me at my Sunday school class? Like the other dads do?"

Elena shook her head. "I don't think he knows where your class is." Rafael had gone on holidays and special occasions, but he wasn't familiar with the layout of the church, except for where the sanctuary was.

"Okay," Izzy said. "But he'll sit with us in church, right?"

"If he comes," Elena answered, "I'm sure he'll sit with us."

When Cesar joined them for breakfast, Izzy announced to him that her daddy was going to church.

"Where is he?" Cesar asked.

"Sleeping," Izzy said. "But he's going to get up. I know he will because I prayed—" She clamped her hand over her mouth.

Cesar asked for the syrup and Elena passed it to him and asked what his plans were for the day. She didn't want Izzy to keep talking about what she wanted. She couldn't bear to hear her granddaughter lament about wanting her parents to get back together again.

Cesar said he was going to mow the lawn and then catch a basketball playoff game on TV in the afternoon. "Just gonna take it easy," he said.

There had been a time when Elena begged Cesar to go to church with her, but she'd figured out that she must let that go. She wasn't being a loving wife or faithful to God when she hounded him. Elena was grateful Izzy didn't say anything to her grandfather about his going too.

Elena was happy that he was going to relax. He'd been working longer hours with his detective position than he had when he was an officer.

On the way to church Izzy talked nonstop about Rafael's joining them. Elena knew Rafael meant to, but she'd heard him come in after three o'clock that morning, and then it probably took him a while to wind down. Izzy kept talking as they walked down the hall to her classroom, her black dress shoes clicking on the linoleum and the skirt of her dress swinging around her knees as she waltzed along.

Sarah was already in the Sunday school classroom when Elena and Izzy arrived, and the first thing the little girl announced was that Rafael would be coming for church.

"Really?" Sarah looked straight at Elena, her gray eyes wide. Elena mouthed, "We'll see."

After Sunday school was over, Elena returned to the classroom and as Izzy gathered her things, Sarah said, "I wasn't going to stay for church, but Izzy really wants me to."

Elena wasn't surprised. It all seemed to be part of her fantasy. Izzy said good-bye to her friend Mateo and then said, "Look for me after church, okay? I have a surprise for you."

Mateo gave her a quick hug and then left with his parents.

As Izzy, Sarah, and Elena walked down the hall, Izzy skipped ahead to the foyer and turned her head this way and that. Then she spun around and looked some more. A surge of people came through, and Elena was pretty sure the little girl could only see the bottom halves of people. But if Rafael came, he would be wearing his ratty jeans and Izzy wouldn't have any problem picking him out of the crowd. He wasn't in the foyer though, and he wasn't in the sanctuary when they entered, either.

"We need to sit at the end of a pew," Izzy instructed. Elena, followed by Sarah, trailed after the little girl. "You sit there," she said to Sarah, pointing for her to enter the pew first. "Then me." Izzy scooted in beside her mother and bumped her little bottom up onto the pew. "Save a place for Daddy between us," she said to Elena.

"Will do," she responded and sat at the end of the pew, praying her son would show up. She continued praying as the congregation filed into the church and then as the organist played the prelude. She prayed as the pastor said the opening prayer and then as the choir stood and sang "The Lord's Prayer" a cappella. Izzy never turned her head to see if Rafael was coming down the side aisle, nor did she seem worried. When the assistant pastor began to give the announcements, there was a rustling behind her but Elena thought it was Mateo who sat two pews back with his parents.

The clearing of a throat startled her and Elena jumped a little when she looked up. There was Rafael, wearing a pair of blue casual pants and a button-down shirt, and wanting to get into the pew. She tucked her feet under the bench as Izzy squealed just a little and then slapped her hand over her mouth. Rafael sat beside her and put his arm across the pew, just behind her head, bumping Sarah's shoulder. Then Izzy grabbed both of her parents' hands.

Elena was filled with relief that Rafael had shown up, but was a little alarmed by Izzy's behavior. Did the little girl really think her parents might still get back together?

After the announcements were over, the congregation stood to sing a song. "I thought you'd fallen back asleep," Elena whispered to her son.

"I did," he said. "And slept through my alarm."

Elena gave him a questioning look.

Rafael looked straight ahead as he answered her. "Dad woke me."

Tears sprang into Elena's eyes, and her throat thickened. Cesar was looking out for his little Isabel. She was thankful Rafael didn't notice her emotions. He was following Izzy's instructions to find the hymn in the songbook. She had taken out her glasses and wanted to read along.

When the kids were dismissed for children's church, Izzy shook her head and Elena mouthed, "Okay." Of course she didn't want to leave her special spot between her parents. Elena exhaled, pleased her granddaughter was happy but still worried that she was setting herself up to be hurt.

After church was over, Elena led the way out to the foyer of the church. Sarah and Rafael chatted for a moment. Elena watched them out of the corner of her eye. Rafael looked at Izzy and then smiled at Sarah, saying something quietly. Izzy spun around and Rafael scooped her up into his arms. As he held her, Izzy reached over to Sarah and hugged the young woman around her neck. Rafael looked a little uncomfortable. A moment later, he said he needed to get to work.

Izzy asked him to wait just a minute and began scanning the crowd from his arms. Her face lit up when she spotted Mateo, coming down the hall from children's church with his mom on one side and his dad on the other.

Izzy pointed to Sarah, whom Mateo already knew, and then to Rafael and then gave Mateo a thumbs-up. His parents made their way over to Rafael and Sarah and introduced themselves to Rafael, who put Izzy down and shook their hands. After they'd chatted for a few moments, Rafael told everyone good-bye. He patted Sarah on the shoulder and then bent down and gave Izzy a hug.

Izzy was fine to leave then and told Sarah good-bye. When they reached Elena's small SUV, Izzy said, "See, I told you God would answer my prayer."

Elena turned around in the car, looking over her headrest at her granddaughter. "And what exactly did you pray for?"

"That both my mommy and my daddy would go to church with me." Izzy's eyes lit up, and she smiled.

Elena reached between the seats and squeezed her granddaughter's leg, but the tears were starting to come again and she didn't dare speak. She turned around. She knew that her granddaughter's long-term hope was still that her parents would get back together. But, in the meantime, she'd asked God that they would both go to church with her. And they had. *Ah, the faith of a child.* Elena swiped at her eyes, reminded to pray her own desire—that Cesar would go to church with her.

Chapter Twenty-Five

UESDAY AFTER WORK, CANDACE OPENED HER closet doors and stared at the handful of dresses in the back. Heath had told her to wear something dressy because they were going out to a nice restaurant in Peoria for her birthday a day early, so she could spend the actual day with her family.

She pulled out a black sheath from the very back and held it against her body. The dress was short-sleeved, shimmery, and fell just above her knees. She'd bought it for her and Dean's tenth anniversary. They'd gone away for the weekend to Chicago, and her mother had watched the kids. Howie had only been one and Candace had missed him horribly. It was the last trip she'd taken with Dean. She put the dress back in her closet.

Beside it hung a sleeveless dress in cobalt blue. She would need a sweater for it today; the fickle spring weather had turned cool again. Next, she pulled out a three-quarter-sleeved black dress with blue and white flowers embroidered on it. She'd bought it last year because it was on sale and she liked it, but she'd never worn it. She held the hanger up to her chin. The dress came to just below her knees. She could wear her black strappy sandals to dress it up a little and she had a shawl with black beads in the fringe that would give it an extra sparkle.

As she turned toward her mirror, her eyes fell on her wedding photo on the table beside her bed. She still hadn't moved it to the living room or the family room.

"Where should I put you, Dean?" she said out loud.

Her mom was right. He would want her to remarry. They'd even talked about it, generally, once. She'd told him she would want him to remarry if she died, and he'd said the same. Life was meant to be shared.

"It's time," she said, out loud again. She walked around the bed and picked up the framed photo. She took it to the living room where she set it among a grouping of other family pictures. She knew that Heath honored the marriage she had shared with Dean and respected the children's need to remember it.

She would never forget Dean. Never forget all they had shared, the marriage and home they had created together, the babies they'd made together. But life was meant for the living. It was time to move forward.

She dressed quickly and pulled her hair back, securing it with a black clip. Tendrils fell around her face and for a second she looked younger, not a day over thirty-five she was sure, but then she leaned a little closer and noted the wrinkles starting around her mouth and eyes.

Oh well. Thirty-nine wasn't that old. She smiled. At least not as old as she'd thought at twenty-nine.

As she applied her makeup, she tried to keep her mind from the obvious, but it went there anyway. *Does Heath plan to propose? Tonight?* As she put on her black dangly earrings, Howie began banging on her bedroom door.

"Come in," she said.

"Brooke said you're going out to dinner with Heath," he wailed. His hair was messed up, as if he'd been wrestling, and it was pushed up from his sweaty forehead.

"*I* told you that. When I got home from work."

"I want to go too." His green eyes were heavy.

She sat down on her bed and he climbed up beside her. "Not tonight. Some other time."

"I promise I'll be good, and I'll wear my church clothes."

Candace stroked his thick hair and was beginning to say again that sometimes grown-ups needed time alone, when Howie heard the sound of a vehicle outside, most likely Heath's.

"Gotta go!" he shouted, bounding off the bed and out the door.

Candace found her shawl, neatly folded on the top shelf in her closet, and her matching black beaded purse. After she transferred what she needed into the little bag, she headed down the stairs. At the main level, she looked down into the family room to tell Brooke good-bye, but she wasn't there. As she opened the door, she registered the sound of a basketball and as she stepped outside, everyone came into view. Heath, wearing a suit, was playing H-O-R-S-E with Brooke and Howie.

The ball bounced right past him when he caught sight of Candace. "Wow—you look great."

Her cheeks burned. "Thanks."

"Ready?" He met her on the porch and offered her his arm.

"Ready." Or was she? Her insides quaked just a little.

Howie ran toward them. "Can I go, pleeease?"

"Not this time, buddy." Heath ruffled his hair. "Tonight's just me and your mom. But next time. I promise."

Instead of taking Heath's Jeep, Candace handed him the key to her SUV and let him drive, since she didn't know where they were going.

Dinner was at a fancy place, a seafood and steak restaurant in downtown Peoria with linen tablecloths and crystal goblets. They sat at a table in an alcove with high-backed chairs. Light from the single candle danced across the tablecloth.

Heath seemed relaxed, and pretty soon Candace found her anxiety easing too. They bantered back and forth over the menu. Heath wanted to order calamari as an appetizer. Candace asked if he expected her to eat it because eating an eraser would be easier. He laughed and told her she hadn't had good calamari before if that had been her experience.

He talked about the fresh seafood he'd grown up on in Washington State: salmon, clams, squid, scallops, crabs. He loved it all. Candace agreed to try the calamari but ordered a filet mignon for her entrée, trying not to focus on the twenty-six-dollar price tag. That led her to thinking about the hospital board meeting that was going on as they spoke. She shivered. Maybe they'd find out tomorrow they didn't have jobs.

"Earth to Candace," Heath said.

She refocused.

"What were you thinking about?"

"You don't want to know." She unfolded her napkin.

"Work?"

She nodded.

"About what's going to happen with the hospital?"

She nodded again and spread her napkin in her lap.

"None of that tonight," Heath said. "Stay with me. Here. Now."

The conversation turned toward summer plans. Heath wanted to go camping. Candace hoped to take a vacation with the kids, maybe to the beach, but that would depend on how things were going at work—

Heath held up his index finger as a reminder against the topic.

Candace laughed, and the subject veered toward Heath's father and how he was redoing the flower beds in Heath's front yard, pulling out all the plants and starting over.

Not once did Heath excuse himself or confer with the waiter or seem secretive in any way. He didn't pat his pocket, nor were there any bulges in his pocket. The more convinced Candace was that a proposal wasn't imminent, the more relaxed she became. By the time they ate dessert—crème brûlée—she was a little disappointed that the evening didn't seem to include a proposal. It was the perfect atmosphere. She looked as good as she was ever going to. Heath was over-the-top handsome in his suit and sky blue tie that perfectly complemented his eyes.

But no proposal came. On the way home Candace dozed a little as a soft rain fell on the windshield and the SUV's heater warmed her. For the first time in weeks she felt cozy and safe, able to let go—to trust Heath with the driving and God with her future.

The next morning, Candace sat down in the computer chair at work and rolled close to the desk.

It was her birthday. She had grown used to having it be a pretty low-key day. Dean used to go overboard with celebration and gifts, making her birthday that much harder to get through the first couple of years after he died. She'd convinced her mom not to make a big to-do about it since then. And it seemed that had worked, because as far as she knew, no one had planned anything to celebrate tonight other than a regular family dinner.

The staff was abuzz about the board meeting that had taken place the night before, but no one had any definite information. A group of nurses gathered behind Candace, and she couldn't help but hear their conversation.

"I heard from Frederick Innisk's niece that the guy from California wanted so much money that his salary alone would force Hope Haven to close."

Candace knew that wasn't true. She tried to concentrate on the charting she needed to do.

"Why would they bring someone in from the outside anyway?" another nurse asked. She bumped into Candace again, this time on purpose. "Candace, isn't the guy a friend of Heath's?"

Candace nodded, her attention still on the computer.

"So what's the scoop?"

She turned toward the women and shrugged. "I have no idea. Your guess is as good as mine, but I wouldn't believe the rumors." *Surely we'll have an answer soon*, she thought.

After work, she hurried home. Heath had asked the night before if he could take Howie and Brooke on a hike. She'd said a week or two before that she seldom had any alone time in the house. Janet had been helping Susan with a gardening project and wouldn't be home until later, so Heath suggested he take the kids out to Bass Lake again and she could relax. "Take a nap if you want to," he had said.

The kids were ready to go when she walked through the door and thankfully the weather was cooperating. It hadn't rained all afternoon. Heath arrived a couple of minutes later wearing jeans and a jacket. Candace waved good-bye as the three of them took off for their adventure.

She took a deep breath, enjoying the stillness in the house and then made herself a cup of tea. But the house was too quiet. It didn't feel right. She couldn't possibly take a nap in such silence.

But she did. She sat on the couch, intending to read, and then decided to rest for just a minute. She woke up to Howie bounding through the front door, shouting, "Mommy, Mommy! We have a surprise!"

By the time he reached the living room, Brooke was right behind him.

"Mommy, Heath—"

Brooke tackled Howie onto the carpet and slapped her hand over his mouth. "Heath told you to wait!" she bellowed.

Candace leaped to her feet, unsettling her teacup and then righting it quickly as she called out with a smile, "Brooke, get off him."

Heath stood in the doorway, trying not to laugh. "Sorry," he said.

Brooke rolled off Howie and, unnerved, the little boy ran to Candace. "We have a surprise!"

"We're supposed to wait until after dinner." Brooke was clearly exasperated.

"Dinner?" Candace stared at her kids. "I haven't even started cooking."

"We're going to go to the Parlor," Howie said. "Heath let me choose." He turned toward Heath. "Do we have to wait to tell Mommy?"

Heath threw up his hands. "No. Now is as good a time as any." He smiled at Candace as he spoke and walked toward the center of the room, then extended his hand across the coffee table. She took it and he led her to the center of the room.

Then he got down on one knee and took a small box out of his pocket and removed a beautiful solitaire. Tears sprang into Candace's eyes.

Howie clapped his hands together. "He asked us first," he shouted.

"Candace," Heath said, taking her hand again, "will you marry—"

The *me* was drowned out by Howie's yelling, "Please say yes, Mommy, please say yes."

"Howie." Brooke clapped her hand over his mouth again.

There wasn't a doubt in Candace's mind. "Yes," she said, glancing at Brooke and then at Howie, before her eyes locked on Heath's. "Yes, I will marry you."

Heath slipped the ring onto her finger, and Candace pulled him to his feet. He embraced her and then kissed her. He whispered, "Happy birthday."

Her eyes welled with tears as they turned, together, toward the kids, who stood ramrod straight and still, Brooke's hand still over Howie's mouth.

"Come here," Heath said, motioning to the children.

They both moved at once, running together, and flung their arms around Candace and Heath.

Our first family hug, Candace thought, and then she was crying, tears of joy and relief flooding over her. That was another thing that she loved about Heath—that he could surprise her and include the kids.

Later, after dinner and cake with Janet and Susan and her family at the Parlor, after the kids were in bed, Heath said he wanted to ask before they knew what was happening at Hope Haven.

"Why?" she leaned away from him a little.

"Because we're in this together," he said and then kissed her again. "Regardless of what happens with the hospital and our jobs, *we're* meant to *be*."

Chapter Twenty-Six

THURSDAY AFTERNOON, JAMES SAT AT HIS DESK checking the status of his unemployment benefits and found out his file still hadn't been updated.

He stretched his back and clicked into e-mail. A message from Joel popped into his box.

Hey Old Soldier,

Made it to Texas with just a few mishaps—my chaplain's not nearly as good at transferring me as you are. Ended up on my butt in the middle of the plane when we were supposed to be disembarking. Besides that, everything else has gone well so far. Started therapy two days ago—my PT makes Polly look like a saint.

Thanks again for your help.

Joel

He read the e-mail to Fern. She left her book in her lap when he finished and said, "It seems to me that God had you lose your job for a reason."

"So I could take care of Joel?"

She nodded.

He'd thought of that too. But now Joel didn't need him any longer. He was jolted out of his reverie by the phone ringing. He stood and ambled into the kitchen. It was Cody, calling to check in.

James kept his voice low. "Do you have bad news for me?" He'd put off calling her all week.

"Nothing definite," she said, "but the man interested in the house has his financing all in order. He might make an offer by tomorrow."

James lowered his voice even more. "If he does, when would the house close?"

Cody cleared her throat. "By the end of May. The sale would move quickly."

It sounded like the man had cash. "Just let me know as soon as you know," he said to Cody.

"Sure," she answered. "And I'm sorry."

James said he understood and hung up. As he refocused on the computer, the phone rang again. This time it was Dr. Hamilton. "Albert Varner wants to talk to both of us, ASAP," he said.

"About?" James stood, bumping the office chair backward.

"He won't say," Dr. Hamilton answered. "And I don't want to guess."

After giving report, Anabelle checked her work e-mail before going home. She had one message—from Leila Hargrave.

Anabelle's heart raced as she opened it. They'd all been waiting for word about the future of Hope Haven. Maybe this was it.

She clicked open the message and read it quickly. Leila instructed her to stop thinking about retiring—there was no need. Nor was there a need for her to lay off Marie. And she should stop worrying about James too because everything was going to work out. Anabelle read the e-mail a second time, a smile growing on her face with each word. She e-mailed Leila back, thanking her and asking what happened for her to change her mind. It would be tomorrow morning before she would hear back from Leila, unless she went down to the HR office on the first floor before she went home. Maybe someone else would have the information she hoped for.

As she headed to the nurses' lounge she spotted Marie in the distance, hurrying down the hall, probably in a rush to get home to her kids. She would never know how close she came to losing her job, even though that was her fear. Anabelle sighed in relief. The woman would be able to support her children. And Leila had been right—Anabelle wasn't ready to retire. She was surprised at how grateful she felt to know she wasn't at that point.

Elena was in the lounge refilling her travel mug with coffee. "Have you heard anything?" Anabelle whispered and then told her about the e-mail.

"Maybe Candace knows."

"Let's go see if she's gone home yet," Anabelle said. "Maybe we can catch her before she leaves."

Candace had stayed late because her patient was giving birth as the shift changed. She cleaned up the baby and made sure the mom was settled before turning everything over to the evening-shift nurse. She hoped Heath was waiting for her in the parking lot. She hadn't seen him all day. During his lunch, he'd picked up prescriptions for his dad but told her he'd find her after work.

She hadn't worn her ring—it was a little big and she needed to get it resized—so she hadn't told anyone her good news. She and Heath hadn't discussed whom they would tell and when. She assumed he'd told his dad and, of course, they'd told Janet and Susan and her family last night, but she would wait to tell anyone else until she and Heath had talked.

Smiling, she started down the hall. Coming toward her were Elena and Anabelle. *Did Heath tell them already?* She couldn't tell by their faces and before they reached her, the hospital PA system crackled and a voice—Heath's voice to be exact—began to speak.

Candace stopped in her tracks.

"This is Heath Carlson and I have an announcement to make to the Hope Haven community so you can share in my joy."

Elena and Anabelle quickened their pace, smiles spread across their faces, and behind them a group of OB nurses had gathered.

Heath's voice continued. "I proposed to Candace Crenshaw last night, and she accepted."

A cheer rose from the nurses, just as Elena and Anabelle reached Candace. The older women hugged her together, cheering. Behind them, Heath made his way through the cluster of nurses, a bouquet of red roses in his arms.

"How did you do that?" Candace asked Heath as Anabelle and Elena let her go, sure her face was the same color as the flowers. "How were you just talking over there—and now you're here?"

"I prerecorded it." Heath grinned.

Everyone began to clap again and Candace took the roses in her arms and then planted a kiss on Heath's mouth as another cheer erupted.

James and Dr. Hamilton stood outside Albert Varner's office, waiting for the CEO to open his door, and both smiled as Heath's announcement sank in.

"It's about time," James said. But before Dr. Hamilton could respond, Varner opened his door and escorted them in, seemingly oblivious to the announcement.

"Sit, sit," he said. "I wanted you to be among the first to know. Skip Mullen accepted the job about an hour ago. We're reinstating the Holistic Cardiac Program and want you both to resume where you left off."

James leaned back against his chair. It looked as if he might get his position at Hope Haven back but not have a home for his family.

As if he could read his mind, Varner added, "Sounds like he's going to live in Princeton instead of Deerford though, but I guess that's a short commute if you've been living in LA."

Relief flooded James for a moment, but then a wave of unsettledness alarmed him and he began to stutter as he said, "I—I don't think I'm the right nurse to lead the program th-though," he said. But as he spoke, he felt surer of what he was saying. "I've decided patient care really is where my heart is. Don't get me wrong. I treasure working with you, Dr. Hamilton, and enjoy interacting with patients to get them ready for surgery, but my heart is in taking care of the same patient several days in a row and working with their families."

"Well." Varner's eyebrow twitched. "Speak with Leila. We'll have a fair amount of juggling of nurses in the next couple of weeks. I'm sure we can get you back on the floor . . . with the same seniority you had before." He turned to Dr. Hamilton. "And Leila will help you find another lead surgical nurse."

Dr. Hamilton nodded and shook James's hand, thanking him.

"If it's official, as far as the CIO's being hired, is it all right if I tell the other nurses?" James asked as he stepped toward the door.

"Tell away," Varner said, pleasure spreading across his face.

James hurried up the back stairs, nearly knocking down Valera Kincaid from the *Dispatch*.

"I've been wanting to interview you," she said to James, flattening against the stairwell. "About being let go from the hospital."

"The story's moved on," James said, still climbing. "I'm gain-fully employed at Hope Haven again."

"Then the rumor must be true," she said. "That Skip Mullen has been hired."

"Ask Varner. He'll give you the details," James called over his shoulder, leaving her behind. He didn't want the celebration in the Birthing Unit to end before he got there.

He pushed through the fire door onto the second floor and bounded down the hall. Just past the nurses' station, a crowd was gathered around Heath and Candace. James nudged his way through into the center and shook Heath's hand and then gave Candace a hug.

"Now we just need good news for you," Candace whispered in his ear.

"We've all got good news this afternoon," he said stepping back, addressing all of the nurses. "Skip Mullen has been hired as the new CIO, and I'm getting my old job—my position in Med/Surg—back."

A cheer, led by Anabelle went up along with another round of hugs.

James stepped back, taking it all in. They had leaned on God—and He had carried them through.

About the Author

Leslie Gould is the author of eight novels, including five in Guideposts' Home to Heather Creek series. Leslie lives in Portland, Oregon, with her husband and four children. Visit her Web site at www.lesliegould.com.

Read on for a sneak peek of the next exciting and heartfelt book in *Stories from Hope Haven.*

Special Blessings
by
Anne Marie Rodgers

EY, LOOK AT THAT!" HEATH CARLSON POINTED into the cool emerald forest that ringed Bass Lake.

"What?" Candace Crenshaw turned her head to peer into the woods on Heath's far side. As she did so, Heath quickly pivoted, capturing her lips with his in a sweet, lingering kiss before starting forward again on the lakeside path.

"Heath." Candace was smiling. "What was that for?"

Her fiancé grinned and shrugged. "Just because. You look very pretty in that green T-shirt. It matches your eyes."

Candace's heart melted. "Thank you." She gestured to the seven people in front of them. "We'd better not get too far behind. Howie has a knack for falling into any body of water he gets near."

Dappled sunlight slipped through the forest canopy above them, and off to their left, sunlight danced across the surface of the lake as a warm breeze lightly rippled the water. The weather in early May in Illinois could be capricious, but today was pleasantly mild. Last year at this time, she and Heath had been on the verge of dating and falling in love. The thought warmed her.

Just the night before, Candace's friend and fellow nurse Elena Rodriguez had hosted a small party for the newly engaged pair. Their family and closest friends—mostly co-workers from Hope Haven Hospital where they'd met—had gathered in Elena's home to wish them well. All the women had exclaimed over Candace's engagement ring—a stunning, round, brilliant-cut diamond with pear-shaped side stones. It was very different from her first ring—the sweet, small solitaire her late husband Dean had given her when they were both poor college students, which she had cherished. She still was getting used to seeing Heath's ring flash on her left hand.

After attending church at Riverview Chapel earlier that morning, Heath and Candace had brought Brooke and Howie to meet some friends for a picnic at Bass Lake State Park, a popular local recreation area.

Ahead of them on the tree-shaded path that encircled the lake were Skip and Margie Mullen, their three young children, and Brooke and Howie. Skip was a friend of Heath's from high school who recently had been hired as the chief informatics officer for Hope Haven. He planned to bring in grants to fund updating the hospital's electronic charting technology capabilities. In turn, that would free up funds to save other departments and jobs that were on the chopping block.

After looking at homes in nearby Princeton, the Mullens had decided instead to build a house in the new development where Candace's friend and fellow Hope Haven nurse James Bell lived. Candace was glad the Mullens would be closer. It would be easier for her to get to know Heath's old friend and his family.

As the group continued their hike around the lake, Heath, Brooke, and Skip took turns carrying the Mullens' two-year-old Violet piggyback-style when she tired of walking.

Afterward, they returned to their picnic site near the lake's sandy beach—a wooden table beneath some fir trees with a nearby stone grill. Heath and Skip did not let Candace or Margie lift a finger and provided the entire feast: barbecued chicken, burgers and hot dogs for the kids, pasta salad and coleslaw from a local deli, deviled eggs, a vegetable plate, and fresh, sliced strawberries. Fudge brownies covered in peanut-butter icing satisfied everyone's sweet tooth.

When everyone was stuffed to contentment, Candace and Margie spread a blanket on the sand and sat watching the children play at the water's edge while Heath and Skip cleaned up the remains of the meal.

"I haven't felt this relaxed in ages," Margie said with a laugh. Brooke was holding Violet's hand to keep her from running into the water, distracting her with a shovel and sand pail. The oldest Mullen child, nine-year-old Indiana, trailed behind them. The little girl had a bad case of heroine worship and hadn't been more than an arm's length away from Brooke all day. Candace had noted with pleasure that Brooke had been exceptionally kind and gentle with the younger girl as well as the toddler. "Your daughter has been doing my job all day."

"Brooke loves children, just like my mother does." Candace hooked her hair behind one ear with a finger to keep the breeze from blowing it across her eyes. "We invited my mom to join us," she told Margie, "but she doesn't care for sand. She said she'd rather relax in solitude with a good book."

Margie laughed. "That sounds good to me too."

"She helps out with my children a lot," Candace confided. "Sometimes I worry that I'm taking advantage of her, but she always swears she loves being with them."

"She probably does then," Margie offered. "My mother isn't the grandmotherly type, and she makes no bones about it. I doubt your mom would willingly spend so much time with Brooke and Howie unless she really wanted to."

The thought was reassuring to Candace.

"And besides," Margie went on, "there's an end in sight, right? The who-picks-up-which-kid-from-what-activity deal will get easier once you and Heath are married and he pitches in."

"That's true," Candace said, smiling. "He's going to be a great father to them."

"Hello, ladies." Heath dropped down beside Candace, interrupting their chat, while Skip sprawled next to Margie. "Cleanup has been conquered."

"Have you heard about the award nomination?" Skip asked Candace and Heath.

Heath shook his head, as did Candace. "What award nomination?" Heath asked as Candace mentally sorted through the disquieting feelings that Margie's comment had provoked.

There's an end in sight. Will it bother Mom when Heath begins to take on some of the child care she's been doing? Skip's voice brought her back.

"Hope Haven has been nominated for the National Outstanding Small Hospital Quest for Excellence Award."

Candace's eyes widened. "I've heard of that award, and it's quite prestigious. How did that happen?"

"Patient nominations." Skip leaned back on his elbows. "Hospitals must be nominated by five or more patients who were admitted for at least two nights during the previous calendar year, and the facility has to have under a certain bed count. Apparently someone in the community was impressed enough with the care our hospital delivered to organize a nomination for us. I haven't even learned who it was yet."

"That's terrific," Heath said. "Even being nominated is an honor."

"It sure is," Skip assured him. "And winning would really give an added shine to our reputation."

"Then I hope you win," Margie said.

"Me too," Candace said. "Hope Haven needs positive publicity."

She couldn't help remembering the recent threat that the hospital might be downsized, not to mention the tense days some months earlier when the papers had been filled with headlines trumpeting allegations of negligence against the hospital and its employees. Thank heaven that lawsuit, which had named her as the primary target, had turned out to be baseless.

"How's registration going for your next childbirth class?" Skip asked Candace. They had received several cancellations in the past few months as people heard that Hope Haven might be cutting some departments. Although the Birthing Unit had not been mentioned, they feared the bad publicity might create an adverse effect on the number of couples choosing to deliver their babies in Deerford.

Candace beamed. "The class is full. I guess the good news that we aren't going anywhere is getting around town." Her smile faded a bit as she thought of one couple she had met recently who would be taking the class. The Nottingtons were significantly older than most expectant parents, at ages forty-eight and forty-five. And while they had been pleasant, she had detected something—some hint of anxiety and stress—that she hoped the couple could resolve. Reading their preadmission questionnaire, she had seen that the couple had two older teens. Perhaps their jitters were simply from the thought of beginning a new parenting journey.

"Howie! Don't you dare pour that on Eason!" Candace raised her voice just as her son began lifting a pail filled with water to douse his six-year-old buddy.

All the adults laughed at the dismay on the little boy's face as his plan was foiled, and Candace's concerns were forgotten. The sun was bright. She lifted her face to its soothing warmth for a moment.

"So where are you two planning on living after the wedding?" Margie asked, turning to look at Candace. "Combining two households of furniture and belongings will be crazy, won't it? We got married right out of college, so we never really had two households to integrate." She smiled at her husband.

Candace didn't answer immediately. She hadn't really considered that Heath might be bringing furniture when he moved in. Silly of her, but in her mental planning, she had just plunked him down in her home as it existed.

"We haven't made any firm plans yet," Heath said, "but Candace's home is a lot bigger than mine, so I imagine that probably will be our first step."

First step? Is he thinking we should sell my house and buy another? She sat up abruptly.

"What's your mother going to do now?" Skip asked her. "Doesn't she live with you?"

"Yes," Candace said. "She moved in with us after my first husband passed away. She's been a great help with the kids."

"She's talking about finding a place of her own," Heath volunteered. "I told her I'd be delighted to have a mom in my life again, but she says there's a big difference between having a mom in your life and having one underfoot when you're newlyweds." He chuckled, as did Skip and Margie.

Candace felt as if she'd been hit in the stomach. "My mother's moving out?"

Heath's blue eyes widened as he recognized the magnitude of the blunder he'd just made. "I'm sorry," he said. "I assumed you knew. You two discuss everything." He shrugged, lifting his hands for a moment in a helpless gesture. "It was just a passing comment she made the other day. Maybe she didn't mean it. She could have been looking for reassurance that I wouldn't mind her living with us." He took a deep breath, obviously aware that he was babbling. "Sorry," he said again.

There was a moment of awkward silence during which none of the adults met anyone else's gaze.

Margie jumped to her feet. "We'd better pack these kids up and head home," she announced. "They're not used to this much sun, and I don't want to overdo it right at the beginning of the season."

"Good idea," Skip said. He also rose hastily and strode toward the water to begin corralling his children, leaving Heath and Candace sitting side by side in uncomfortable silence.

To read *Special Blessings* in its entirety,
you can order by mail:
Guideposts
PO Box 5815
Harlan, Iowa 51593
by phone: (800) 932-2145
or online: shopguideposts.com

A Note from the Editors

Guideposts, a nonprofit organization, touches millions of lives every day through products and services that inspire, encourage, and uplift. Our magazines, books, prayer network, and outreach programs help people connect their faith-filled values to their daily lives.

Your purchase of *Stories from Hope Haven* does make a difference! To comfort hospitalized children, Guideposts Outreach has created Comfort Kits for free distribution. A hospital can be a very scary place for sick children. With all the hustle and bustle going on around them, the strange surroundings, and the pain they're experiencing, is it any wonder kids need a little relief?

Inside each easy-to-carry Comfort Kit is a prayer card, a journal, a pack of crayons, an "I'm Special" wristband to wear alongside the hospital-issued one, and a plush golden star pillow to cuddle. It's a welcome gift and has a powerful effect in helping to soothe a child's fears.

To learn more about our many nonprofit outreach programs, please visit www.guidepostsfoundation.org.